THE MYRTLE BEACH MYSTERIES

Color Her Dead
Stripped To Kill
Dead Kids Tell No Tales
When Dead Is Not Enough
Hurricane Party
Sanctuary of Evil

OTHER BOOKS BY STEVE BROWN

Black Fire
Radio Secrets
Carolina Girls
The Belles of Charleston

THE
CHARLESTON RIPPER

THE
CHARLESTON RIPPER

Steve Brown

Chick Springs Publishing
Taylors, SC

First published in the USA in 2007 by
Chick Springs Publishing
PO Box 1130, Taylors, SC 29687
E-mail: ChickSprgs@aol.com
Web site: www.chicksprings.com

Library of Congress Control Number: 2007904492
Library of Congress Data Available

ISBN: 978-0-9712521-0-3

10   9   8   7   6   5   4   3   2   1

AUTHOR'S NOTE

ACKNOWLEDGMENTS

For their assistance in preparing this story, I would like to thank Mark Brown, Sonya Caldwell, Sally Heineman, Missy Johnson, Capt. Jackie Kellett of the Greenville County's Sheriff's Department, Kate Lehman, Jennifer McCurry, Kimberly Medgyesy, Ann Patterson, Chris Roerden, Robin Smith, Susan Snowden, Louise Watson, Dwight Watt, and a very special thanks to Sgt. Mike Sherman of the Charleston Police Department, and, of course, Mary Ella.

For Sir Arthur Conan Doyle

Whoever fights monsters should see to it that in the process he does not become a monster.
—Friedrich Nietzsche

AUGUST 7TH

The killer stood in the hallway darkness, waiting for the woman to leave her apartment. Only moments before he had smashed out the overhead light and everything he wore tonight—and the kill must be done tonight—was black: shoes, socks, trousers, and hooded top from a pair of sweats. The scarf around his neck could be pulled up so all you saw were his eyes and remained handy to wipe blood away. His eyes were covered by dark contact lenses. He had to be covered from head to toe. He was anticipating a lot of blood.

For weeks he had stalked this woman, watching as she left for work, mostly at night, and hurrying from one of the houses in the Ansonborough section of Charleston. In this neighborhood, there were plenty of escape routes, and given the state of lighting on the streets of Charleston, you could disappear almost immediately.

Martha Turner was a high-class prostitute who advertised on the web. She would have been a call girl when hookers were referred to as call girls, a courtesan well before that, but what it came down to was this: Martha was an enterprising young woman who learned early in life that she could make more money modeling clothes than assembling burgers at the local Hardee's, even more money if she went down on a man. Her other job, clerking a few hours a day at Victoria's Secret, gave her a front, and an opportunity to sample the merchandise.

Martha was run by no pimp, no organization, and had no one to protect her. She had come to Charleston for an education and never returned home, which was Newberry, South Carolina, where the people were nice enough but a bit gossipy. Still, Martha's days as a freelancer were near an end, and not because of her imminent demise at the hands of the killer waiting outside her door.

After New Orleans had been buried under a lake of water, organized crime, like any other large operation, had its own hookers to employ and independent contractors would no longer be tolerated. For those looking for a good time, Charleston was now the premier coastal city with the history, charm, and access to plenty of beaches and golf courses. And Charleston residents feared no hurricane, as did its sister cities along the coast. The Holy City had taken Hurricane Hugo straight on and reveled in its resiliency. So New Orleans had been left in the dust, rather the mud, and more storms would simply shake out the wannabes from those devoted to this city by the sea.

Martha was one of those devotees to Charleston, and on the night of her death, it never occurred to her that someone would hate her so much that he'd repeatedly stab her—thirty-nine times!

If she'd had time to think about it, she would've wondered why this was happening. Everyone loved her. Men adored her, and women were quite rightly envious of her figure, her clothes, and her lingerie. But no one hated her.

Or did they?

Martha came out of the ground floor apartment and turned to lock the door. Martha never allowed her "dates" to know where she lived and always met them at hotels. First-timers she met in restaurants, her motto being "If you have to ask how much, I'm too expensive for you." When she turned around to drop her keys into her purse and to see why the foyer was in darkness, the killer was on her.

Forearm across her chest, he slammed Martha into her apartment door, shutting off any scream. When his arm came off, Martha mistakenly thought she'd broken free and didn't scream. She should've screamed, because when she looked into the face of her assailant, she realized there was no face, just a hood and a black mask covering everything but a pair of . . . black eyes?

Her keys fell to the floor as she felt the first blows from the knife and the pain in her abdomen. No chance to scream, no chance to catch her breath—the blade slamming into her over and over again. And the killer counting.

"Twenty-one, twenty-two, twenty-three . . ."

This was no robbery. This was not rape.

What was this?

And Martha's last thoughts: Why are you doing this? Why is this happening to me?

CHAPTER ONE

I was browsing through the regional section of the bookstore when Mary Kate Belle said from the other side of the freestanding rack, "So Chad is dead to the world?"

"Pretty much dead to me," I said without any humor. I was bent over on the other side, running my finger across the spines of the nonfiction. Not much here I hadn't read.

The store had closed minutes ago, but the manager allows us to linger as a favor for friends who work late and need to pick up something to read ourselves to sleep. Besides the manager, a couple of college girls hustled around, putting the store to bed. Mary Kate and I were off the job; me an agent for SLED, the State Law Enforcement Division, South Carolina's equivalent of the FBI, and Mary Kate Kelly a reporter for *The Post and Courier* who goes by her maiden name, Belle, because, in Charleston, it opens many more doors.

MK had been named for competing grandmothers:

Mary Kate and Mary Jane, so she became Mary Kate Jane Belle so either grandmother could choose whatever part of Mary Kate's name that particular grandmother favored. And Mary Kate was a real clotheshorse. Tonight she wore a floral bias-cut silk dress, shoes from Seychelles, and carried a flap wallet by Elliott Lucca. But the girl was just as dedicated to her job as I was to mine, which was why she and her husband, a ne'er-do-well by the name of Kelly, no longer "shared the same accommodations," as Mary Kate put it.

From her side of the book rack, she said, "You're not the only woman who works long hours. Chad should cut you some slack. Where does he stand on the boat?"

"Says it's a poor allocation of our meager resources." Despite my attempts at neutrality, I frowned.

"That's pretty lame. Everyone knows boats are holes in the ocean you pour money into. If you want a boat, you buy a boat. You don't go around rationalizing the purchase. No boat owner I know is ever in short supply of people who'll tell them they've made a bad decision."

"I'm taking a slow count on the issue."

"Then you must be counting higher than ten." Mary Kate stood on tiptoes and peered over the shelf, at least that's what it sounded like. "Just because Chad works on boats all day is no reason for him to deny you the pleasure of going sailing."

"That's not the only pleasure he's denying me." I forced a chuckle, trying to lighten the mood.

"Okay, okay, so he helped build *Spirit of South Carolina,* and that frigging tall ship can sit out in the middle of the harbor where everyone can ogle it. Who cares. Any free time he has, he should spend with you."

Continuing to run my fingers along the spines, I said, "It's difficult for a SLED agent to demand equal time. We give so little ourselves." Still, I made the effort by driving back and forth to the state capital where I worked cold cases, and that was more than a two-hour trip and took more than a couple of Red Bulls to stay awake.

Mary Kate came around the corner of the rack and stood hands on hips. "You have money, don't you? You know, from when you . . . lost your other boat?"

"Don't mince words. When *Daddy's Girl* was blown to smithereens. Yes, I could buy something."

"Well, you should."

"And how many of your relationships have worked out when you've been so pushy?"

"Hey, don't turn this around on me."

"Why shouldn't I?" I straightened up and looked at her. "Isn't that what this is all about, you judging me? I have a lover. What about you?"

From out of the stacks walked a guy well over forty, almost six feet, going bald, and wearing his remaining blond hair in a ponytail. "Did I hear someone mention love?" he asked with a smile and teeth whitened beyond anyone's expectation. His eyes were a brilliant blue, he was richly tanned, and he wore a shirt open to his navel, exposing not only a good bit of chest hair but quite a bit of bling bling.

"Ask me anything," he said, still smiling and showing off those teeth. "I'm an expert in matters of the heart. Been married three times." He stuck out a manicured hand. "Darryl Diamond. I'm a movie producer from the

West Coast, and you are . . .?"

"Susan Chase." I shook his hand.

"From Myrtle Beach? I think I've heard of you." When he released my hand, I could see that his shook. "Sorry, but it's been a long day and I need a drink."

"Or a hit." I stepped back, evaluating the condition of his eyes, arms, and especially his nose.

The move placed me beside my clotheshorse friend, and my off-the-rack pantsuit, gray with a thin chalk stripe, put me at a distinct disadvantage. All the clunky equipment that goes with the job was strapped around my waist: phone, cuffs, and a couple of pistols. Thankfully, my jacket covered most of that gear, and for that very reason women in law enforcement rarely carry purses but purchase suits with lots of pockets.

"If you need a hit," said Mary Kate, "that would make you a real Hollywood producer."

"Well, I—I've been under a great deal of . . . financial pressure and may have to sell my house on Rainbow Row." He extended his hand to my friend.

"Charleston ladies do not shake hands," said Mary Kate, "and I can't say that I'm sorry you'll have to sell your home, but trophy hunters aren't welcome in Charleston."

He looked at me. "What happened to that famous Charleston hospitality I've heard so much about?"

I held my hands up in mock surrender. "Don't look at me. Ask her. She's a Belle of Charleston."

And Mary Kate Jane was definitely a Belle. You could see it in her blue eyes, pale skin, and raven hair. Often called Black Irish, plenty of French Huguenots inhabit Charleston, most of their forebearers arriving after the revocation of the Edict of Nantes by the Sun King. Back in those days, you either became a Catholic or were marched off to the galleys; the women sent to convents.

"Ah, Miss Belle," said Diamond, "so very nice to meet you. I purchased the rights to *The Belles of Charleston.* You must have a role in my new movie. Most of it will be filmed right here in Charleston."

"Is that how you win over the locals, by putting them in your movies?"

He grinned. "Well, it's worked in the past. Would you have access to the Belle home on High Battery?"

"Of course. I grew up there."

"Then perhaps we might be able to film there. I go for as much authenticity as possible."

"Sorry, but my family has strict rules applying to the media."

"You're related to Simms Belle?"

"I am."

Behind me, I heard a knock on glass, then the opening and closing of the bookstore door.

"Mr. Diamond," said Mary Kate, "if you're really from L.A., you must understand what it's like to have reporters showing up on your doorstep at all hours."

I turned away, trying to suppress my own grin. Evidently, Darryl Diamond's research didn't extend to who reported for *The Post and Courier.* When I turned away, I saw James Stuart weaving his way through the stacks in our direction. The store manager locked the door and followed him over, and why not? Stuart towered over most people with his dark hair and eyes, and year-round tan. And he knew how to dress: expensive silk suit, light blue shirt, and rep tie sporting the colors of the Citadel, tied in a Windsor knot, of course.

My breath quickened and I brushed back my hair. James Stuart was more than eye candy. A retired army colonel who'd been hired to run Charleston's Department of Homeland Security, he'd whipped that outfit into shape seemingly with ease, and now turned his attention to learning the ropes of the homicide division of the Charleston Police Department. Medal of Honor winners can pretty much write their own ticket. Stuart's only visible scars from twenty years' military service were where a roadside bomb had plowed a furrow along the side of his head and a notch in his ear.

"Miss Chase. Mary Kate," said Stuart, nodding at us in turn.

"James . . ." replied my friend, who had grown up with the Stuarts on the Battery and knew his family history, the latest tragedy being a home invasion gone terribly wrong. His wife—pregnant with twins—had died while he was overseas.

All in all, James Stuart was "the man" in Charleston, and he wanted to have a cup of coffee with little old me. At least that's what he said. Such a Mickey Mouse code might fool a movie producer but not any decent reporter, so after making our good-byes to those in the bookstore, Mary Kate followed us out of the building, down the steps, and to the street. Parked at the curb was Stuart's 1965 Wimbledon white Mustang coupe with a 260-cubic-inch V-8. Something else to drool over.

Mary Kate fought me for shotgun and ended up in my lap. After all, I'm taller and have the shoulders. Then Stuart wheeled around on Meeting Street and headed in the direction of the crime scene.

CHAPTER TWO

The crime scene was in Ansonborough, named for George Anson, a British naval officer who patrolled the waters off the Carolina Coast and defended Charleston during the Golden Age of Piracy. Later, in a high-stakes card game, this dashing sailor won title to the lands that would later become the first suburb of Charleston.

Knowing we'd have to run the media gauntlet, I was out of the car and heading toward the yellow tape at a brisk trot. Crime-scene tape enclosed the sidewalk, several skinny trees, a couple of lampposts, and the entrance to a two-story building. Charleston is not well lit—ambience, you know—but at every crime scene you could always count on TV to provide enough light for reporters to do their stand-ups and cops not to stumble. The reporters saw us coming and headed in our direction, shouting questions and burning their lights into what was left of our night vision.

"I'm with them," I heard Mary Kate say as we broke

through their ranks and ducked under the crime-scene tape.

When the other reporters objected to Mary Kate's preferential treatment, Stuart took his cousin by the arm and steered her back toward the tape, but only after Mary Kate had completed a full turn, holding out her arms, and singing: "All the other reporters push and pull, but they'll never get inside . . ."

I didn't have to see any more to know she'd disappear into the crowd, looking for one of her many contacts inside the police department. By tomorrow morning, Mary Kate would know more about this incident than the gossipmongers at the Greenberg Center, so named to honor one of the most popular former chiefs of police in modern-day Charleston.

Though I held up my lanyard ID, the uniformed patrolman still stopped me, taking my ID and examining it. I was allowed to proceed only with Stuart accompanying me: CPD policy. Another patrolman stood near the stoop of a two-story house, and a young couple was being questioned by two Charleston homicide detectives: one skinny, the other carrying way too many pounds.

The fat one, whose name was Abel Waring, lowered his pad and asked, "What are you doing here, Chase?"

Glancing at James Stuart, I said, "Take it up with the colonel."

"Colonel?" asked the thin man. That would be Sam Gadsden.

"Why don't you ask the mayor," said Stuart.

"Why don't I ask the chief," said the fat detective. "This isn't some John Jay field trip," a reference to where Stuart had studied online after learning of his wife and unborn children's murder, and well before his discharge from the army.

Waring fumed as he stalked off. "Every Tom, Dick, and Harry . . ."

"Harriett," I corrected before he disappeared into the darkness and left the questioning of the couple to Gadsden. Evidently Waring had someone on speed dial because he began bitching about me right away.

One of the burly guys standing off to the side snorted, saw me look in his direction, and turned away. They were members of the coroner's office and there to do the heavy lifting.

On the stoop I fitted on a pair of paper booties. "Colonel, remain out here and learn what this couple has to say."

Instead, Stuart finished his own booties, opened the door, and held it open for me.

"Oh, please!" I said, charging into the building and almost stumbling over a red-headed technician kneeling before the body.

The foyer was lit by a light on a tripod that gave out enough light to blind you and was plugged into the wall behind the coroner. The coroner wore a white linen suit and would do so until Labor Day. He nodded at me when I looked up from my abrupt halt behind the tech and her crime-scene kit.

I returned his nod and knelt beside the tech. Jacqueline Marion wore her red hair in a boyish cut and had on a crime-scene jacket and a pair of blue nitrile gloves. Paper sacks on the victim's hands told me how far along they were in processing the body. The victim was a Caucasian in her mid-twenties, brown hair, brown eyes, smartly dressed, and her abdomen had been slashed to pieces.

Bobby, literally Jacqueline's partner in crime, lowered his video camera and smiled at me from the other side of the body. A third tech—a blond guy I did not know—processed the door to the apartment, and a lone fly buzzed around. Trapped in the small room was a rancid smell that permeates every homicide scene, especially those with open wounds and seeping body fluids. The air-conditioning was fighting a losing battle.

Jacqueline said, "I tried to call you."

"I had my phone off."

"That's why they sent someone. I suggested the bookstore." Jackie smiled up at Stuart. "How'd I do?"

"Right on the money," said Stuart, leaning over us.

Jacqueline's face was covered with freckles, and whenever she heated up, her freckles became a solid sheet of red. A former forensics officer from Horry County, Jacqueline had left the Grand Strand for more money and experience. The city of Charleston had provided both.

"Susan spends too much time with books," added Jacqueline. "She has an inferiority complex regarding her education."

"As do I when it comes to police procedure," agreed Stuart, taking out his pad and pen.

"Colonel," I said, interrupting their prattle, "I asked you to interrogate the couple outside."

"No, you didn't. You told me to listen to what the homicide detectives learned. I can read that in the file tomorrow, but this . . . this is OJT."

I returned my attention to the dead woman. Oh, well, I wasn't going to train him, or any other man, in a matter of days.

The victim lay in a pool of blood, eyes open in disbelief, and she had several defensive wounds on both hands and forearms.

Good. You never liked to see a dead woman who hadn't put up a fight.

Playing out the formality calling him to the scene, the coroner said, "Miss Chase, this is Martha Turner and she's still warm to the touch. I did a liver temp. My estimate is that she's been dead less than a half hour."

I pulled on a pair of the new nitrile gloves and scanned the foyer, stairs, and walls, all covered with an enormous amount of cast-off spatter. There was something else, and I don't mean the fly buzzing around. The lobby was so small, with only the narrow steps to the second floor, you could almost feel the woman's presence, her soul searching for a way out.

I glanced at the storm door that closed automatically behind us, then looked up the narrow steps. "Would you mind opening a window?" I asked the coroner. "And let in some air."

The coroner appeared puzzled but did as I requested, and as he went up the narrow stairs I noticed that the overhead light had been busted out. Shards of bulb lay on the floor around the body. Some pieces stuck up through the pool of congealed blood.

Jacqueline said, "The couple being interviewed outside say Turner lived on the ground floor and they live upstairs."

The male tech—the new guy I didn't know—snapped a piece of translucent tape from the doorjamb. "And we'll be ready to go inside in just a moment."

Jacqueline enlightened me. "The landlord's been sent for and the key is on its way."

I heard the coroner opening a window, then the storm window. He returned down the steps, fell back, and took a hard seat on the stairs.

"You okay?" I asked, smiling up at him.

"Yeah . . . I guess. It felt like something brushed . . ." The coroner looked upstairs, bewildered.

Now the foyer felt roomier, and I could breathe, and the fly was gone.

"Thanks," I said, getting to my feet. "We appreciate that."

With Stuart on my heels, I stepped outside.

The fat homicide detective was nowhere to be seen, but the skinny one was stepping up on the building's stoop.

Raising a hand, I stopped him. "Gadsden, you need to decide what you're going to do in the next few minutes."

The skinny man said nothing. No surprise there. Gadsden used words as if he was being charged by the syllable.

"The victim's been dead no more than a half hour. You need to decide if you're going to shut down the city and try to catch this guy." I gestured at Stuart. "The colonel can help with that."

Stuart glanced at his watch and shook his head. "Been too long, and it would only irritate the tourists."

"Your other option is to put out an APB for someone,

anyone who might be spattered with blood. Or someone who might've seen someone covered with blood. Or seen someone carrying a plastic bag, a suitcase, or backpack that might contain bloody clothing."

"That's the way to go," said Stuart, nodding, "and you don't upset so many people."

"Colonel," I said, turning to Stuart, "what we need to form is a net. Nets usually take time to set up and pull personnel away from their usual routine, but I recommend you get all on-duty officers out of their cars or off their mounts and have them move in this direction, paying special attention to the alleys, dumpsters, any dark corners."

"As if walking abreast," said Stuart, nodding again.

"You're gonna miss a lot . . ." said Gadsden.

"We're going to miss people anyway. What we're trying to do is get everyone facing Ansonborough and moving in this direction, with the goal of closing the circle." Glancing at the street, I reached under my jacket and unhooked my cell. "And the quicker the CPD gets the media involved, breaking into their regularly scheduled programs, the better."

Gadsden said, "I don't know . . ."

"I'll take responsibility," said Stuart, pulling out his own phone, flipping it open, and touching a button.

As Stuart's phone ran through its speed dial, the skinny man asked, "Who you calling?"

"The mayor."

"But the chief has to check with the mayor."

"I'm cutting through all that red tape. You can call the chief, if you'd like."

Gadsden did not like. The chief was a tough black

woman you did not want to cross, a real Dragon Lady.

"You know," I said to the skinny detective, "to speed this along, we really could use the keys to Turner's apartment."

"Waring's on it," said Gadsden, referring to his partner.

As Stuart explained the situation over his cell, the mayor cut him off, asking what Stuart proposed to do. It wasn't long before we heard the mayor yelling, "Do it, do it!"

I flipped open my phone, speed-dialed Mary Kate, and glanced in the direction of the herd of reporters. "Has the public information officer arrived?" I asked into my phone.

"No," came my friend's angry reply, preceded by an unnecessary vulgarity. "No one's here, Susan. No one at all."

"Okay, I'm sending someone out." I flipped the phone shut. "You need to do this, Colonel, and watch your choice of words. This is a tourist town."

He nodded and headed for the police line.

"Colonel," said Gadsden, taking a few steps after him, "let's wait for the public information officer."

But Stuart was gone.

I returned to the foyer, knelt beside Jacqueline, and told her what we were doing.

"Excellent," she said, using a pair of disposable tweezers to raise pieces of the dead woman's clothing.

Near the victim's feet lay a pair of black heels. No hose. An envelope purse lay near the stairs, unopened, and a strand of pearls remained around the victim's neck, unbroken.

"Susan, you're not going to believe this, but I've counted over twenty entry wounds, and I haven't had the opportunity to get her on the table."

"That makes it personal," said Gadsden, looking over our shoulders and taking notes in his pad. He, too, wore nitrile gloves and paper booties.

"Over twenty?"

I got to my feet so quickly I almost knocked Gadsden into the storm door. People say I take situations like this personally, and they would be right. Women, children, I'm there for them. Men can take care of themselves.

Looking at the new tech bagging the purse, I said, "If Turner has any sort of home office, I want that processed first. If we're lucky, we'll have this guy before he can leave town."

The male tech looked at Jacqueline, who nodded.

"Hey, cowboy," I said to the newbie, "you don't look to her for confirmation. You do what the investigator says, understand?"

"Yes, ma'am." And he slid the envelope purse into a baggie, followed quickly by the pair of black heels.

"Want us to pop a lock and go in through the back?" I asked Jacqueline. "It's pretty evident the crime occurred outside the apartment, and I really want to get after this guy."

"No problem," she said, standing. "Body's ready to be moved."

The coroner left the building and returned with the two burly guys. Once the body was in the bag, and the bag out the door, Jacqueline and Bobby snapped and videotaped the crime scene while the new tech bagged a set of keys that had been hidden by the body.

"Finished," announced Jacqueline.

Staring at the baggie, I said, "I'd really like those keys."

"Don't need them," said Stuart, coming through the door behind me. He inserted a key in the lock, turned it, and twisted the knob. Using the barrel of his .45, he pushed back the door.

By the time the door swung open, the lights came on, illuminating the living room, a kitchen and dining nook, and a hallway leading to the rear of the apartment. The illumination startled us, causing everyone to pause at the entrance.

"Smart girl," I said.

"For all the good it did her," said Jacqueline.

Gadsden had taken up a position opposite Stuart. Now the thin detective shouted into the apartment, "Make yourself known. Charleston police coming through!"

CHAPTER THREE

Gadsden and Stuart cleared the apartment so that Jacqueline and Bobby could do a walk-through. The newbie toted the crime-scene processing kit through the door and placed it in the middle of the living room, a sterile-looking place, its only color being a newly reupholstered Queen Anne chair. Probably handed down through Turner's family.

I was headed for the kitchen refrigerator, looking for names and phone numbers, when an unfamiliar voice said, "She had the lights wired special."

I turned around to see an elderly man following us into the well-lit living room. He was slight of frame and wore a sweater, as if his pants and long-sleeved shirt were not enough to keep him warm on these long summer nights. His hair was salt-and-pepper and worn in a brush cut.

The fat detective trailed the elderly guy into the apartment. "This is Turner's landlord, Mr. Edgar."

I said, "Please put your hands in your pockets, Mr. Edgar, and keep them there."

The landlord attempted to comply, but he'd seen the blood pool as he came through the foyer, and before that, the body bag hauled out of the building. Not only did he fail to put his hands in his pockets, he also insisted on sitting down. I couldn't blame him. All the color had drained from his face.

"Clear!" came the sound of Gadsden and Stuart's voices from the rear of the apartment.

Jacqueline and Bobby were moving around, one snapping photos, the other with the video cam, and the new tech had disappeared into the rear of the apartment.

Stuart came up the hallway, put away his weapon, and frowned when he saw Edgar. "Computer in the spare bedroom. It's a home office."

Jacqueline looked up from her camera, saw the landlord, and screamed, "Get him outside the perimeter!"

The landlord turned to go, moaned, and collapsed in the doorway, facedown—rather, chin down—in the pool of blood. Once down, the elderly man did not move.

Jacqueline's freckles flashed scarlet. "What the hell's going on?" She stopped taking snaps—the camera fell to the length of its lanyard—and she rushed to the doorway. The heavy cop beat her there and reached down to pull the landlord out of the blood.

"Stop contaminating the crime scene!" Jacqueline clamped a hand on Waring's arm and pulled him away.

The fat detective stumbled back into the living room, and as Jacqueline brought him with her, she moved aside and allowed Waring to trip over his own feet, go down, and land flat on his back.

The skinny detective rushed down the hallway and past his partner. The fat man was grabbing air and sputtering, but instead of going to his assistance, Gadsden grabbed Jacqueline's arm.

"Get your hand off me!" My friend shrugged off his hand, lifted the camera to her eye, and began snapping shots of the landlord lying in the doorway, his chin in the pool of blood. Over her shoulder, she asked, "Bobby, are you getting this?"

Bobby joined her at the doorway with his video cam, and Jacqueline stood aside as he videotaped the corrupted crime scene, meaning the old guy with his chin in the pool of blood.

Gadsden helped his partner to his feet, and Waring came up bitching. Mr. Edgar was groaning and swabbing the hall floor with his chin, and about to reach out to push himself to his feet—well, at least to his knees—but to do that he would have to stick his hands in the blood, making him a poor subject for any interview. And time *was* a factor, probably why Waring had disregarded crime-scene protocol.

Waring and Gadsden tried to get my attention, but I ignored them and said to Jackie, "I need that guy out of the doorway."

"In a moment."

"You've had it. Colonel, move that guy out of the doorway."

Before the landlord could reach out and place his hands in the blood pool, Stuart grabbed Edgar by the belt, lifted him off the floor, and brought him to his feet. He had to assist the man to stand.

"Can he sit in this chair?" Stuart asked Jacqueline, referring to the Queen Anne chair.

"Don't even think about it!"

I quickly huddled with my red-faced friend. "Look at him," I said, gesturing at the trembling man. "This guy's not capable of going anywhere and we need answers now."

Jacqueline stared at the landlord—who could only remain on his feet with Stuart's assistance. She looked around the room and nodded, and Stuart deposited the landlord in the Queen Anne chair. Very quickly paper towels materialized, and Stuart wiped the blood from Edgar's chin. By the way Stuart examined the soiled paper towels, I could see he realized why we investigators always wear gloves at any and all crime scenes.

Waring was adjusting his tie. "I thought you might want to interview him. I didn't know he was going to pass out."

Jacqueline said something, and I told her to hold that thought. The new tech, the one I did not know, had wandered back down the hallway and stood there, staring. And something was wrong with Turner's living room and kitchen. I just couldn't put my finger on it.

I asked the new guy, "Can you crack the computer or do we need to send for a tech?"

"I haven't processed the room yet."

I stood, hipshot, hands on my hips. I may have begun to tap my foot.

"What?" He looked at Jacqueline, then, remembering what had happened in the hallway, his head snapped back to me. "What?"

Jacqueline bailed him out. "Susan didn't ask you if you'd processed the room. She assumes you'll do that. It's your job."

The kid was still confused.

"I asked if you could crack Turner's computer."

"Sure," he said to me. "Most people have their code written down somewhere in the same room."

"Then process the room," said Jacqueline. "Bobby will help you, and then get on that computer. Agent Chase wants anything that will catch the killer before he runs to ground."

"Er—yes, ma'am." He hurried down the hallway with Bobby trailing along and grinning over his shoulder.

I called after them. "I want an address book, anything that would tell me who this woman knew, and I want it now."

This caused Sam Gadsden to follow the two techs to the rear of the apartment.

"Martha didn't have any gentleman callers."

We all looked at Edgar. The landlord appeared to have recovered, but to maintain eye contact I had to take up a position between him and the blood pool in the hallway. Jackie handed Stuart a baggie for the soiled paper towels. Stuart stuffed them in the baggie, returned the baggie to Jackie, and took out his pad and pen.

"Never?" I asked. "No one ever slept over?"

"If they did, I never saw them."

"Colonel, could you see if you can find Turner's car?"

Stuart reached for the baggie containing the keys that lay on the crime-scene processing chest.

"Not so fast!"

Jacqueline snatched up the baggie and left the living room with Stuart right behind her. In seconds we heard a couple of squawks from Turner's car, parked down the street.

Jacqueline returned to the living room. "He didn't use Turner's car for his getaway."

"Then there's a chance he's still inside the net."

"And I may win the lottery." Jacqueline headed for the kitchen to check the door of the fridge.

"So Martha Turner didn't have a steady beau?" I asked the landlord.

Edgar shook his head.

"Attractive woman, good clothes . . ." I looked around. "Nice place." Still, something was odd about the living room and kitchen. Something was missing . . .

"Clothes in the closet are nice, too," said the skinny detective coming down the hallway. "Couple of bras hanging in the shower from Victoria's Secret." Gadsden smiled as he handed me an address book. "Found this in the nightstand."

"That's where Martha worked," said the landlord. "Victoria's Secret."

"On King Street?" I opened the address book and started flipping through it. For decades, lower King had been the fashion mecca of Charleston.

"That's the one." Edgar tried to look out the door, but I stood in his way. "Terrible thing to happen to such a nice young lady."

I turned to the fat man. "Could you ask a uniform to drive by Victoria's Secret and pick up the security number on the front of the store? I may want to talk to her boss."

"Yeah," said Waring, who was simply standing in the middle of the living room. "I suppose so."

"Would you rather dispatch send someone?" I asked, putting an edge into my voice.

"No, no, Miss Chase, I can handle it." Waring took out his cell and left the building.

Stuart dodged him, returning to the apartment. "Turner's car is a silver Accord. I left it with a uniform taping off the car."

I flipped through the address book. Nothing but out-of-town addresses, most of them in Newberry.

I bent down where Jacqueline could see me over the counter separating the living room from the kitchen. "Can we open the purse?"

"Let me." Jackie returned to the living room, took the baggie holding the purse, and, returning to the kitchen, laid the baggie on the counter under an overhead light. Soon I heard the snapping of her camera.

"So, Ms. Turner was single?" I asked the landlord.

Edgar nodded.

"Any impression she may have been a lesbian?"

"Martha? No. She was far too nice to be . . . that way."

"Did she have any enemies that you know of?"

"Of course not."

"Injunctions against stalkers?"

I had to explain what I meant.

"No, no," said Edgar, shaking his head, "not in this neighborhood."

I glanced at the skinny cop.

"I'm on it."

Gadsden joined Jackie in the kitchen where he

opened a line on his cell and called in the particulars. Jackie, using another pair of disposable tweezers, held up the paperwork from Turner's wallet.

"What about friends?" I asked Edgar.

"Not that I can remember." He appeared puzzled. What gal doesn't have girlfriends?

"No one from work ever stopped by?"

"No." He thought for a moment. "Maybe when her car wouldn't start. She had to call someone to pick her up, you know, during the wintertime."

"Mr. Edgar, where do you live in relation to Martha?"

"Directly across the street."

"Directly?"

"Yes."

"So you were in a position to see Martha coming and going?"

"Very much so." He straightened up in the chair. "But I wasn't spying on her . . ." He peered at the lanyard hanging around my neck and added, "Miss Chase. Martha asked me to keep an eye on her place when she wasn't here."

"Then who did you see?"

"Pardon?"

"Mr. Edgar, we're trying to get an idea who could've done this terrible thing and that means we need to know who you saw, whether they appear important or not."

Edgar tried to look into the hallway, but I remained in his way. Instead, he rubbed his chin where the blood had once been.

"Mr. Edgar?" I asked.

No reply. The old guy just sat there, rubbing his chin.

"Mr. Edgar!"

He focused on me. He had not been startled, only reached.

"Yes?" he asked.

"You said you watched Ms. Turner's apartment, that she asked you to. What did you see?"

More thinking by Edgar, and I was about to prompt him again when he finally said, "The usual people . . . meter reader . . . mailman . . . paperboy . . . UPS . . . policemen in patrol cars . . . trash collectors."

"Anyone else you can think of?"

He shook his head.

Still, I was impressed by his list. Maybe by tomorrow he would remember even more. But I needed answers tonight.

"Mr. Edgar, for this crime to have worked, the killer would've stalked Martha, and you can't remember seeing anyone out of the ordinary, such as people walking their dogs more often than usual, new residents in the neighborhood, someone sitting in a car, or perhaps a van? Vehicles with tinted glass?"

"I'll . . . I'll have to think about it."

I waited for as long as I could stand it. "Could you think a little faster?"

"Young lady, I'm not as young as I once was."

"None of us are, and while you're taking your time, Martha's killer is getting farther and farther away."

He only sat there, staring at me.

I counted to ten. Okay, okay, I got as far as four. "Tell me, Mr. Edgar, if we were to check your place, would we find a pair of binoculars near the window?"

"No." He shook his head and frowned. "Why?"

"Do you mind if we check?"

"Certainly not." He rose from his seat.

"Later," I said, waving him back into the Queen Anne. "When did Martha generally come and go?"

"Usually afternoons and evenings."

"You never saw her leave in the morning?"

"I didn't pay much attention. It was daylight then."

Abel Waring returned from having a patrol car drive by Victoria's Secret. The fat man handed me a slip of paper.

"Why don't you handle that?" I asked with a smile.

"Gotcha. By the way, I forgot to tell you. The wife from upstairs said Turner had nothing to do with her, and she learned to have nothing to do with Turner. Well, nothing more than a howdy. I guess they didn't hit it off."

"I don't know . . ." I was thinking of Mary Kate. What woman owns attractive clothes but doesn't show them off, not even to her girlfriends?

The thin detective returned from the kitchen. "Martha Turner has a sheet."

I nodded, finally understanding. "For prostitution."

"Martha was a hooker?" Edgar struggled out of the chair and got to his feet. "I certainly didn't know that or she wouldn't have lived in this neighborhood."

"And why's that?" I asked with a wan smile. "Working girls have to live somewhere, too."

"Well, they can damned well live somewhere else. The good people of Charleston have put in fifty years restoring this neighborhood and we're not going to let it be run into the ground by a bunch of deviates."

Outside, I spoke to the couple who lived upstairs, hoping they'd seen something, anything. They knew nothing, had seen nothing, and the lack of information was beginning to annoy me. I could feel the killer slipping away. The first twenty-four hours are so critical . . .

Once the couple had been cleared to return to their apartment, I spoke again with the two homicide detectives. "Do either of you buy the idea that this was a random killing?"

Waring asked, "Do you really think—"

"I asked whether you thought it was random or not."

"Not random," volunteered Gadsden. "Planned."

The fat man looked around, his gaze coming to rest on the reporters standing behind the crime-scene tape. "Nobody saw nothing, and this isn't gangbanger territory. Yep," he agreed, nodding, "this was planned."

"I'm glad we're in agreement because we need to canvass the neighborhood, beginning with this street."

"Which side?" Gadsden asked his partner.

Waring glanced at the throng of reporters. "Not this one, that's for sure." To me, the fat man said, "You know, Miss Chase, you're going to have to feed the jackals."

"Not my job." I pointed to the public information officer coming under the tape and having his name written down by the patrolman. "That's for that guy to do."

Gadsden smiled. "So, what do they pay you for, Miss Chase?"

I favored him with one of my few smiles of the evening. "I thought you knew by now, Detective Gadsden. To make things happen."

CHAPTER FOUR

It's not good for tourism to keep an active crime scene in the historical district, so a couple of hours later my phone buzzed as I was sliding into a seat at the Noisy Oyster, where the windows are rolled up and people walking by on the sidewalk practically join you at your table. The restaurant stands at the end of the public market and just down the street from the old Exchange and Provost Building.

When George Washington visited Charleston, a grand ball was held in his honor on the second floor, the second floor of the Exchange Building, not the Noisy Oyster. Opened for business in 1771, the Exchange Building was built to meet the growing demands of a flourishing shipping industry in the Southern colonies. It also served as a public market and meeting house, and in protest of the Tea Act of 1773, the offending tea wasn't thrown overboard, as done in Boston, but confiscated and stored inside the Exchange Building. I suppose the people of Charleston, then, as now, were a bit more genteel than those living in New England.

The phone call was from Jacqueline Marion, who joined me a few minutes later and waved off the waitress's suggestion for some tapas. The waitress returned with Jacqueline's Frascati and asked if I'd like another Amarone. I told her no thanks.

"Bring her another," insisted my freckle-faced friend. Her cell phone had been dropped on the tabletop and now she wrapped both hands around her wine glass. She squeezed the glass so hard I thought she might shatter it.

"I don't think so . . ."

"Do it," said Jacqueline, waving the girl away. When the waitress was gone, Jacqueline took a long pull from her glass, coughed, and cleared her throat. "The final count of entry wounds on Martha Turner's body was thirty-nine."

"Jeez!" I sat up, almost knocking over my glass. "For real?"

Her head bobbed rapidly. "I—I was there when the final count was made. There were a few defensive wounds but they're not part of this count."

Noticing that several couples sat at the bar, a few more at tables scattered across the room, I lowered my voice to ask, "But why . . . ?"

"Not my job to find out, Nancy Drew, but yours."

"Yeah, right, but Nancy never had to figure out why some woman would be stabbed thirty-nine times at the doorway of her own home."

"Thank the Lord or I never would've finished that series." Jackie shuddered. "And to think I have to raise children in this world."

I reached over and gripped her forearm. She glanced at my hand, looked up, and forced a smile, and we sat there considering what we knew, which was damned little. A woman without friends, possibly no enemies, had been stabbed thirty-nine times in downtown Charleston.

I took my hand off Jacqueline and polished off my own glass. The attack didn't make sense, and it certainly didn't make sense that nothing had come of the investigation. Martha Turner appeared to have no close friends, and her family lived in Newberry, on the Woodpecker Trail, so named because before the days of numbered highways, the Trail, marked by a silhouette of a woodpecker, was the route snowbirds followed from Washington, DC, to Florida.

Once the waitress left my new glass of Amarone and took away my empty, Jackie asked, "What'd you find in her address book?"

"Nothing but relatives," I said, downing half of my glass in one single gulp and forgetting about the full body of any Amarone.

"Business associates?" asked Jacqueline.

I coughed and had to clear my throat to speak. "All . . . all college girls, and most have roommates, or they'll wish they had. Probably weren't able to get back to sleep after being interrogated by Waring or Gadsden."

"I know the feeling. Sometimes the people I process return for an encore presentation—in my dreams, and I'm sure I'll meet Martha there. Thirty-nine times . . ." She shook her head, looked out the window, and stared down the street.

From where she sat, Jacqueline could see the public

market, and contrary to what tourists believed, this wasn't where the slaves had been sold. That was farther down East Bay.

She shook her head. "Having some nut running around loose in the historical district isn't going to play well with the Chamber of Commerce."

"Yeah," I said. "Why couldn't Turner have been killed by one of her johns? Maybe in a hotel room so we could hint at *their* lack of security."

Her head whipped around to me. "God, but you're cold."

"Not cold. Thirty-nine strokes and no suspects. We don't even know the right questions to ask. The killer could be anyone, set off by anything, and slaughtering Turner practically in public. Is someone trying to send us a message, you know, like us gals aren't safe anywhere?"

"Well, not until we get home and throw all the locks." She shivered and took another sip of her Frascati. "What became of the net you threw up around the historical district?"

"We picked up a traveling salesman whose car had broken down and he was hoofing it to his hotel, several college boys on bicycles and wearing backpacks, and a few homeless folks who, according to the city, don't technically exist. But no bloody clothing."

Outside the window, a girl laughed as she and her guy pal walked by. Jacqueline and I glanced at the passersby, found it impossible not to smile, but we didn't smile long.

Thirty-nine strokes and no leads.

"Did any of her fellow employees at Victoria's Secret know Turner was a working girl?"

"Nary a one."

"Anything from the computer?"

"I left Stuart working on that." I pulled out the cell phone on my waist and glanced at the dial.

"Why'd he bring you in on this case anyway?" asked my friend.

"I have no idea." I smiled. "But I did enjoy the moment."

"No kidding. Don't you think you were a bit rough on my new tech?"

"A bit rough? What does the little twerp think he's doing, working for a paycheck?"

"Oh, come on, Susan, don't give me that advocacy crap."

"Hey, I work for the victim. How many times do I have to tell you that?"

"You work for the state, like I work for the city. They cut your check."

"And this has to do with what?"

"He wasn't disrespecting you, Susan."

"You knew Stuart was bringing me in, why didn't you warn him?"

"And tell him what: the bitch is on the way, so look busy?"

I couldn't help but laugh, and very soon Jacqueline joined me. Having a shared history from the Grand Strand made it tough for us to remain annoyed with each other. But her point was taken, and I'd make nice at my next crime scene, which I didn't think was going to happen anytime soon. I was headed back to cold cases in the morning.

"Speaking of a beat-down," I said to Jacqueline, "I've

never seen you explode like you did at Abel Waring."

"Are you kidding? He brought the landlord inside the tape."

"Yeah, and you practically lifted him off the floor. Where did that come from?"

"He's an idiot." Jacqueline's freckles flushed, and she glanced at the few tourists remaining on the street. "Are you sure Martha Turner had no boyfriends? No guy friends at all?"

I turned my wine glass by its stem, with thumb and forefinger, staring at the remaining liquid. "There were two. Both left Charleston, one over a year ago, one several months ago. Neither said Martha was much fun, which to guys means there wasn't much sexual activity. We contacted them and their alibi witnesses. One was from Spartanburg, the other from Raleigh. Neither one's been in Charleston in the past ninety days."

"What about Turner's church? Did she know someone there?"

I reached over and patted her arm. "There's nothing, Jackie, nothing at all." Straightening up, I added, "Oh, there might be a break when someone interviews the meter reader or the paperboy or whoever picks up the trash or cuts grass in that neighborhood, or some braggart in a bar, but we've got nothing more than a good excuse to bother a few more people."

"Then what's your best guess?"

"I don't have one."

"Susan, please . . ." There came Jackie's plea again, and contrary to what people believe, forensics personnel are not the sarcastic people portrayed on TV, not with a monster on the loose and you being the only one standing between you and your ex-husband raising your two kids. Jacqueline's ex was a jealous guy, which definitely limited her ability to hook up.

I ventured an opinion. "If I had to guess, I'd say Turner was a recluse."

"A recluse? How's that? She had to go out to meet guys. She was a working girl."

"Not if she used the web." I took another sip of the Amarone. "I checked with several bartenders on my way over, and as you know, the turnover in bartenders is horrendous, but the guy at the Blind Tiger and the one at the Charleston Grille understood what type of web-based business Turner ran and could produce her business card, once I leaned on them."

"So she didn't have to leave her house to solicit?"

"Not once she got her operation up and running."

"Gosh," said Jacqueline, leaning back on her side of the booth. "I don't think that's what *Time* magazine had in mind when they named those golden geeks 'Man of the Year.'"

"Yep. Nowadays when you think of smut on the web you think of pedophiles." I gazed out the window. "I really need to hit the streets and work my network." I was thinking of the dealers, prostitutes, and general all-around hustlers that I was wired into on the street. Some of them would inform on their own mothers for a smile from a pretty face. Evidently I was that face. Whores generally demanded money.

"But a recluse . . ."

"Think about it, Jackie. Turner had tons of DVDs, and her bedroom had been converted into a home theater where she could sit in bed and watch movies, and the movies she liked were chick flicks. You know, where the guy and the gal ride off in the sunset together. I was trying to figure out what was wrong with her living room and it finally dawned on me. No TV in the living room, no black-and-white portable on the kitchen counter, as there were no condoms in the nightstand or the dresser. But she had tons of contacts on the web, and I don't mean her johns. She spent gobs of time online, in and out of one chat room—or virtual world—after another."

"She didn't have a basic need to talk with a live person?"

"Jacqueline, I've known marriages to break up because the husband or wife would rather chat online than spend time with their spouse. It's my opinion that Turner lived a self-contained life, her only contact being with those college girls at Victoria's Secret and her relatives in Newberry."

"What about Newberry? What's going on there?"

"I roused the chief of police out of bed and learned that Turner still had friends living there, one of them a boyfriend who just happens to be the chief's nephew. The chief's going to dig a little deeper in the morning, but at the moment, the boyfriend has an alibi."

"Did they know Turner was a hooker?"

"They didn't believe me. It took Stuart to make the chief a believer. I guess hearing that some little girl you knew grew up to be a hooker is more believable coming from a guy than a gal."

One of the male waiters approached us and gestured at the open window overlooking the sidewalk. I slid out of the booth to give him access to the rope, and he slid across, pulled down the window, and slid back out of the booth.

"About to close," he said to me.

After returning to my seat, I said, "The only thing I can figure is Turner saw herself as the next 'Pretty Woman,' which, incidentally, was one of the DVDs on top of her player."

"Waiting for a sugar daddy to come along?"

"And keeping the boyfriend in Newberry as a fallback position."

My phone buzzed, and I told Stuart where we were. Ansonborough was not that far from the harbor.

When I flipped the phone closed, Jacqueline asked, "He's meeting you here?"

I was brushing back my hair and checking my reflection in the window. "Just like us, he probably has to wind down before going home."

Jacqueline arched an eyebrow. "And who does Stuart go home with?"

"Just about any woman he wants to. The girl from Channel Five thinks she has the inside track, but it won't happen. She's been trying to score Stuart ever since he returned from overseas and hasn't made it to first base."

"And how do you know this, about the Channel Five reporter?"

"She told me."

"Oh, yeah?" said Jacqueline, chuckling. "Was that before or after she learned you were being bird-dogged by Stuart?"

"Before," I said with a smile.

Jacqueline became serious. "Susan, you'd tell me if Stuart hit on you, wouldn't you?"

"What? Sure. Where did that come from?"

"Oh, come on, Susan . . ."

"Hey, I know he's a lost puppy when it comes to investigative techniques, but that doesn't mean we have to hook up."

"But you do share a common interest, not like Chad, who appears to have lost all interest in sailing."

"Well, Chad does spend his days building boats."

"And never looks toward the harbor entrance and wonders what it would be like to sail the open sea?"

Stuart's Mustang pulled to the curb and he climbed out.

I sighed. The guy was still a hunk, and he was ambling in my direction, and flashing that cat-who-ate-the-canary smile. I couldn't help but return his smile.

"If folks didn't think you were hooked up before, they'll think you are now because of this solid he's done for you. You owe him, don't you?"

My hands moved around aimlessly. "I don't know what you're talking about. I thought you recommended me to him."

"I did," said Jacqueline, sliding out of the booth and taking her cell phone with her. "You *should* be working the streets. Well, got to go. There'll be a ton of paperwork tomorrow and endless meetings. This was not a good day for the city of Charleston." Checking her reflection in the window, Jackie fluffed her hair.

I glanced behind me, saw Stuart flirting with our waitress, and felt a pang of jealousy.

Wait a minute. What did Jackie know that I didn't know? I was in love with Chad, right?

When Stuart reached our booth, he asked, "Am I too late to buy you ladies a drink?"

"Thanks, Colonel," said Jacqueline, "but I want to get some sleep before the kids wake up."

Stuart visibly brightened. "Want me to take them sailing? You don't have to go along if you don't want to."

Last time out Jacqueline had fallen asleep on Stuart's boat and returned with a terrible sunburn.

"Sorry, Colonel, but what part of my reputation I still have, I want to keep."

Stuart watched her leave, and then took her seat on the other side of the booth. Through the closed window, he watched Jackie climb into her SUV, the black and white one provided by the city.

"You know," he said, "since returning stateside, I didn't think appearances were all that important in Charleston."

I couldn't help but laugh. "You may be right. We just had a woman butchered in the historical district, so I'd say, yeah, just about anything goes in this burg, and any woman's reputation could be suspect if she hooked up with you."

He tried to protest, but I cut him off. "And if you had half a brain, Colonel, you'd never allow yourself to be alone with any kid. Or any two kids, no matter who they belong to, or whose permission you have to take them sailing."

"Now what the hell does that mean?" His glare reminded me that not so long ago James Stuart had been well placed in the army's chain of command and not used to being questioned.

Yeah, yeah, like any guy could intimidate me.

"Perverts, Colonel, someone accusing you of being a pervert. Or some woman looking to score a few bucks off you."

"I've already had that. The woman said she was carrying my child." He looked out the window, but the SUV was gone. "I don't know what this country's coming to if I can't take a couple of kids sailing. Jacqueline Marion's all alone in this world. You know that as well as I do."

"There's her mother," I said with a smile. Watching men ride to the rescue of damsels in distress always amuses me.

"You think women can raise children alone?"

"That's the pot calling the kettle . . ." I flushed, lowered my head, and stared into my empty wine glass. Too late. I'd already stuck my hand in the tar baby.

He thumped the table, forcing me to look up.

"Don't be afraid to say it. It's public record that I was overseas when my family was murdered."

"I'm . . . I'm sorry. I didn't mean anything."

Stuart glanced around. Few patrons remained in the restaurant. Still, he lowered his voice to say, "But what everyone does not know, and I'll depend on your discretion in this matter, is that I've been tested more than once and can never father children. That's why the woman couldn't squeeze a dime out of me."

My mouth was still hanging open when the waitress brought Stuart's bourbon and water and a new Amarone for me.

Looking at the wine glass, I said, "Uh . . . I'm pretty sure I don't need this."

Stuart smiled that cat-who-ate-the-canary smile of his again, leaned back on his side of the booth, and said, "Don't be silly, Susan. Drink up and tell me how a wild child from Myrtle Beach evolves into the professional investigator I saw at the crime scene tonight."

So I leaned back, drank from my glass, and, until they finally kicked us out of there, matched him lie for lie.

AUGUST 31ST

Mary Ann Nichols and her husband climbed out of the cab once it pulled to a stop on the Battery. Counting out the fare, Bill Nichols wondered if he could afford a tip. This long weekend was about to break him.

"Come on, Billy," said his wife, striding out on the stone promenade. Not far from where Mary Ann strolled lay Pirates Point, where Charleston had hung pirates in the past, at least those who failed to contribute to the economy of Charleston.

The cabbie leaned over to the window. "Want me to wait?" He glanced at Bill's wife, hunched against the breeze off the harbor. "Getting kind of chilly." *Translation: It won't be long before your wife gives this up.*

Bill looked at his wife, then past her, toward the harbor entrance, the moon shimmering out to sea. Nothing like this back in Columbus. He shook his head and told the cabbie not to wait.

The Nicholses were in Charleston for a romantic weekend, and after settling in at their hotel, they'd begun to visit every historical spot in the city. That was two nights ago, and each night they ended the day with an evening stroll along the Battery, where Bill had proposed marriage sixteen years before. After all, you couldn't spend all your time in bed, and there'd be questions about what they'd seen and done.

Mary Ann's friends would ask those questions. Her husband's buddies would want to know if he'd been able to squeeze in a game of golf. Well, not this trip. He'd promised Mary Ann that they'd see the sights, and to tell the truth, Bill loved Charleston as much as his wife. Yesterday, they'd seen the Confederate submarine *Hunley,* the day before they'd toured Fort Sumter, and each evening they'd enjoyed a late dinner on Market Street, a carriage ride, and a romantic walk along the Battery.

The killer had been tracking Bill and Mary Ann for the past two nights. He knew where they were staying, and knew they would return to the same place, at the same time, and on the correct date. All he had to do was cruise the Battery until they showed up. Must be where the guy had proposed to his wife was all the killer could figure.

And there they were!

The killer scanned the stone promenade and then zeroed in on his prey. With a stiff breeze off the harbor, few couples were strolling along the rock citadel, though the view was spectacular: the moon low in the night sky, its reflection shimmering out to sea.

He couldn't have picked a better setting.

Mary Ann thought she heard someone . . .

"What?" asked her husband, turning his head.

She felt Bill's arm jerked from around her waist and saw him pitch forward, a bicycle driving hard between her husband's legs and riding Bill down.

"Sorry," said the rider, as he let go of the bike, dropping it to the promenade and Bill Nichols with it.

Mary Ann stifled a cry. For a moment, she'd been frightened, but it'd been nothing but a silly accident. A young man with long blond hair stood over her husband, a student wearing jeans, sweatshirt, and backpack. At his feet lay a twenty-one speed.

But instead of helping her husband to his feet, the young man clubbed Bill over the back of the head with his fist. Bill gave a small "Uh" and went down a second time, collapsing on the cobblestones. Mary Ann opened her mouth to scream, but the cry died in her throat when the young man—now she could see he was much older—drew a knife from under his sweatshirt.

Moonlight flashed off the blade.

Down at the harbor the watchman stepped out of the kiosk, stretched, and checked the key secured to his waist. Time to make his rounds, and the place he always started was where kids sometimes climbed the fence and sneaked down to the ships. But when he faced inland, he was horrified to see that a fire had broken out behind a row of containers lining the road running parallel to the harbor. Dropping the key, the watchman raced back inside the kiosk and dialed the fire department, then the harbor patrol. Fires like this could get out of control and in a hurry.

Bill Nichols sat up on the walkway. His neck and butt ached. What had happened? What had hit him?

The lights of a passing car revealed Mary Ann lying beside him. Had they been mugged?

Clumsily, he crawled over and shook his wife's shoulder. When he did, he thought he saw Mary Ann's head roll across the cobblestones. Bill Nichols began to scream and didn't stop screaming until he stumbled into the street where a passing car almost ran him down.

CHAPTER FIVE

The incessant ringing of the bedside phone woke Eugenia Burnside and she fumbled the instrument into her hand. As she rose up, she noticed that her husband had yet to come to bed. Phone in one hand, she slammed her fist into the bed where her husband should be.

Rotten bastard. Dirty rotten bastard trying to sabotage her career. Every night he drank himself into a stupor, and it wasn't a case of whether he was in his cups, but where he ended up in his cups.

She composed herself and said into the phone, "Burnside here."

"Chief, you said to call you if there was another bad one."

"What is it?" Burnside tried to remember what instructions she'd issued and to whom. She'd just fallen asleep.

"It's pretty bad from what I'm told," continued the watch commander.

"What do you mean?" Burnside swung her long, dark legs over the side of the bed. An elegant black woman, who with good looks and good brains had earned a law degree from the University of South Carolina while walking a beat for the city of Charleston, Eugenia Burnside had climbed the ranks to chief, but only after taking a job with the police department in Durham, North Carolina. Sometimes you had to leave town before the locals realized how valuable you were.

"It's the guy with the knife again," continued the watch commander. "Head rolling around on the sidewalk is what I was told. Those on the scene say the victim's an out-of-towner."

Burnside shuddered. Labor Day weekend was practically upon them. How many tourists would be coming to Charleston when they heard this?

"Where'd it happen?"

"White Point Gardens."

Burnside groaned. The city's main tourist attraction, where kids climbed on Civil War cannons and parents stared over the harbor, trying to figure out which island was Fort Sumter. "Send a patrol car. I'll be ready in twenty minutes. Who's on the scene?"

"Gadsden and Waring are on the way. McPherson asked to be given a call and he's headed there, too." McPherson was her acting captain of detectives.

"Tell them no one's to touch anything until I arrive, and to make a lane. I'm not going to speak to the media the moment I arrive, nor do I care to be seen blowing them off. Move the perimeter out if you have to."

But before Burnside could leave the house, she received another call about a fire that had broken out on the docks of Charleston harbor.

"It appears to be vandalism," said the watch commander, "but I thought you should know."

"Well, at least that allows me to set my priorities."

In cyberspace, that nebulous world of wisdom, knowledge, and misinformation, web crawlers, or bots, never sleep but are always busy collecting odd pieces of information and linking them according to rules laid down by their masters. The report of a fire on the Charleston docks would be picked up by only one news service, but it took only one, and the following day that stupendous collection of data on the web would include not only the harbor fire, but also reports of a woman who'd died of multiple stab wounds. The Charleston police would link the killing in Ansonborough to the murder on the Battery, but certain web crawlers had already linked that murder to an earlier one that same year, also in Charleston.

When Burnside arrived at White Point Gardens, the air was muggy and the moon hung low over the junction of the Ashley and Cooper Rivers. Vehicles crowded Murray Boulevard and South Battery and lights flitted around. Local TV was there: an attractive-looking black woman and an equally attractive white guy doing stand-ups, another station scrambling to set up.

As the patrol car parted the media, and the crime-scene tape was lifted, Burnside took the mic from the dash and called the watch commander to make sure that the public information officer was on his way. The PIO was, and then, considering where this murder had taken place, Burnside placed another call, this one over her cell phone, to someone living on Lake Murray.

It was a short call, and the guy living on Lake Murray said he'd be on his way once he called the highway patrol. Then, with the light bar still flashing and one of the uniforms opening the car door, Burnside stepped out. The chief of police didn't appear at many crime scenes, and once everyone had gotten their look, the uniforms were content to enforce the police line and ignore questions shouted at them from the media. But the reporters wanted more, like what would bring the chief out this late at night.

Two women butchered in the last three weeks, why wouldn't she be here?

Not to mention the people of Charleston needed to know she was on the job, that a woman could handle this job, that a black woman could handle this job. Still, once she'd passed under the yellow tape, she was aware that she'd invaded the turf of a bunch of homicide detectives and would have to deal with all the Dickless Tracy comments made behind her back.

A large man with a buzz cut and wearing a rumpled suit handed her a pair of nitrile gloves. Burnside took the gloves, fitted them on finger by finger, and ignored the media, including Mary Kate Belle. Still, Burnside couldn't help but notice that Belle wore a red satin sheath with the fabric hooked by a large brooch at one hip and layers of satin below the waist. Burnside couldn't make out her earrings, but Belle's hair was pulled back into a bun, a feather-sized bang of black hair falling to one side. On each wrist was a variety of gold bracelets. In contrast, Burnside wore a dark business suit with a white blouse. Her only color: a periwinkle scarf.

God, how that Belle woman irritated her!

Flashlight beams whipped around, and the people who lived along the Battery, one of the most vocal interest groups in all Charleston, stared from the porches of their antebellum homes.

A proper Charlestonian would never gawk, but then, not many proper Charlestonians still lived along the Battery with all the Yankees moving in.

A hundred years ago, Eugenia Burnside would've been prohibited from strolling along the Battery at this time of night. And, of course, a black woman, or any woman, would never have been appointed chief of police. Still, with much of the city proudly frozen in time, the city of Charleston also took pride in its progressive ideas.

"What do we have?" she asked her acting captain of detectives. Burnside's captain of detectives was home, dying of cancer.

"Body's over here," said McPherson, gesturing toward a small crowd of personnel armed with flashlights. "Victim's Mary Ann Nichols from Columbus, Ohio." He handed Burnside a flashlight, then gestured at a van. "Husband's with the EMS."

"The husband was injured in the attack?" asked Burnside.

"Yes. It appears both victims were knocked to the pavement."

"So the husband isn't a suspect?"

"More likely an innocent bystander."

Burnside stopped. "With his wife knifed to death right in front of him?"

"Husband says he was run down from behind and knocked to the ground. Never saw a thing."

"And you believe him?"

McPherson took a three count. Why was this woman here? Matter of fact, why was a woman his boss in the first place?

Michael McPherson was a Jersey guy, but after being discharged from the navy, he had applied for and won a position on the Charleston police force and started his climb up the same ladder as the chief. Actually, McPherson had begun his climb a few years before the woman who was now his boss.

McPherson was also a member of a church that had saved his family from complete disintegration when all Mac had been able to think of was The Job, or going out to a cop bar to wind down after a long day on The Job. But that same church fueled his dislike of gays and feminists, and why the word "acting" remained in front of his title long after everyone knew their former captain of detectives would never return to his job.

"Chief," said McPherson, containing his irritation, "I told the husband we could move this investigation along if he wouldn't mind dropping his drawers and letting me check his backside. Nichols did so immediately—in the EMS with the doors closed. Appears he was run down by a bike, just as he said."

"A motorbike?" The chief hated bikers, and especially hated the way they rode their hogs through the historical district, without regard for life or limb.

"No. A bicycle."

"Are you serious?"

"No reason to doubt him." McPherson pointed at the

cobblestones with his flashlight. Small yellow triangles marked the location of two narrow black streaks, one right behind the other. "Bicycle stopped here. Twenty-one speed or something like it. Narrow tires, not wide ones like those used on the beach."

"Am I getting this right? Someone ran down the husband, then went after his wife?"

"Right on the money," said James Stuart, joining them. Stuart's family owned a house on South Battery, and seeing the crowd, the former officer had wandered over. In his hand was a narrow pad in which he'd been sketching, and under his custom-made suit, Stuart wore a shoulder rig holding a Colt .45, which Eugenia Burnside believed the former military officer was a little too eager to use.

"Speaking of money," asked Burnside, "what was the motive, robbery?"

"Nope," said McPherson. "Both wallet and purse are intact."

Burnside looked from the streaks on the cobblestones to the EMS van, doors open to reveal the husband sitting on one of the metal benches, head in hands. As she watched, the mobile crime lab's doors swung open and several techs leaped out and hurried in their direction with sets of halogens. A cord was pulled, and after a few feeble starts, the sound of a generator filled the night air. A technician nodded at the brass while continuing to unwind a long orange cord from a turn that whirled on a stick.

"Since robbery wasn't a motive," said Stuart, "this murder links with Martha Turner's."

"Now don't jump to conclusions, Colonel."

The captain of detectives had the greatest respect for James Stuart as a soldier, but when it came to working a crime scene, Stuart was just another novice. And McPherson suspected that Stuart only hung around to crack the case involving his dead wife and kids. And the first thing Stuart had learned was a fact as old as the act of murder itself: with a high-profile killing, such as a pregnant Eleanor Stuart, investigators had allowed everybody and their brother to tromp through Stuart's home on South Battery; hence, the status of the case: cold.

Burnside asked, "You're *sure* there was no altercation between the two men before the attack, such as over a parking space?"

McPherson shook his head. "The last person the husband remembers arguing with was at work, four days ago, back in Columbus."

"So this attack came out of the blue?"

"Just like Ansonborough," said Stuart, looking at McPherson. "No slur intended, Mac, but this all might make more sense to a different investigator." He gestured at the body near the curb. "And save lives. This guy is definitely not through."

"Not Chase again," groaned McPherson. "I can't be babysitting—"

"Three murders, Mac," said Stuart, and when the white man and the black woman looked at him, he explained. "Chase believes she's found a case from back in April that links this one tonight and Martha Turner's. The woman was tied up and left under a house. She eventually died from peritonitis."

"But there was no bondage in either of these two murders," argued McPherson.

"I understand, Mac, but Chase says the victim had to be restrained so she would die of peritonitis."

"Wait a minute," asked Burnside, frowning, "are you saying the April murder victim *had* to die from peritonitis?"

"Chief, really, I'd rather Chase lay it out for you."

"Okay, okay," said Burnside, waving off any further discussion. "I'll make time to speak with her, but only after we process the current scene."

Burnside walked to where the body lay. Standing over the victim was the coroner in his white suit, and kneeling beside the victim was a red-headed woman wearing a black windbreaker. Several other techs and detectives stood about, taking another look when the halogens came on, spitting and popping in the night air.

The victim's head was barely connected to her body, and on the right side of the face was a bruise, not visible until the halogens popped on. The victim lay on her back, hands at her sides, legs open. She wore a long-sleeve blouse tied off at the waist over another dark garment and skirt; flats for walking, face and legs pale in the sudden glare of the light. Eyes locked open in shock.

"I did a liver temp, Chief," said the coroner. "She's been dead less than a half hour." Few people commented about the coroner's white suit, as this was Charleston and many of its inhabitants had an image to project.

"Less than a half hour?" asked Burnside.

"Correct, Chief. Just like Martha Turner."

Turning to Stuart, she asked, "And the net?"

The former officer almost came to attention. "Per your

instructions if this situation ever happened again, the city was immediately shut down. The highway patrol closed the interstate and the sheriff's department shut down all surface roads leading out of Charleston."

McPherson nodded. "If he's out there, we'll find him."

A fat detective, Abel Waring, read from his notepad. "Bill and Mary Ann Nichols were staying at a bed-and-breakfast, but Mr. Nichols didn't remember the name."

"Who can blame him," said the tech kneeling beside the body. "This was one hell of an attack." The red-headed tech extended a metal tape measure. "I make her at five-foot-three or four." She retracted the tape. "Should come in at one hundred twenty to one hundred thirty pounds. Race: Caucasian. Cause of death: slit throat. Or the umpteen stab wounds to the abdomen. Either one would've done the job."

"Then why both?" asked Burnside.

When the tech stood up, the chief could see the young woman's face was covered with freckles. "Somebody didn't like this woman, Chief. Her throat's been cut down to the vertebrae, though how you can get that ticked off at some tourist . . ."

Her voice drifted off as she saw McPherson shaking his head. Lately, crime scene techs had begun to consider themselves real detectives, and it had begun to annoy people, especially homicide detectives. Blood oozed from the victim's mouth and two vicious cuts to the throat.

The tech began again, sticking to the facts. "Either the killer used a small knife and had tremendous arm strength, or used a very large knife—like a butcher's knife. Nothing exotic."

The dead woman's clothing had been pulled up and bunched around the waist, leaving the lower part of the torso exposed, legs splayed. More yellow triangles led off down the street. Off to one side, almost in the curb, lay the woman's purse.

"Was this woman sexually assaulted?" asked Burnside.

"Doesn't appear to be," said the tech, but only after glancing at McPherson.

"How long did it take, the attack, I mean?" Burnside was using her flashlight to follow the yellow triangles down the cobblestones. "Someone had to have seen this . . . this butchery."

"Less than a minute."

"Less than a minute? Sweet Mother of God . . ."

One of the patrolmen walked over to see what could be seen under the recently lit halogens. As usual, anyone working in law enforcement had an unnatural interest in the dead. The patrolman was sent away.

"Any blood spatter on the husband?" asked the man in the white suit.

Everyone stared at the coroner. They'd forgotten he was even there.

"Just asking."

Burnside understood his concern. A monster was loose in the historical district and it was their job to catch him. James Stuart seemed to believe this Chase girl could help. Well, they'd need all the help they could get. Typically, monsters like this were tripped up by some inconsequential act, like the Son of Sam's parking ticket. But the CPD couldn't wait. You wait in Charleston and the tourists go elsewhere. But, on the plus side, if you caught the guy, it added to the folklore of the city.

Waring added, "Blood across the left arm of the husband's jacket would be consistent with the husband's back being turned during the attack, or already being facedown when his wife was attacked."

Burnside scanned the cobblestones, left and right, up and down, her frustration growing. "Then where's the blood? I see only droplets here and there."

"My guess is that it was soaked up by her clothing," said the red-headed tech. "We should find more soaked into the body, into the tissue, once we get her on the table."

Burnside looked from the dead woman to the growing number of the media held back by the police line. Television would want something for the eleven o'clock news, and that was only minutes away.

"Anyone see or hear anything?" asked Burnside, looking around the tight circle of personnel. "Any noise of any kind? Odd lights? Any witnesses of any sort? City employees on the job? Other strollers? Anyone involved in illegal activities? No drunks? I'm having a hard time believing no one saw or heard anything."

"Chief," said Abel Waring, "besides a couple of guys doing their thing in the bushes and a few couples with stars in their eyes, we got nothing."

"It's chilly," said Sam Gadsden, speaking for the first time.

"I've got the uniforms checking the area," said McPherson, looking from one antebellum home to another. "I can have the colonel take another run at them tomorrow. After all, they're his people."

"Then do it," said Burnside, returning the flashlight to McPherson. "And before that, have everyone in my office tomorrow morning at nine o'clock sharp."

"Don't you mean eight?"

"Nine o'clock, Mac." Burnside noticed the public information officer coming under the yellow tape. "Before that, you and I will most certainly be meeting with the mayor."

CHAPTER SIX

Someone was knocking at our front door.

I stopped unbuttoning my blouse.

Chad rose up in our bed. "What? Who's that?"

It was just after midnight. I was undressing in the dark so as not to wake Chad. And drinking a glass of wine to celebrate a successful surveillance I'd just finished across the river.

Still, there was that knock at the door.

I picked up one of my weapons and stuck it in my waistband. "Go back to sleep. I'll see who it is."

Chad and I owned one of the ramshackle buildings near the College of Charleston. With his shipbuilding skills in high demand, and my need to commute to Columbia daily, the two of us generally crashed early.

Chad sat up, sheet tangled around him, blond hair in his face. The boy slept hard, and I envied him.

He glanced at the clock. "You just coming in?"

"From Mount Pleasant."

"Susan, you're going to get sick pulling all these hours. There's a bug going around." And he turned over and immediately went back to sleep.

I rebuttoned my blouse, hefted my weapon, and padded barefoot down the hall. Crossing the living room, I released the safety, then stood to the side of the door and rapped on it.

"Hey! What you want?" I did not stand in front of the door, nor did I use the peephole.

"Susan, you in there?"

Now I looked through the peephole. Despite the late hour, James Stuart looked sharp and imposing, wearing another one of his fabulous suits and looking completely out of place among the dead plants and old bicycles hanging from our porch ceiling.

My legs weakened, and I faltered, not wanting to believe what his presence meant. I reached out, leaned into the jamb, and steadied myself, bowing my head and trying to catch my breath. There was only one Mary Ann Nichols in Charleston County, and I'd sat on the steps leading to her upstairs apartment until well after midnight.

But here was James Stuart.

I finally regained control of my breathing, straightened up, and then, holding the weapon down beside my leg, flicked on a porch light, then a living room light, and opened the door.

Stuart saw the weapon but said, "Your blouse is misbuttoned."

I glanced down. The former military officer was correct, so I fitted the safety on my weapon, stuck it in the waistband my jeans again, and stepped back, allowing him to enter the living room.

"Am I interrupting something?" he asked.

"At this hour of the night I would hope so, but no such luck."

"So what are you doing in Charleston?"

"I live here." By the look on his face, I could tell this did not compute. "I come home each night to keep the home fires burning." Turning away, I re-buttoned my blouse.

When I faced him again, Stuart was checking out the beat-up furniture, the worn couch, and the area rug that didn't cover much area. Well, I've never been much of a homemaker.

"Jackie said you lived here, but I didn't believe her."

"What do you mean? Are you and Jackie hooking up?"

"No, no, she told me at the crime scene. You need to come with me. There's been another murder."

I gritted my teeth. "Mary Ann Nichols."

"Er . . . right."

"Was there a fire in the harbor?"

"I didn't hear anything about a fire."

"Trust me, if Mary Ann Nichols is dead, there was a fire in the harbor."

"Anyway, I've worked it so you can put forth your case to the chief. She's at my place."

"Burnside is at your house?" Stuart lived on South Battery with his grandmother and she was really old school.

When I made no move to leave, he asked, "Well, are you coming or not?"

"Of course," I said, shaking off my surprise. "I wouldn't miss this for the world."

CHAPTER SEVEN

On the way over to his place, Stuart took calls from both the police department and the county sheriff's office. No one wearing bloody clothing or packing bloody clothing had been stopped by either department. And the city remained shut down.

He flipped closed his cell phone. "This means the killer is still in Charleston."

"Of course," I said, my voice flat. "Why would he leave? He's not finished."

Stuart glanced at me while negotiating the narrow streets, made even narrower by parallel-parked cars. After a few more turns, he approached his home on South Battery, where, with the touch of a remote, he opened a low gate and steered the Mustang into the courtyard. The house, one of the finest examples of Georgian architecture in the city, and built before the Revolutionary War, dominated the street with its four stories and matching stone stairs to a second-story front door.

I stepped out before Stuart could come around and open the door for me. The front of the house remained in shadows, and I thought I saw Abel Waring at the top of the matching stone staircases before we walked around to the rear. There, Sam Gadsden acknowledged us with a nod, and we climbed the rear stairs and entered the house.

More than two hundred years ago, the city's rich and powerful had filled in Oyster Point, so named for the shells found there, and built a wooden wall, later replaced by one of stone, to protect their homes from the occasional hurricane. In the cool of the evening, families of the elite, which would certainly include Stuart's ancestors, strolled along that promenade, the Ashley River on one side, the Cooper on the other, and it didn't take long, as the money and influence piled up, for those strolling along this rock promenade to come to believe that Charleston was the center of the universe.

Stuart opened the door to a mud room, and I scrambled inside and held open the next door for him. The issue of equality-in-opening-doors settled, I allowed him to lead me through the house.

I got a quick look at a huge kitchen with a large stove, cooking utensils hanging from racks, and a sleepy-looking black woman standing at the stove, hair covered by a scarf. We passed through the usual hallway with its hardwood floor, old furniture, and generations of Stuarts staring down at us from the walls. A worn runner ran the length of the hall.

I was ushered into a room where three people sat at the far end of a cherrywood table that could easily seat twenty. Heavy curtains shut out the light and the sounds of the Battery, and despite the hour, Stuart's grandmother fluttered around, asking if anyone wanted coffee or tea. Everyone declined. They were drinking from Styrofoam cups brought over from the crime scene.

An attractive black woman, the chief of police, whom I knew only by reputation—a real hard-ass—wore a dark suit and sat at the far end of the table flanked by two men. Burnside told Mrs. Stuart not to make any fuss, that they only needed her dining room for a few more minutes. McPherson, the captain of detectives, a bullet-headed man who thought all women, cops or otherwise, were incompetent, sat at Burnside's right. At her left was a guy with hunched shoulders, dark hair over the collar of his turtleneck, and nicotine-stained fingers drumming on the cherrywood tabletop. Drumming on the tabletop, that is, until Stuart tossed him a silver ashtray, causing his grandmother to gasp.

The nervous man fielded the ashtray, nodded his thanks, and lit up. Jerry Tobias was another person I knew only by reputation. If your candidate was found in the wrong bedroom or caught doing a bit of blow, or your candidate's wife or children were found in the wrong bedroom or doing a bit of blow, Tobias was the guy you called. What looked like legal pads and pens lay in front of Burnside and McPherson, but in front of Jerry Tobias sat an opened laptop. Tobias's face appeared strained, possibly simply from driving down from the state capital. Behind me, Stuart slid closed the pocket doors between the dining room and a parlor.

Forcing a smile, Stuart's grandmother asked, "Would the young lady like a hot chocolate?"

"A scotch," I said, "Neat." I was in an irritable mood, and angry enough to take it out on anyone's grandma. I'd failed to protect Mary Ann Nichols. Or at least one of them.

"Oh, no, young lady," said Mrs. Stuart, "you're much too young to be drinking."

"You're on duty, Chase," broke in the black woman from the other end of the table, "so there'll be no drinking."

"Actually, Chase," said McPherson, scowling in my direction, "I'm all for taking you to the Greenberg Center and interrogating you there."

As Stuart ushered his grandmother out of the room, I smiled at the captain of detectives. "You make it sound as though I could leave this place in handcuffs."

"Absolutely. Nothing would please me more."

Looking around at the assembled personage, I said, "You'll need more people."

Tobias chuckled. "Very ballsy, Ms. Chase."

McPherson pushed back his chair, but Burnside checked him with a hand on his arm. "Ms. Chase, are you aware of where we've been?"

"The crime scene where Mary Ann Nichols was killed." I searched the faces at the far end of the table. "Where was she from? Out of town?"

Foreheads wrinkled at the question, or the fact that I knew more than they had suspected.

I gripped my end of the table and leaned into it. "I asked where she was from." I could hear my voice rising.

"Columbus," offered Stuart. He pulled out a chair for me, and I didn't object. "Ohio."

I collapsed into the chair, shoulders slumped, staring

at my lap. This hurt. It really did.

"How did you know her name?" asked McPherson.

I continued to stare into my lap. "He's copying Jack the Ripper, isn't he?"

"What?" asked more than one of them.

I raised my head. "Was there a fire at the harbor?"

Those at the far end of the table looked at each other.

"How do you know all this?" demanded McPherson.

From his seat next to me, Stuart gestured at the other end of the table. "Tell them what you know, Susan."

"Tell them what?" I snapped. "It's in all the books."

"What books?" asked the three at the other end.

"Books about Jack the Ripper."

They just stared at me.

Mrs. Stuart returned with a cup of hot chocolate and placed it in front of me. I thanked her but didn't speak again until the elderly woman had left the room.

"Get on with it, Chase," said McPherson, an edge of impatience coming in his voice. "We have a murder investigation to conduct."

"You know, Mac," said Jerry Tobias, leaning forward so he could make eye contact with the captain of detectives, "we're here to gather information, to learn what Ms. Chase knows."

McPherson glared across Burnside at Tobias. "I don't even know why *you're* here."

"Now, boys," said Burnside.

While waiting for the testosterone level to fall, I stared into my lap and beat myself up again over the death of Mary Ann Nichols. From Columbus, Ohio. How did the bastard even know she'd be in town?

"Susan?" asked Stuart from beside me.

Without looking up, I began, "On April third of 1888, Emma Smith—"

"Did you say 1888?" interrupted McPherson.

"Mac," said Stuart, "why don't you let Susan lay it out for us. Then we can make a judgment on the merits of her information."

"I don't see what 1888 has to . . ." McPherson looked hard at me again. "Is this Charleston you're talking about?"

"Not yet," I said from under my eyebrows.

"Mac," said Burnside, patting her subordinate's arm, "let Chase explain what she's learned from her books so we can move onto more serious matters."

More serious matters? Three women murdered—then I realized Burnside was handling him as most women do their men, in business or otherwise.

McPherson leaned back in his chair. "I'm all for that."

"Ms. Chase," said the chief, a tight line that could be mistaken for a smile crossing her face, "please continue. You won't be interrupted again."

Yeah, right.

Still, in response to her attention, I sat up and said, "On the third of April, 1888, in London, England, Emma Smith was attacked by three street thugs who robbed and beat her, ripping off an ear in the process, and jammed a blunt instrument up her vagina, causing a rupture of the peritoneum and other internal organs. These days such an attack would be called an object rape. The peritoneum is a smooth transparent serous membrane lining the cavity of the abdomen. It folds inward over the abdominal and pelvic viscera. Both men and women have this membrane."

McPherson appeared puzzled, Burnside troubled, and Jerry Tobias began punching keys on his laptop. Charleston has a WiFi network for those who take an excessive interest in their computers while on vacation.

"Since Emma Smith failed to get the proper medical attention, she later died from peritonitis in a London hospital."

"And this was done by street thugs?" asked Burnside. "Not Jack the Ripper?"

"Gangbangers, if you like, but because Whitechapel District was all white in those days, the term doesn't really apply."

"Then," said Burnside, tapping her #2 pencil on her pad, "I want to make sure I'm getting this straight: Emma Smith was not killed by Jack the Ripper."

"Correct."

She made a note and at the same time asked, "And this relates how to our two murders in Charleston?"

"Three murders. The death of Emma Smith in 1888 London is relevant to the deaths of both Martha Turner and Mary Ann Nichols because a woman by the name of Emma Smith was killed in Charleston on April third of this year, and by the same method as in Whitechapel, 1888. With a piece of wood shoved inside her."

Jerry Tobias let out a smoke-filled breath. "She's right."

Everyone looked at him.

"Charleston and Whitechapel District have these murders in common. The death of Emma Smith was part of a police report filed on April third of this year. Someone notified the CPD that there was a person restrained under a house who had a piece of wood jammed inside her." Tobias gave the street address where the body was found, followed by the time of day. "The coroner verified that Emma Smith, the Emma Smith of Charleston, that is, died April third of this year."

McPherson leaned forward to see around Burnside. "You have access to police files on that computer of yours?"

"Well," said Tobias, looking a bit chagrined, "I wouldn't be much help if I didn't."

"But you're a civilian."

"Whitechapel District?" asked Burnside.

Tobias punched more keys. "I'm sending a file to your computer, a whole file about Jack the Ripper. It'll be at your office and your home."

That did not please the chief. "I don't want that crap in my house. I still have a teenager living at home. Send it to the office."

Tobias nodded, and a few strokes later, he took his cigarette from between his lips and said, "Done."

"Whitechapel District?" asked the chief again, looking at me.

"The stomping grounds for the original Jack the Ripper."

"Right," said Tobias, "but there's a problem with the second victim." Looking over his laptop, he said, "Ms. Chase, the second victim's name—"

"Wait a minute," said McPherson, pulling his chair forward, "just wait a damn minute. First victim, second victim. Dammit, use names, locales, and dates. And if you and Tobias insist on having a coded conversation, I have better things to do."

"Use the back door when you leave," said Stuart. "There was no media out there when Susan and I arrived."

It took Burnside to bring everyone together. "I think Mac's idea is an excellent one. Otherwise, we'll spend the rest of the evening asking if we're talking about Whitechapel or Charleston."

"Thank you," said McPherson, jerking his head into a nod, "but I want it on the record that I think all this Jack the Ripper nonsense is nothing but a bunch of hooey."

"So noted," said his boss without making a notation on her pad. "But I have to meet with the mayor in a few hours and this may be the only lead we have."

"You'd tell the mayor we've put out an APB for Jack the Ripper? With what description? Top hat and cape?"

Again Burnside ignored him and looked down the table. "Ms. Chase, would you explain, and succinctly, please, what the three murders in today's Charleston have to do with Jack the Ripper who operated in 1888 London"—she glanced at her pad—"in this Whitechapel District."

"The guy you're looking for is copycatting Jack the Ripper, beginning with the death of Emma Smith, who, back in 1888, was considered one of the Whitechapel murders but not someone actually killed by the Ripper. So, it follows that the modern-day Jack will kill four more women unless he's stopped, just as four more women were murdered in Whitechapel."

McPherson shook his bullet head but said nothing.

"Look," I said, leaning on the table, "if you can have all kinds of copycats reenacting previous kills of other serial killers, why is it so hard to believe someone wouldn't get around to copying the original serial killer? The only thing slowing him down would be how difficult it would be to plan and execute all the necessary murders. The later ones get very tricky, especially if law enforcement knows what you're up to."

Burnside only stared at me.

I ticked off the victims on my fingers. "April third, Emma Smith; August seventh, Martha Tabram—"

Stuart asked, "Martha Tabram?"

Tobias explained. "Martha Tabram was the first confirmed kill by Jack the Ripper. After her husband threw her out for excessive drinking, Martha went to live with Henry Turner for another twelve years before she was murdered by Jack the Ripper."

I nodded. "That's why the death of the first victim, and here I'm speaking of the Charleston victims—"

"Thank you," growled McPherson.

"That's how the death of Emma Smith from peritonitis, and found under a house in Charleston, is linked with the second victim, Martha Turner in Ansonborough, and the victim tonight, Mary Ann Nichols. And you had to have a fire at the harbor. A fire broke out on the London docks the same night Mary Ann Nichols was murdered in Whitechapel."

Burnside nodded slowly. "The watch commander said something about a fire when he called."

McPherson sat up. The captain of detectives appeared to finally be taking an interest. Golly, gee. I'm sure the families of the victims will be pleased to hear that.

Burnside asked Tobias, "So who's next?"

The political fixer put down his cigarette. "Ann Chapman," he said, letting out a smoke-filled breath.

"Ann Chapman?" asked McPherson.

"The next woman killed by Jack the Ripper."

Burnside looked from one man to the other. "It can't be this easy, can it?"

"Easy?" asked Stuart from where he sat next to me.

"All we have to do is surveil every Ann Chapman in Charleston County, even those flying in or registering at one of the hotels, and wait for our killer to show up." Burnside had another question for Tobias. "What's the date of the next attack?"

"September eighth."

"Eight days from now." Burnside studied her pad, then raised her head. "Ms. Chase, how did you make the connection between Martha Turner and Jack the Ripper? From what you've told us"—she tapped the yellow pad with her pencil—"there's nothing here to justify such a leap. It's not even the correct name."

"I work cold cases for SLED, and with the new computers you can ask questions such as: What murder victims suffered thirty-nine stab wounds? One of the cases that showed up was Martha Tabram, or Turner, in Whitechapel District, which linked to Emma Smith, who died from peritonitis. That's when the computer really pays for itself by connecting the death of Emma Smith of Charleston County, who died April this year, with the death in April 1888. From there, you follow the thread to Tabram, or Martha Turner, with the thirty-nine stab wounds, and on to Mary Ann Nichols, which will appear tomorrow morning on my screen when I go into work."

"And the fire at the harbor?" asked Burnside.

"That's something I picked up from reading details of the murders in the case reports and newspapers of the day." I shrugged. "Something I assumed the CPD was doing."

Stuart snorted and leaned forward, arms resting on his knees.

"Colonel," said the chief, looking down the table, "if you have anything to add . . ."

Stuart merely shook his head and stared at the floor. On the way over, Stuart had told me that after the murder of Martha Turner, he'd run my theory of a copycat Jack the Ripper by the captain of detectives and had been laughed out of his office. But to give McPherson his due, Stuart was also the one who touted the use of bees and wasps to detect bombs and drugs coming through the port of Charleston.

I know, I know. Don't ask.

While the chief had been quizzing me, Tobias was extracting more data from the web. Finished, he said, "All the victims of the original Jack the Ripper were white."

Everyone looked at him.

"What I'm saying is there are three Ann Chapmans listed in the Charleston DMV records, voter registration, or city directory, and two of them are Caucasian. Either one could be the Ripper's target September eighth."

"Because serial killers don't kill outside their race," said Stuart, straightening up in his chair.

"Actually," I said, "serial killers don't kill outside their comfort zone."

"So the next victim should be white," said Tobias, running with the idea. "That is, for the modern Jack the Ripper to continue his game."

"Game?" asked the chief, a look of severity appearing on her face. "A game is something my boys play on their computers."

Tobias let out a smoke-filled breath and snubbed out his cigarette. "Eugenia, I can tell it's been a long time since you've been in a bookstore. There are shelves of role-playing books and paraphernalia in any bookstore these days." The political fixer inclined his head in the direction of my end of the table. "And if what Chase says is true, a new role-playing game has been created right here on the streets of Charleston."

"What about the media?" asked Stuart. "Something like this is going to be everywhere, even on the web. Probably already is."

And that started a discussion about what a pain in the ass the media could be. McPherson wanted to shut down everything, but Tobias was all for opening it up and letting the public assist in finding the killer.

The political fixer added, "You'd be surprised how many role players there are out there."

"You can't tell everyone," groused McPherson. "You'd have all kind of nuts running around shooting their neighbors."

"There *are* all kinds of nuts running around shooting their neighbors," said the chief. "This is, after all, Charleston."

"Oh," I said, smiling from my end of the table, "it's

going to get much worse if you don't give this guy a name, and you can't call him the Ripper. You don't want people in Charleston connecting our murders with the ones in Whitechapel."

"I thought Jack the Ripper only killed prostitutes," said McPherson.

"Correct, but the object of the game—sorry, Chief, but Tobias is right. The object of *this* game is to recreate the murders from Whitechapel District 1888 with a simplicity any gamer can grasp. Focus on the big picture, such as the victims and dates of death, then the thirty-nine stab wounds, a case of peritonitis, and harbor fire become the authenticators."

This was way too much for those at the far end of the table. They were silent as I babbled on.

"Perhaps, for the media's sake, you could call him The Slasher?" I nodded at my own brilliance. "Yeah, that would work: The Slasher."

"No one's going to speak to the media, Ms. Chase," said the chief, "and that includes you."

But I was on a roll. "And I won't even charge you a trademark fee."

"That will be all, Ms. Chase." Burnside's smile was flinty now. "We certainly want to thank you for bringing this matter to our attention."

I blinked. "Pardon?"

"Captain McPherson will be in touch with SLED if we need any further assistance."

The bullet-headed man smiled down the table at me.

"Eugenia—" started Tobias.

"Later, Jerry."

I stood up and looked down at Stuart, who remained seated.

He pushed back his chair. "I'll give you a lift home."

Burnside nixed this idea. "Mac, didn't you post Sam Gadsden outside?"

"Yes, I did," said McPherson, again smiling at me. "Detective Gadsden will see you home, Miss Chase. And remember, none of this is to leave this room."

Though I was ticked off at being excluded from further involvement in the case, it turned out that it really didn't matter. A few days later, the Ripper was dead and I ended up working in a whorehouse.

THE WEEK PRIOR TO SEPTEMBER 8TH

Just as the chief of police and her captain of detectives had learned some astonishing information pertaining to the recent murders in Charleston, so had a variety of men living in different cities and different time zones. These men peered at their computer screens and could hardly believe what they saw.

The relevant highlights:

April 8: Emma Elizabeth Smith, of Charleston, South Carolina, dead from vaginal trauma and peritonitis resulting from lack of medical treatment.

August 7: Martha Turner, also of Charleston, dead of multiple stab wounds and found in a pool of her own blood in the entryway to her home. Someone in a chat room, who bragged that they had seen the crime scene photos, said "Thirty-nine stab wounds were found on Turner's body," and the web crawlers (bots) traced this message to a server located along the coast of South Carolina.

Finally, August 31: Mary Ann Nichols, again in

Charleston, but a resident of Columbus, Ohio, dead from multiple stab wounds that practically severed her head from her body.

And the coup de grace, as far as these men were concerned: The same night Mary Ann Nichols died, a fire had broken out in Charleston harbor.

In San Jose, California, Luke Rogers peed in his pants at what he saw on his computer screen. He simply could not move. He was that excited, and he sat there until the dampness finally got to him. Then he reached over, pulled a dirty T-shirt off a stack of CDs, scattering CDs to the floor, and stuffed the tee under him.

Luke didn't hear the falling cases. He'd been listening to Judas Priest and had the volume cranked—in his headset, that is. Still, he could not believe what he was seeing. Luke really wanted to get up because the pee had begun dripping to the floor, but he could not stop staring at the screen. Luke wet his lips and culled through the links provided to *The Post and Courier.*

Someone had finally done it! Someone had finally told the thrill killers to put up or shut up! And how did the Charleston Ripper know the other killers would receive his invitation?

Because thrill killers had their search engines constantly combing the web for their own kind; Goths were so yesterday. Of course, none of them actually knew each other, but they met in chats where you learned who could out bullshit who.

But, there had always been this one guy, Jack, who would pop in once a month to let everyone know that he'd made another kill, and provide newspaper links as evidence. Sometimes even police reports. Lately, there'd been nothing because Jack had said he was going to be busy setting up the ultimate role-playing game. Just keep your computers warm, boys, Jack had told them, and your bots active. Soon the fun would begin.

And now the game had begun, and Luke so desperately wanted to play along. But Luke was only fourteen, still lived with his parents, and occasionally peed in his pants at what he found on the Internet.

In Boulder, Colorado, John Perry sat behind a dumpster at a Starbucks and hooked his stolen laptop into the store's WiFi. If anyone from Starbucks saw him back here, they'd run him off. The people at Starbucks knew guys like John Perry stole info off their customers' computers while their owners were inside enjoying a latte. And it was well known among such thieves that those who had recently connected to the web did not usually turn on their computers again until several hours later. So John downloaded the information he needed, waited for someone to sign off, and then checked the status of what was being hailed as the greatest role-playing game ever.

And there it was! Someone had finally done it. Someone had set up the game to end all games, and if John had the nerve, he'd soon be on his way to Charleston.

John shook his head in wonder. It was like having your own private gang, similar to the one he belonged to in Boulder. Except this gang connected with computers, and John would've been into computers big time if he'd only had a home where he could plug and play. Now all he had to do was screw up the courage to leave his old gang, the only family he'd known since age twelve, and join this new gang operating on a much larger playing field.

Dean Kline read the same information, and also realized that someone was inviting him to Charleston. So he went upstairs, picked up a bag packed for just such occasions, and before shutting down his computer, sent a final e-mail.

Dean worked at home in the healthcare industry, and he worked efficiently and politely, answering each customer's query, though there were not enough hours in the day. This final e-mail informed the home office that he would be out of town for a few days. His mother, in a retirement home, had tripped and fallen. Luckily, nothing more than a bone in her left foot had been broken, but she would not be ambulatory for a couple of weeks, and everyone knows how people treat the elderly in retirement centers. Knowing how devoted Dean was to his mom, the people who read the e-mail would be surprised to learn that Dean's mother had died more than ten years ago, and with a little help from her son.

Two women read this e-mail: Dean's immediate superior, a woman who said there couldn't be many young men like Dean Kline in the world, and her secretary, who said, "Sure there are. They're called fairies."

Dean's supervisor sighed. Everyone would be old one day, and you simply hoped someone as sweet as Dean Kline would be there for you.

Both women were wrong. Dean Kline was no fairy, nor was he sweet. Dean Kline was a monster, and, after sending this final e-mail, he was off to Charleston to join the hunt.

Then there was Jones—not his real name—who lived off the land and avoided as much human contact, well, as humanly possible. Jones was a hunter who trapped and killed animals, and the occasional Boy Scout who intruded into his territory. When he wanted a woman, he snatched one from the rest areas and disappeared with her into the Everglades.

Jones had once lived on the street, like so many other runaways, but, intrigued that no member of law enforcement ever hassled you in the Everglades—just some fish and wildlife people checking licenses and limits—Jones hitched a ride to the 'glades and never looked back. It was a tough transition, changing from the streets of Miami to the waterways of the Everglades, but, to tell the truth, Jones had become too old to be a street kid. When you were over eighteen and they sent you away, you did hard time.

Jones paid $4.95 a month to be able to "read" his e-mail over the phone when he came out of the 'glades for supplies. Jones had little interest in computers, but a guy he'd met in a biker bar introduced him to the Undernet, and if there was a more perverse group of people, Jones had never heard of them: queers, porn freaks, and more than one child molester. Jones had met fourteen of the sons of bitches, under one ruse or another, and killed them all. Just a little payback for the way he'd been raised.

From a pay phone at a marina, Jones was given the name of a new victim, Ann Chapman, and the challenge to be the first to complete a series of tasks, or kills, that would qualify him for the hundred thousand dollar grand prize being held in a bank in the Caymans. And you were welcome to call and check out the offer. A toll-free number had been set up for just that.

Jones hung up the phone, left his canoe—with a hundred grand he could always buy another canoe— and hiked to the main road, where he caught a ride into Miami. There, Jones cleaned up in a storage unit he kept in the city, and since the building was temperature controlled and an excellent place to store trophies, for luck, Jones tapped each jar containing a human head; then he hiked over to I-95 and began hitching his way up the East Coast.

CHAPTER EIGHT

Trying to head off the fourth attack, which would give me no small degree of satisfaction, I redoubled my efforts on the streets, trying to get a line on anyone with a sadistic streak. I talked with pimps, whores, dealers, users, bikers, gangbangers, thieves, bartenders, ropers, parking lot attendants, and street kids—which has lately become a hot topic at PTAs or PTOs. And I tell those parents never, ever, let your children hang with street kids because those kids are not children, though they almost always get a pass from the local cops.

And why is that?

Because your average American doesn't feel threatened by some kid acting out roles from Nintendo.

How could they? Their own children play the same games on their home computers.

But for street kids, role-playing is a way of life, and their rage at being left out of the mainstream is fueled by crack cocaine and the energy of being a young male, making it easier for them to bash gays, straights, or anyone buying or selling drugs.

You'd be surprised at the number of suburbanites who are using, and sometimes my message, meant for their kids, reaches their mom and dad.

While working the street, more than one guy put a move on me. The lucky ones had friends to warn them off. A perfect example would be when I entered a biker bar in North Charleston, called North Chuck by the locals, and a guy wanted to "do" me.

When I walked in, all conversation ceased and a variety of drugs and drug paraphernalia hit the floor. Not to mention a path cleared all the way to the bar. Everyone took their beers and scooted down a few feet, opening a space for little l'il ol' me.

After the bartender told me what was going down in his small corner of paradise, he warned off a guy who had sidled up to me.

"Stay away from her," snarled the bartender.

"And why is that?" The biker wore lots of leather, and his skin was all muscle and tattoos.

"Because Chase would just as soon shoot you as to take you in. SLED doesn't let her out of her cage unless something important is coming down."

The biker gave me another once-over. "You're kidding me." That wasn't what he really said, but the city fathers try to keep Charleston G-rated because of the tourist trade. "She's just a kid."

"Hey, take your best shot," said the bartender, returning to his glasses, "but whichever way it turns out, you're going to be gone an awfully long time, either out of state or up at Lieber."

The biker recognized the reference to one of the two hard-core prisons in South Carolina, but still, he studied me. The patrons held their breath.

"Just how old are you, girlie?" he asked.

I shook my head and smiled. "A lady never tells her age."

He returned my smile in spades. "It wasn't a lady I was looking to spend the night with."

"And I doubt you ever will."

I walked out of the bar to the catcalls and whistles of the patrons.

Chad complained I wasn't getting enough sleep and said I'd come down with something. Actually, I'd been more concerned about falling asleep driving back and forth to Columbia to put in a day's work on the cold case squad. But it was during these hours on the streets that I learned the escort services were being terrorized by a mean-spirited bastard who liked to play rough with his dates.

The night I caught up with the bastard, I lay snoozing on a chaise lounge in a book-lined study of one of the homes overlooking Harleston Green, the home of the first golf course in Charleston, and for that matter, the rest of the country. The phone rang constantly and made me wonder whether I was in the right line of business or not.

I lifted the book from my face, *The Yemassee*, William Gilmore Simms' most popular historical romance, and looked across the room. The woman at the desk, who'd gotten herself worked up at every call, took a drag off her cigarette and stared at the phone, letting it ring.

"Answer it, Dixie," I said, rising up on my elbows.

She clunked her glass to the desk and scotch slopped over the sides. In her late fifties, Dixie Bishop had peroxide blond hair, a rich, deep tan, and spoke with a raspy voice, the victim of one too many cigarettes or other unimaginable horrors.

"I can't," she said, staring at the phone. With each call the tension had been growing, and I'd been here several nights. Dixie was coordinating this effort.

I sat up, closing the book with a thump. "Dixie, answer the damn phone!"

"I'm—I'm scared. You saw what he did to Kristy."

"Hey," I said, swinging my feet off the chaise lounge, "you're not the one going to meet this guy. Now pick up the damned phone, and don't forget to put it on speaker."

Dixie swallowed, cleared her throat, and picked up. "Hello." Belatedly, she punched the button so I could hear what the other madam said on the other end.

". . . there?" came a shrill voice. "I'm not sending one of my girls out unless Susan promises to meet her in the lobby." And she gave us the name of the hotel.

"Sure this is the guy?" I asked from across the room. "We've had lots of dry runs."

"You bet your bippy," said the woman on the speaker, "and he's changed hotels again."

"Okay." I got to my feet, stretched, and rolled my shoulders.

Dixie told the caller, "She'll be there."

"Good," said the voice. "Denise is supposed to meet him in thirty minutes. But she won't be going upstairs alone."

"Smart girl," I said, crossing the book-lined study.

"I can't believe it," continued the voice from the speaker. "The bastard actually asked if she 'liked a little rough stuff.'"

Glancing over my shoulder, I saw Dixie shiver, probably remembering how Kristy looked in the hospital. Pardon the expression, but Dixie had paid through the nose to make sure Kristy's parents didn't learn the extent of their daughter's injuries.

"She'll be there." Dixie's deep rasp described what I wore.

"You know," said the woman over the speaker, "we've got to do something about Susan's look."

"Tell me about it," said Dixie, touching the button and breaking the connection.

I rolled my eyes as I slid *The Yemassee* back into its slot. Brushing dust off my hands, I asked, "Ever read any of these, Dixie?"

"Not a chance, darling. Bought them by the pound."

Dixie puffed away and watched me strap my equipment around my waist, mostly to the rear of my hips. I may have to dress like a business woman, but I don't have to look like a cop.

"We appreciate what you're doing, Susan."

"Yeah, well, if my boss ever learns about this . . ."

"Well, he won't hear about it from us."

Settling my pistols behind my back, I looked at her from under my eyebrows. "Word on the street is that Susan Chase has become a working girl."

Dixie shook her head. "Not in those clothes, honey."

Dixie was referring to the dark pants, white blouse,

and dark jacket. For some reason, I never got style points for my two pistols. I shrugged into my jacket and headed for the door.

"You know, Susan, they have some nice flats out this fall. I saw them in a window over on King Street."

At the door I faced her. "I really doubt I could afford them."

She shrugged. "Well, you always know where you can make a little extra money if you ever need to."

"Yeah, and probably why those working girl stories will never die."

CHAPTER NINE

I met the girl in the lobby of a hotel that, despite being fought tooth and nail by the local preservationists, had become one of the anchors of the historical district and led to the rise of modern-day Charleston. Two bellboys stood at the glass-door entrances of the portico, and at the registration desk, a clerk checked in a family of late arrivals, small children clutching blankets and leaning into Mommy. There were few guests in the lobby, and those that were stared blankly at the chandelier or matching curving staircases leading to the mezzanine level.

Sitting in an upholstered chair with her back to Market Street was a pretty brunette, and whatever the girl wore was hidden by a long black coat; buttoned up tight, no fabric or cleavage showing. A bit much for summer Charleston; still, a pretty enough face: brown hair in curls, narrow face, and an elegant curve to her neck.

Stopping in front of her chair, I said, "I'm Susan.

Tell me, what's your name?"

"Denise," said the girl, standing.

"No, no, your real name."

"Emily."

I took her arm and walked her over to the elevators, and we got to stepping. Mary Kate Belle sat in the Calhoun Club, chatting up some guy. The club has a low wall between it and the lobby, and before we disappeared behind the circular staircases, Mary Kate was on her feet and heading in our direction.

"What's the room number?" I asked.

She told me, but stammered getting it out.

I punched the button more than once, resisted looking over my shoulder, and tried to focus on the job at hand. "Emily, this isn't going to work if you don't relax. I need access to the room, and as you can see, I'm not dressed for the occasion."

Thankfully, the girl didn't comment on my attire. "I—I don't know if I want this to work. I had to take something."

The bell rang and a set of doors opened. Behind us. I wheeled Emily around and steered her onboard. A voice called my name as I punched the Door Close button. That was followed by punching the button for the mezzanine floor, then three more floors above it.

"What'd you take?" I asked.

"I took a 'lude," said the girl.

Thankfully, the doors finally closed and the elevator began to rise from the lobby.

"How long ago?"

She told me, her chin jutting out.

"No sweat. It'll kick in before we get upstairs."

"I—I just don't want to get hit."

"There's nothing to worry about. I'll be right outside."

"And I'll be in the room." She shook off my hand. "Why do you need me? You're a cop, aren't you?"

"Yes." The elevator doors opened on the mezzanine. "Now walk with me."

I took her arm and we walked to the fire door at the far end of the wide hallway. Flanking us were the conference rooms and ballrooms.

When I pushed through the fire door and into the stairwell, Emily asked, "Why aren't we taking the elevator?"

"What was the room number again?" I asked, tugging her up the first flight.

She repeated the number, and climbing the stairs, she asked, "Why don't you just bust him?"

"On what grounds?"

"For beating up working girls." The echo of her footsteps on the stairs told me that she was right behind me.

"I doubt either you or your coworkers would get much sympathy from the courts."

"It could bring our situation into the public eye."

"Sorry, but for that to happen, it would take quite a few dead whores."

She stopped on the third-floor landing. "I don't like that word." When she realized I wasn't going to lecture her about her choice of occupations, she continued up the stairs. "What you're saying is the john has all the rights and we have none."

"Pretty much."

By the fourth floor, she had to catch her breath. "You

know . . . we don't have to sneak around like this. It's not like . . . the hotel minds the service we provide."

I pushed open the door on the fourth floor, glanced down the hallway, and then looked up for the security camera. At the same time, I reached for the telescopic steel baton under my jacket. Turned out I wouldn't need the baton. For some reason the security camera tilted upwards, filming the ceiling, not the hallway. Now that was a nice break.

Emily had caught her breath well enough to ask, "You have women working vice, why don't you use one of them?"

"Emily," I said, my arm across the doorway, "your fear has made you stupid. I don't want to book the guy. I want to teach him a lesson."

She looked past me down the hall. "But you haven't told me how to signal you."

"Don't worry. Five minutes after you go through the door, I'll be in there."

"A lot can happen in five minutes."

"There is one thing . . ."

"Yes?"

"Unbutton your coat. I want you slipping out of your coat as you cross the room. That way he'll be checking you out instead of the hallway."

"Gotcha." She unbuttoned her coat and put both hands under her breasts and lifted them, situating the cut of her red dress to reveal maximum cleavage.

"How's that?" she asked with eyes much older than the college student she was purported to be.

"That should do it. And slide out of your coat whether he offers to take it or not. Make him follow you across the room." I took a thin, flexible, and transparent piece of plastic from inside my jacket. "That way I can wedge the lock open."

She glanced at the colorless piece of plastic. "I can do that."

"And once you're inside, be forward, demanding."

"I always ask for the money upfront."

"Whatever. Just make sure you draw him across the room."

"He'll slap me." A glance down the hallway made her shudder.

"He won't get the chance." Making a last attempt to bolster her resolve, I took my arm off the jamb and pulled her close. "Emily, you were picked for this job. I asked for the toughest gal they had whether you were the john's type or not."

It took a moment for her to process this, and she came to her own conclusion. "This is for Kristy, isn't it?"

"Yes, it is." I released her and started down the hallway.

She followed me, our footsteps soundless on the padded carpet. Still, she lowered her voice when she said, "Kristy and I had some classes together. The rumor is there was some—uh, facial damage."

"Nah," I said, lying through my teeth, "she was just slapped around."

"Well, I guess I can take that."

And we were there.

I stood out of the line of sight, and Emily took a deep breath and knocked on the door. At the same moment, the cell phone on my hip vibrated.

I ignored the phone and remained flattened against the wall. When Emily disappeared inside, I reached over, slipped the shim between the lock and jamb, grabbed the knob, and pulled the door firmly shut.

"Hey, baby," I heard the guy say. "Let me take your . . ."

Down the hall, a young couple came out of a room and headed for the elevator. Because I was a gal, they didn't give me a second glance. Turning away from the room, I slid the phone off my hip and checked the readout: Mary Kate Jane Belle.

When I returned her call, she asked, "Susan, was that you who went up in the elevator with that prostitute?"

"What prostitute?" I asked, whispering. "Wait a minute." I walked away from the door. "How'd you know where I am?"

"I was in the Calhoun Club downstairs. Where are you now?"

"What are you doing here, Mary Kate?"

"I asked you first. Got anything new on the Slasher?"

"The Slasher?"

"Yeah. The guy who killed the two women."

I couldn't help but smile, and as I turned around and headed toward the john's room, a guy from room service, several doors down, returned my smile, startling me. He carried a tray with a bottle of champagne and two glasses, and he'd had trouble finding a hotel jacket small enough to fit him.

I hustled back to the john's door and stood there, shielding the shim from the room-service guy. A puzzled look crossed the small guy's face as he came down the hall, but then he stopped, knocked on a door one room away and announced "room service."

In hushed tones, I asked Mary Kate, "Is that what you guys are calling him—the Slasher?"

"I came up with the name and it kind of stuck. But what are you doing upstairs, Susan?"

"Using the restroom on the mezzanine floor," I said, but only after turning my back on the room-service guy. "Man, I shouldn't have eaten that last chili dog. Look, Mary Kate, I'm not doing so well up here, but I'll drop by the Calhoun Club on my way out. Just give me a few minutes."

I clicked the phone closed, settled it back on my hip, and returned to the john's door. The room-service guy had disappeared, so, from the other side of my hip, I took the telescopic steel baton, and flicking my wrist, extended the shaft.

Once the rod locked into place, I gripped the plastic shim with my left hand, leaned a shoulder into the door, and pushed my way into the john's room.

CHAPTER TEN

The guy had his back to me and held Emily by one hand. One side of her face was red, but she wasn't crying. Kudos for her. To the left was an open bathroom door, and beyond Emily, a king-sized bed, her coat lying across it. On the dresser by a wallet sat a bottle of good scotch and a single drink poured, along with some male jewelry, chains mostly, and some white powder scattered across a small sheet of plastic.

The john appeared to be well over two hundred pounds, in his forties, and had a blond ponytail over the collar of his aloha shirt. He didn't notice me enter the room or hear the door click shut, but when he raised his hand to strike Emily again, I jabbed him in the back with the metal shaft. I was aiming for the guy's kidney, but he must've seen something in Emily's eyes and started to turn around. I was prepared for that, slid to the left, and still hit my target.

His back arched and he cried out, one hand reaching behind him. I grabbed his wrist, jammed that arm higher—he yelped again—and ran him into the wall next to the bathroom.

"Assume the position!" I placed my forearm against the back of his neck and kicked his feet out and away from the wall.

"What's . . . going on?" With one side of his face jammed into the wall, he couldn't see who hit him, only the dresser and bathroom door.

Emily snatched up her coat, slipped into it, and headed for the door. Along the way she downed the single glass of scotch and riffled the man's wallet.

"Hey," shouted the guy, seeing what the girl was up to. "Put down my wallet."

I jabbed him with the shaft again. He gasped and fell against the wall.

"I said 'assume the position!'"

From the corner of my eye, I, too, saw Emily at the dresser. "Out the door, honey. You're finished for the night."

"But I didn't get a proposition," said the girl, knowing the rules of entrapment and using the explanation as a stall to steal the john's credit cards.

"Leave the plastic, take the cash, and use the stairs. There's someone in the lobby you don't want to run into tonight."

"She's right," said the john, wheezing. "You've got nothing . . . on me . . . I didn't have . . ." He canted his head. "Susan . . . that you?"

It was the movie producer Darryl Diamond.

For a moment I lost my focus, and he was able to leverage himself off the wall. I stumbled back and sat down hard beside the bed. Because Diamond couldn't bring himself to kick a woman while she was down, he bent over and reached for me. When he did, I brought the steel baton up between his legs.

That made him holler, and when he stumbled back, I spread my feet in front of me, set both feet at angles, my arms and shoulders cocked back, and threw the top of my body forward, springing to my feet like a rapper finishing a street dance. By the time I'd regained my balance, Darryl was staggering toward me, one hand holding his crotch, the other reaching for my throat. Before he could touch me, I broke several of his ribs.

He groaned, fell back, and bumped into the dresser. Unable to keep his balance, he stumbled forward again, went to his knees, and while he was down, I stepped around him, put my foot on his back, and pushed him into the carpet. He shrieked as he landed on the broken ribs.

But he wasn't done, and as I moved even with his shoulders, he grabbed one of my ankles, causing me to swing the baton again. Instead of a scream we got a whine. Darryl Diamond was nothing more than a big bully who picked on girls and wasn't used to getting a dose of his own medicine.

I leaned down while he sobbed into the carpet. "Listen up, Darryl. We have enough perverts in this city without you out-of-towners adding to the case load. Get out of Charleston before word gets around that some girl kicked your butt."

Through a red haze filling the room, I heard a voice say, "Sweet Jesus . . ."

I thought I'd heard someone earlier, but after being knocked on my butt, it was all I could do to keep the perv off me. Stepping back to put some distance between me and the guy lying on the floor, I looked around. The world had slowed down. Now it picked up speed. When I moved toward Emily, steel baton in hand, she headed for the door.

"No, no. I'm outta here."

"You're not the only one."

I went out the door right behind her, wiping the knob for prints, and bringing along the scotch glass, which I dropped in a trashcan down the hall. The plastic shim that I'd used on the door and collapsible metal rod that I'd used on Diamond were inside my jacket by the time I caught up with Emily, who was stabbing the elevator button. Grabbing her arm, I turned her around.

She shrank back. "No, no, please don't hurt me. Please don't . . ."

I got in her face. "You had no good reason to remain in that room once I came through the door."

The bell rang, but neither of us heard it, and me, I was once again mired in that red fog, ears roaring.

"I know, I know," she said. "Just please don't hurt me."

I was leaning into her when the elevator doors opened and we fell into the car. Emily landed on her back with me straddling her. Jarred back to reality, I reached behind me and punched the button for the mezzanine floor, then realized we weren't alone. The couple I'd seen in the hallway earlier stared down at us, looking properly horrified.

Getting to my feet, I asked the guy, "Could you give me a hand here?"

The couple looked at Emily, then at me.

"I need to get my sister home," I said, focusing on the

gal, "before our father finds out who she's been with."

"Help her with her sister," said the woman to her guy friend.

The guy and I got Emily on her feet at the same time the elevator doors opened on the mezzanine floor.

"Sorry about this," I said, tugging Emily out of the elevator, "but my sister has a real talent for picking losers."

"Tell me about it," said the woman.

"What?" asked her guy friend.

"Not you, honey," said his girlfriend, smiling and putting an arm around him. "Every guy who came before you."

As the elevator doors closed, I heard him ask, "And how many were there?"

Emily was incoherent and unstable on her feet. She jabbered in my ear and slobbered on my shoulder as I walked her toward the ladies' room. Thankfully, we passed only one other couple; they, too, with love on their minds. Evidently this *was* the place to spend a romantic weekend.

In the ladies' room I pushed Emily down the stalls and opened the last one, the wider one for the handicapped. There I made her take a seat, but I couldn't make her stop crying.

"Get a grip, girl!"

"But—but," she said through her sobs, "you beat him up really bad."

"I don't know any other way to do it." I ran off a handful of toilet paper and handed it to her. "I tell you to leave the room and you stop for the money. I tell you to use the stairs and you go for the elevator. You want to run into that reporter downstairs? That reporter knows you, and she knows you're a whore."

Emily shook her head wildly. "No, no, no . . ."

"And because you hung around, you've become an accessory."

"What?" She stopped dabbing at the corner of her eyes.

"That's how the law reads."

"Oh, no," she said, shaking her head. "It can't be."

"You just had to take his money, didn't you?"

"I—I'm sorry." She looked up, tears streaming down her cheeks. "I truly am." She dabbed at her eyes again, this time smearing her makeup.

"Prove it!"

"What—what?" She stopped dabbing again.

"Prove you're grateful that I pulled you out of that room before *he* put *you* in the hospital." I got in her face again. "I lied about Kristy. There was considerable facial damage. If you had any brains you'd get out of this business."

By the time I'd straightened up, the cold-hearted whore had returned. "Okay. I'm grateful. Now, what do you want me to do?"

"Tell anyone who asks—"

"Susan?" called Mary Kate as she came into the restroom. "Are you in here?"

I put a finger to my lips, and Emily froze. Even her tears stopped running.

Inclining my head in the direction of the voice, I whispered, "That's the reporter I warned you about, and if you don't want to end up as Whore of the Month on MySpace.com, you'll do as I say."

More nodding, and rapidly, too.

"Susan?" asked Mary Kate again.

Continuing to whisper, I went on, "Make sure everyone understands you left the room before the action began."

"Susan," came the voice, opening stall doors and moving in our direction. "Are you all right?"

"I will, I will," whispered Emily. "I left before anything happened." And the stupid twit crossed her heart and hoped to die.

"You damned well better."

"Susan?" asked Mary Kate, practically at our door.

Emily glanced in MK's direction, pulled her feet up on the john, and wrapped her arms around her knees.

I brushed down my blouse, opened the door, and staggered out of the stall, pushing my way past Mary Kate. "My God, MK, can't you let a person have any privacy. I was dumping my guts out in there."

I hurried past the stalls to the washbasins, but didn't spend much time there, just enough time to rinse my hands and check my hair, then I was out the door before MK could ask any more questions. Though my hair and makeup were in good shape, I can't say the same for my face. There's something about The Job that sours any woman. Or perhaps it comes from kicking some guy's ass.

Mary Kate caught up with me as I strode down the hallway past the ballrooms and conference rooms. By the time we reached the matching circular stairs, people were running through the lobby and screaming that a man had just leaped to his death from the hotel roof.

CHAPTER ELEVEN

The body lay near the portico turnaround, and it took only a glance in the direction of the fourth-floor landing to realize the jumper had simply walked out on the swimming pool/tennis court level and flung himself over the side. It takes only forty to fifty feet to kill yourself and the fourth floor was high enough to do the job.

The jumper lay with one arm under him, and the way he'd hit had flattened one side of his head, causing a trickle of blood from that side, both eyes, and his nose. In the light of the portico, I could make out his aloha shirt, slacks, and his remaining hair in a ponytail.

Darryl Diamond.

Oh, my God, what had I done?

Not as affected by Diamond's death, Mary Kate walked around taking snaps with her camera phone.

I gathered myself together, took out my own phone, and called dispatch. "And send an investigative team. You've either got a guy who fell over the side or a suicide on your hands." I closed my phone as the hotel's night manager joined us on the cobblestone turnaround.

"Oh, my Lord!" he gasped. "Is he—is he a guest?"

Mary Kate pointed her camera phone in the direction of the fourth-floor level. "Remember that guy we met in the bookstore, Susan? I think this is that guy." Mary Kate lowered her phone and bent over to take a closer look. "What was his name?"

"Darryl Diamond," I said, refusing to look again. Instead, I trembled. What had I done? *What the hell had I done?*

Mary Kate noticed me tremble. "You okay?"

"Just wondering if I'm going to have to revisit that mezzanine bathroom again."

"Oh, the tough as nails Susan Chase is going to puke." Mary Kate laughed. "Can I go along and take snaps?"

"Back off, Mary Kate, and stay away from the body."

The manager bent over and peered at the body, one of his bellboys looked a bit pale, and the other was tossing his cookies behind a huge potted plant next to the matching glass doors.

I flashed my SLED ID and pointed at the nauseous bellboy. "Get your guy some medical assistance, but before you do . . ." I pointed at the cabs parked in a staggered row. "Send one of those cabs down to where this alley joins Meeting Street and block that entrance." Gesturing at the exit alleyway, the one beyond the parking garage, I told him to do the same thing with another cab.

"But—but," stammered the manager, "how will our customers gain access to the hotel?"

"Use the doors on King and Meeting streets. Post employees there to assist them."

"But the guests' cars?"

"Come on, fella, you think this is the first time someone's had a parking problem in the historical district?"

He nodded and set off to do what I'd asked, first telling a middle-aged couple in a carriage that they had to disembark on the other side of the building. He got a bit of an argument from the guy until his woman realized a body lay in the turnaround. In the distance I heard sirens. A few minutes later EMS and a prowl car were allowed to enter the turnaround, now blocked by cabs.

One of the officers was a sergeant who knew me from my days of running around the historical district. Actually, downtown Charleston is one of the safest areas for kids, and occasionally the locals dump their bikes on the sidewalk and race inside a store to make a purchase.

The sergeant, a graying guy by the name of McKelvey, who loved working the street as much as I did, smiled at me. "Little Miss Susan Chase, and what kind of trouble have you gotten yourself into this time?" Trailing him was a young patrolman.

Pleased to be able to release the crime scene to the CPD, I said, "Sergeant McKelvey . . ."

I scanned the portico and the turnaround. Mary Kate had disappeared. "Oh, crap!"

"Now, Susan, don't be using such language."

But I was gone, asking McKelvey to throw up a privacy shield around the dead guy. "Got to go! Got a girl to catch."

As I hurried for the glass doors, I heard the young patrolman ask, "What is she—some kind of lesbian?"

I raced to the elevators, and as I was punching the button for the fourth floor, I realized I wasn't supposed to know which room belonged to Darryl Diamond. Or have a key.

Jeez!

I raced across the lobby, flashed my ID, and was told the room number. Puzzled, the young man behind the counter made a second key and mentioned that the other officer was already upstairs. That would be Mary Kate.

This time I took the stairs, reaching the fourth floor out of breath, and raced down the hallway. Stopping to catch my breath, I slid the key in Diamond's door, pushed it open, and found Mary Kate going through the dresser drawers.

She looked up and smiled. "Feeling better?"

I held out my hand. "Give, Mary Kate."

"Hey, what you don't know can't hurt you. Why don't you go down the hall and come back in a few minutes?"

"Mary Kate, I don't have time for this."

"How'd you know which room was Diamond's?"

"Don't change the subject." I showed her my key. "You went through Diamond's pockets while I was giving instructions to the hotel manager, then charmed the room number out of the guy behind the desk. If you don't want to go downtown, you'll submit to a body search."

"But we're friends."

"Not enough to conspire to break the law."

"You and I aren't friends?"

"Oh, put a cork in it, MK. CPD detectives are only moments away." Gesturing at her dress, I said, "Show me what you've got under there, unless you want me to call a matron." I took out my phone and opened a line to the Charleston Police Department.

The watch commander said, "Leave the room, Miss Chase. This is not SLED business."

"You misunderstand. I'm standing guard at the door while Sergeant McKelvey and his partner are taping off the crime scene." I closed my phone. "Mary Kate, if the Charleston police don't want me here, you can imagine what they'll do about you." Again I flipped open my RAZR. "Want me to call back and ask them to bring along a matron?"

"Okay, okay," said Mary Kate, crossing the room. "I don't need the hassle, since I already have the story." She flipped me the entry card and headed for the door.

I let the card fly, took her by the arm, and swung her around to face me. "Mary Kate, I want what's under your dress—"

"Most do," said Mary Kate with a smirk, "whether they be guy or gal."

"Mary Kate, if you don't take off your top and raise your dress, I'm going to cuff you and have someone perform a body search."

"Susan, you wouldn't dare!"

I reached behind me, under my jacket, and took out my handcuffs. "You force me to cuff you, then someone at your paper will have to add text to those photographs you sent over your cell, and *their* byline will appear below the story, as will yours, but as the photographer."

Reluctantly Mary Kate lifted her skirt, took out a folded sheet of paper, and gave it to me. She turned around so I could see nothing else was hidden underneath her skirt. How could there be? Mary Kate wore a thong.

She had her blouse unbuttoned and was holding it out and away from her body when detectives Gadsden and Waring walked in. The scene was enough to make Gadsden exceed his quota of words for the day.

"Are we interrupting anything?"

Through the doorway two patrolmen peered, make that leered, at us; make that leered at Mary Kate.

I told Gadsden that Mary Kate and I had found the jumper and that she had somehow talked her way into Diamond's room.

"And we know how," said Gadsden, glancing at MK's chest.

Waring appeared dumbstruck. Mary Kate's breasts were held in place by a lacy black bra by La Perla.

No one seemed to care about the note I'd laid on the end of the bed. Written on hotel stationery was the following:

To whom it may concern:

I killed those three women. May God forgive me. I've been living in hell ever since.

And he listed the victims' names.

Jiminy. I was off the hook.

At the moment, though, it was Mary Kate who was the center of attention.

She hung her head. "I've been a very naughty girl."

I wanted to ring her neck, but we needed out of here.

Gadsden asked, "Sure this is everything, Chase?"

I pointed at the sheet of paper on the end of the bed. "Suicide note. Picked up by Mary Kate and handled by me."

Gadsden glanced at the note and asked MK if this was true.

Mary Kate held her hands out, palms up, and shook her ass. "Hey, these hips don't lie."

I sighed, put a hand on my friend's back, and pushed her out the door. It was only going down the hallway that she finally pulled her blouse around her.

One of the uniformed cops, a hunky-looking guy, came after us, rather, after Mary Kate. "Can I have your digits?"

"Call me at the newspaper," said my friend, buttoning her blouse. "And bring money. I'm high maintenance."

I moved ahead of them, all the time wondering how long it would be before this was all over the Greenberg Center, not to mention SLED headquarters in Columbia.

Tucking her blouse into her skirt, Mary Kate caught up with me at the elevator. "So Darryl Diamond was the Slasher?"

"It would appear so."

"Oh, come on, Susan. Why'd he kill those women? Nothing in the note explains that."

"Probably liked to beat up whores." I punched the button, then used that arm to lean into the wall. A sense of relief had washed over me, still, my legs had weakened.

Mary Kate was straightening her blouse in the sheen of the elevator door. "Beating up whores would apply to Martha Turner but not Mary Ann Nichols. She was a suburban mom."

I pushed off the wall. "MK, you know how little I think of armchair psychologists, but in this case it's pretty obvious that the murders of Martha Turner and Mary Ann Nichols were a cry for help. Darryl Diamond had an urge he couldn't control."

"Well, he sure as hell didn't have to come to Charleston to cry out."

"I imagine the cops in L.A. were closing in on him."

"And you stumbled on Diamond by accompanying that hooker upstairs?"

"Actually, I stumbled on Diamond after a local madam told me that her girls were being knocked around by some guy who used different names and stayed at different hotels."

"Diamond never took them to his place on Rainbow Row?"

I shook my head. "Possibly because he thought he might lose complete control. But I can tell you this: if you attribute anything to me that happened tonight, even reporting my being on the scene, I'll never speak to you again. I didn't have proper backup to follow up on such a lead."

"I can do that. For a friend."

"We are friends, Mary Kate, but you crossed the line by stealing that suicide note. And impersonating a police officer."

"I wonder who the first woman on Diamond's list was, this Emma Smith."

"Maybe someone murdered in L.A. I imagine you could learn more from your friends at the *L.A. Times.*"

As we waited for the elevator, the hallway filled with people, who first stuck their heads out of their rooms, then wandered into the hall. I have to say I was relieved that Mary Kate had her top back on. Nothing angers another woman more than being in the company of a woman who isn't afraid of taking advantage of her cup size.

Lowering her voice, she said, "Susan, I want to thank you for not telling anyone I stole the key off Diamond's body."

Finally, I looked at her. "That's why you didn't tuck in your blouse until we were down the hall, isn't it?"

"Hey, we all know guys become stupid in the presence of a choice pair of boobs." She glanced at my chest. "I doubt if you'd have the same effect."

I felt my eyes narrow. "That so?"

The bell rang, the elevator doors opened, and we made way for Jacqueline Marion and her fellow techs. The techs looked puzzled until I pointed in the direction of Diamond's room, then we stepped aboard and the elevator doors closed.

"Oh, come on, Susan, I'm just like you, only prettier."

In my defense I can only say that I was damned embarrassed about being found in a hotel room with a half-naked woman. I shot back, "Uh-huh. Someday we'll have to find out about that."

Mary Kate straightened her shoulders, thus raising the attitude of her chest. "Oh, you mean like in a wet T-shirt contest?"

"Oh, grow up, Mary Kate."

Thankfully, the doors opened in the lobby, and I was able to get away from the bitch. Still, I had only one question on my mind when I got home, took off my clothes, and dozed in a chair while Chad snored away.

When the alarm went off, Chad stirred, then reached over and turned off the buzzer. He spotted me sitting in the rattan chair, a towel under me.

"Susan, you up already?"

I got out of the chair and walked over.

"What's going on?" He realized I wore no clothing.

"I changed the alarm so we'd have a few minutes together. Don't forget to change it back." I climbed in bed on top of him.

"Are you kidding?" he said as I got comfortable. "After this, I won't remember a thing."

"Really," I said, wiggling my own set of hips. "You won't remember anything?"

CHAPTER TWELVE

Afterwards, I lay in his arms, unwilling to move, and afraid that if I did, it might remind Chad that he was late for work. Still, I needed to talk.

"Hon, can I ask you a question?"

"Uh—what? Sorry. Think I fell back to sleep."

Using an elbow, I jabbed him awake.

"Okay, okay, I'm awake."

"Watch what you say, fella, especially when I ask you the following question."

"Is it a real tough question? I'm kind of exhausted. My girlfriend gave me a real workout."

"Hey, I'm serious here."

"Me, too."

"Come on, Chad."

"I think I've already done that, too."

I ignored the sexual innuendo. "Do you think Mary Kate's attractive?"

He almost threw me off the bed sitting up. "My gosh, Susan, she's way hot! Totally! A real babe!"

My face scrunched up and I felt as if I might burst into tears. "Are you . . . are you serious?"

"Sure," he said, smiling and returning his head to the pillow. "I've already gotten laid. What's there to lose?"

I reached under the sheet, and he was quick to learn what he might lose—to a woman scorned. And that led to me telling him what'd happened last night. By the end of my story, Chad had all the pillows, while I sat cross-legged wearing my tee.

He asked, "So the guy who leaped to his death is the same guy you saved this whore from?"

"Emily didn't like being called a whore."

"What?"

"Sorry." I smiled. "Go on."

"Well, what do you expect, Suze? You know I don't like you putting yourself in tight spots. Cops are too quick to pull their pistols these days—"

"Weapons."

"Sorry. Cops are too quick to pull their weapons these days, and it worries me that you might use yours to get out of a tight spot."

"It's a nasty world out there, hon, and the bad guys have to respect our gang."

"But what's this got to do with Mary Kate?"

I told him.

"So, you didn't talk your way out of there. Mary Kate's chest led the way."

I slapped his arm. "Chad!"

"Hey, I call them as I see them."

"Yeah, and I know what you'd like to see more of. You really think Mary Kate's hot?"

"I guess so, but she's not my type."

"But you know a hottie when you see one?"

"What guy doesn't? We're experts in such visual matters."

I plopped back on the bed. "So you don't know who's the cutest, me or Mary Kate."

"Sure I do."

I waited, but he said nothing.

"Chad?"

"Oh. Sorry. Must've fallen asleep again."

Very quickly I threw the covers back and straddled him. "Boy oh boy, but you're going to pay!" I began pounding him with my fists.

He threw up his hands to protect himself, and when I let down my guard, he slipped his hands under my tee and went for *my* chest.

Surrendering to his charms, I fell over on my side. "What about work . . . ?"

"I'll call in sick and we'll stay in bed and fool around."

"Hmm. You'd do that just for me?"

"Well, yes, but as usual I'll be thinking of Mary Kate."

And, as usual, I took that as a challenge.

"So," he asked a bit later, "what's this all about, Suze?"

I nuzzled against him. "That I love you, is that so hard for you to understand?"

"You jumped my bones. Twice. When was the last time you did that? You work too much."

"Hey," I said, raising my head. "I'm the girl. Don't be stealing my lines."

He grinned and pulled me into him again. "So what's bothering you?"

"Well, I acted like a guy, and from what I'm told, it's not very becoming."

"But you were in a tight spot."

"Maybe, but I went to Diamond's room to kick some ass, and that violates the first rule of being a woman: Don't be rude."

Actually, the first rule of being a woman is: What's wrong with me? But I hardly ever go there.

"You need a baby, that's all."

"What!" I sat up and pulled the sheet over my bare chest.

"You think you'd be out there kicking ass if you had a baby?"

My voice softened. "You really want a child, don't you?"

"More than one, but you're having too much fun running around Charleston, kicking ass."

"So you don't think I did anything wrong tonight—I mean, last night?"

"Sure I do. You didn't have backup when you went to see Diamond. Actually, you shouldn't have gone to see him at all. What concern is it of yours if a few whores get kicked around?"

"I thought he might be the Ripper."

"And surprise, surprise, he was. How can I reason with you since you're so damned lucky? But if you're asking me to like it, I never will. Speaking of that, what do you think Mary Kate will do with the information in the suicide note?"

"The morning paper arrived while you were asleep.

There's nothing in it about Jack the Ripper, just that the Slasher is dead and that he suffered such remorse, he leaped to his death."

"Three mutilated women, and the media hasn't made the connection with 1888 London?"

"Well, there's a problem with one of the names of the victims only a qualified Ripperologist could explain."

"Ripperologist?"

"Someone who takes an avid interest in Jack the Ripper."

Chad sighed. "You do meet the most interesting people . . . What did the CPD tell you?"

"I got a call on the way home. McPherson told me if I ever wanted to work with the CPD again, not to speculate on what the note might've meant."

Chad snorted. "They ought to be worried about their own detectives spilling the beans."

"I assume Waring and Gadsden have been told that they'd better have one hell of a movie deal and be booked on Larry King because they're going to lose their pensions if it can be proved a CPD detective talked out of school."

"So what about tomorrow? Tomorrow is September eighth, the date of the next murder."

I rolled off the bed and landed on my feet. "Me? I'm going to work. I'm not some bum who lies around in bed all day with his girlfriend."

"Aw, come back, Suze," said Chad, trying to grab my bare ass, "and tell me what you've got planned for tomorrow night."

"Uh-huh. I'm not getting back in that bed. You just want me barefoot and pregnant."

"Who said anything about barefoot?"

SEPTEMBER 8ᵀᴴ

In West Ashley, Detective Abel Waring was drinking coffee and eating a donut with sprinkles when Ann Chapman came under attack. But Chapman was too quick for the killer, slipping out of his grasp and screaming "Officer down! Officer down!"—which stunned her attacker and gave two plainclothesmen a chance to leap out of the bushes and wrestle her attacker to the ground.

Waring had been sequestered in Chapman's house all day, and after a double take at the donut, he dropped it back into its box and raced out the back door. The Intel report said the Ann Chapman killed in 1888 had been found in a backyard, so that's where they'd planted the girl from vice, and when Waring stumbled down the back steps, he found a chunky woman and two plainclothes detectives wrestling with a guy.

One of the plainclothesmen rolled off and clasped a hand on his forearm. "Watch it! Watch it! He's got a damn knife!"

"Sap the bastard!" shouted the decoy, who was trying to hold onto her assailant's legs without being kneed or kicked in the face. "Sap the bastard and do it now!"

To Waring, it was all elbows and assholes, and for that reason, he pulled his weapon crossing the backyard. The other plainclothesman, a guy who'd played ball at Clemson, lay facedown across the Ripper, forcing their assailant into a spread-eagle position, arms out and away from his body, knife hand twitching.

The Ripper was trying to figure whether he should drop the knife and try to pick it up off the ground or flip the knife in the air and catch it, hoping he'd catch the handle and not the blade. While he was making up his mind, the plainclothesman who had been cut stepped around the scrum and kicked the hand holding the knife. The Ripper yelped in surprise and dropped the knife. The wounded plainclothesman kicked the knife away and followed that with a good swift kick to the guy's head. The Ripper went limp.

"What'd you do that for?" asked Waring.

The plainclothesman continued to grip his arm where blood seeped through his sweatshirt. "I'm subduing this asshole, what you think?" But all the plainclothesman could think about was whether his tetanus shots were up to date. God did he hate shots!

"But I don't think—" started Waring.

"Of course you don't. You weren't the one he cut." The wounded cop looked at the chunky woman sprawled across the unconscious man's legs. "You okay, Danielle?"

"You took . . . too long," wheezed the woman. She looked up at the fat detective. "You want to blame someone for sapping this guy, blame me. Everybody knows how scared we girls are of you really tough guys."

The other two cops laughed, and Waring, conscious of having drawn his weapon, holstered it.

The plainclothesman lying across the Ripper rolled off, scrambled to his feet, and pulled Danielle up. Danielle brushed grass from her clothing, an old pantsuit kept in her closet for just such occasions.

The injured cop was holding his arm and evaluating the unconscious guy lying at his feet. Young guy. Teenager. But carrying a knife that could take down any adult, and he'd fought in an absolute frenzy. Must be on something.

Waring knelt beside the unconscious teenager and cuffed him.

"Well, Abel," said the wounded cop, laughing, "I guess you've done enough to earn this collar."

*   *   *

On Daniel Island, Ann Chapman sat in a lawn chair, arms slack from too much beer, head lolling against the back of the aluminum chair. Surrounding the chair and a white foam cooler were an army of empty beer cans. Light spilled from the back porch and beach music played from a boom box. From time to time a neighbor shouted for the music to be turned down, but another voice, a woman's, hollered for her husband to shut up, that she liked a little beach music now and then.

Dean Kline stood in the shadows between the two houses. September 8th had come and was almost gone, so Dean took one last look around and pulled his ski mask down over his face. From inside his shirt, Dean took a knife from its leather sheath and walked purposely across the backyard toward the unconscious woman. Approaching her from the rear, he plunged the knife into the woman's chest. Then he was on her, knocking beer cans left and right, crushing the cooler, and slicing and dicing the woman's abdomen—until he realized there was no blood.

Dean straightened up.

No blood? He'd planned to wash up at a service station only a few blocks away. There, he'd stashed a clean set of clothing in a dumpster, clothing purchased for this particular mission.

But there would be no need for clean clothing because there was no arterial spray, and as Dean stood there, Detective Sam Gadsden turned off the beach music, stepped down from the back porch, and said, "Gotcha!"

Dean glanced at the dummy and chair, both lying on their sides, then broke for the street. The cops might catch him, but they'd have to work at it.

As he ran between houses, the guy who'd complained about the beach music stepped out on his rear stoop, raised a weapon, and shot Dean with a dart-like electrode. Knocked to the ground, Dean lay there, shivering and shaking, as the SWAT team member walked over to take a look at him.

Later tonight, the SWAT guy would be on the phone to his father, a huge fan of the teenage inventor Tom Swift, and who had passed along his collection of Tom Swift books to his son. The SWAT team member would tell his father that, once again, he'd brought down another suspect with Thomas A. Swift's Electric Rifle. After turning off the TASER and watching Sam Gadsden cuff the man, the SWAT guy wondered what the sentence was for stabbing a dummy to death.

*   *   *

James Stuart sat on the porch of a small house in a part of Charleston jammed with small houses and large families, an area commonly called the East Side. Beside Stuart sat an elderly black man, Melvin Ott, who was Stuart's pass into the black community living in the shadow of the new Ravenel Bridge.

People walked by, and occasionally a car or two passed by, but neither Stuart nor Ott, who had been sitting on the porch since the sun went down, could be seen in the shadows. The two old friends were watching a stocky young girl with dreadlocks juking and jiving her way up and down the sidewalk to the sound from her iPod. First she juked down a couple of houses, then she jived back their way. Boys she blew off; adults, she totally ignored, and although she'd passed Stuart and Ott several times, she didn't appear to notice them sitting in the darkness across the street.

Miffed at not being included in the surveillance of either of the two white Ann Chapmans, James Stuart had found his own Ann Chapman, and the damned girl had to be on drugs the way she danced up and down the sidewalk. With the iPod's earbuds, there was no way she could hear anything.

But Jones could see her and he watched Chapman

make another return trip up the sidewalk on his side of the street. Wearing Miami Heat sweats and face painted with a black camouflage stick, Jones had been lying in wait since the sun had gone down. Now it was time to make his move.

First, grab the girl, slit her throat, and then run away from the harbor area. But run only two blocks, then turn ninety degrees and run hard another two blocks. Make another hard turn and begin sauntering along that street in his Miami Heat sweats. Five minutes after the attack, he'd be over a mile away, stripping off the sweats and wiping his face free of the camouflage stick.

From his vantage point across the street, Stuart saw Jones crawl from under the house. Leaving his seat and moving to the steps, Stuart watched Ann Chapman jive her way up the street, and, as she did, the former army officer drew his weapon from a shoulder rig made by a leather shop in the Market area; so when Jones grabbed Chapman, Stuart hustled down the steps, crossed the sidewalk, and stepped into the street. As he did, he brought up his weapon, a custom-finished .45 with a special trigger and barrel porting that kept the weapon on target while firing several shots.

"Halt! Police!"

Stuart's eye never left the sight, and since James Stuart had qualified expert with the Colt Model 1911, a weapon he always kept with the hammer back and ready to fire, it just might be the last thing Jones ever saw.

"Sorry," shouted Jones, grinning over the shoulder of the young black girl, "but I don't believe you can make the shot."

And the knife came down . . .

Stuart fired, blowing off Jones's head.

Blood, brains, and pieces of skull sprayed the girl, who went completely ape shit. First, she collapsed to the sidewalk with Jones, and then she was clawing her way free, all the while screaming. She did one hell of a lot of screaming.

Melvin Ott placed a call to EMS while crossing the street, and then both men knelt beside the hysterical girl, gripping her shoulders and telling her that everything was all right.

But nothing would stop her frantic efforts to wipe the blood and brains out of her eyes, out of her hair, and off her face. The gooey substance simply wouldn't go away.

People left their homes and moved toward the shrieking girl, some calling to their neighbors, others trying to locate their own children. Still the girl screamed and thrashed about.

Ott got to his feet and tried to explain to the growing crowd that this white man had just killed someone trying to cut the throat of one of their neighbors, but with the girl's continued hysterics, Ott's explanation wasn't enough.

Stuart knew he had to face these people. But the girl? What about the girl? It was all he could do to hold her down, blood and brains running into her ears and eyes, trying to get into her mouth. She simply would not calm down.

Stuart sighed, cocked his fist, and knocked the girl out. The EMS arrived later, while Stuart was being jacked up by the residents for bringing violence into a neighborhood they had worked so hard to clean up.

CHAPTER THIRTEEN

Michael McPherson, Eugenia Burnside, Jerry Tobias, and Hugh Fenwick, who was running the Intel Unit, and a SWAT lieutenant, all sat around McPherson's desk eating pizza, drinking sodas or bottled water, and waiting for the results of their sting.

Middle-aged, brown hair going gray, Hugh Fenwick carried a paunch from eating too much junk food, a hazard for any detective cursed to spend long hours at his desk. So his wife, concerned with Hugh's health, sent him off to work each day with a vegetarian meal, a lunch Fenwick could count on his secretary eating. The secretary, a year older than her boss, had a remarkable figure for a woman her age.

Michael McPherson brushed off his hands after finishing another slice. "You know, I'll give this Diamond character the knowledge of Emma Smith and Martha Turner, or Tabram, but how'd he know the third woman would be in town, and on the correct date? Mary Ann Nichols flew in from Columbus, Ohio."

Everyone looked at Fenwick. The Intel chief had seen that look before, and it was a good thing he had a flypaper mind.

He put down his half-eaten slice. "I sent Isaac into Diamond's house after the crime-scene people finished processing it. Diamond had a program on his computer allowing him access to the manifests of anyone arriving in Charleston by plane, ship, or a rental car. All the hotels were there, too."

"Is that possible?" asked Burnside, dabbing her mouth with a napkin, then brushing off her fingers. "I mean, for a civilian to have such ownership?"

"Well, Chief, anything Homeland Security can do doesn't take long to hit the Undernet."

Again everyone stared at Fenwick.

"It's an alternative IRC," he said. "The access is limited, and it's usually used for private conversations."

"It's AOL with nothing but chat rooms," explained Jerry Tobias. "It's full of freaks, perverts, and shady deals. You can find anything or anyone on the Undernet."

"But that didn't matter," countered Fenwick. "This guy had a spare Martha Turner living on Upper Tradd in the Charlestowne neighborhood, and there was another Mary Ann Nichols across the bridge in Mount Pleasant, if you consider Mount Pleasant part of the Greater Charleston area. The Mary Ann Nichols in Mount Pleasant has a walk-up on top of a massage parlor."

Unlike McPherson, Hugh Fenwick wasn't bothered by Eugenia Burnside being his chief, as he, too, had left patrol as soon as possible and moved into a job shuffling paper. And there was one hell of a lot of paper to be shuffled on the admin side. A few months after Fenwick began shuffling that paper, the CPD began inquiring as to who might be willing to learn how to operate a computer. Both Fenwick and Burnside had volunteered.

The chief put down her bottled water. "What else, Hugh?" Burnside knew from long experience of working with Fenwick that he did not always tell you everything first time out, which made him an excellent choice for Intel chief.

Fenwick glanced at his pizza. "Well, it seems the Mount Pleasant Police were called to Mary Ann Nichols' apartment the same night that our Mary Ann Nichols was killed on the Battery. When the patrol car arrived, guess who they found sitting on Nichols' steps?"

No one had an answer. No one even guessed.

"Susan Chase," said Fenwick.

That set off another tirade by the captain of detectives, finishing with, "Just because she's a SLED agent doesn't give her the right to butt her nose into everyone's business."

"And what would you have us do?" asked Tobias. "Are you prepared to file a formal complaint about Chase that would, sooner or later, reveal that the CPD failed to protect a tourist in one of the most popular sections of Charleston?"

McPherson ignored him and spoke to Burnside. "You know as well I do, Eugenia, Chase is a loose cannon."

Fenwick quickly broke in: "The odd thing about this whole affair is there's nothing in Diamond's past that points to him being a psychopath. From what Isaac retrieved from his computer, the guy didn't employ a shrink, which is pretty much SOP for those West Coast types. He had no history of drug use and had a steady girlfriend who couldn't make the trip to Charleston because she was on location, and his last movie did okay numbers. And he's got a ton of money stashed in the Caymans. I don't know how much is down there, but there've been a lot of recent transfers. Might be as much as a hundred grand."

Tobias took out a cigarette and lit up. "Okay numbers aren't good enough to get your current project green-lighted these days."

"Green-lighted?" asked the SWAT lieutenant, fumbling around for another napkin. Burnside furnished a napkin for him.

"Do you have to do that?" McPherson asked Tobias. "Smoking *is* prohibited in this building."

Tobias looked at the cigarette as if surprised to find it in his hand. "Sorry. My bad."

He pinched off the tip, reached down to rub his fingers on his socks, realized he wore no socks, and took the paper napkin offered by Burnside to wipe his fingers.

"Green-lighted?" repeated the SWAT lieutenant.

Tobias examined his fingers. "It means to have your project given the go-ahead to film or make plans to film."

"What's that got to do with anything?" asked the SWAT guy.

Tobias sucked his fingers, then said, "Serial killers aren't the draw they once were."

"Damn," said McPherson, "there's a serial killer on TV every night, and it takes only an hour to catch him."

Once everyone had stopped laughing, Tobias said, "That's the problem. Serial killers are everywhere. There's no difference between any of them."

"Don't tell me," said the SWAT lieutenant with a groan, "Diamond brought back the original serial killer to prove there was still interest."

"Actually," said Tobias, returning his snubbed-out cigarette to his cigarette pack, "once Katrina leveled New Orleans, we inherited his project, and if he hadn't lost his nerve and jumped off that building, he just might've pulled it off."

"If Diamond was the Ripper," groused McPherson.

At *The Post and Courier* Mary Kate's editor complained that it was an especially slow night on the police band. Mary Kate said summer was over, so what'd he expect? Besides, she was leaving. She'd accepted a dinner invitation from the uniformed cop she'd met the night Darryl Diamond leaped to his death. Still, MK had her feelers out, and people inside the police department told her some kind of sting was on the agenda, and with a sting it wasn't all that unusual for things to be handled on the q.t.

So, Mary Kate went to dinner with an extra cell phone tucked in her purse. At Magnolia's, when her date said he didn't have a clue anything was going down but promised to make a few phone calls after dinner, Mary Kate only smiled, handed him the extra cell phone, and told the waiter it would be a few minutes before they would be ready to order.

Back at *The Post and Courier* Mary Kate's editor looked up from editing yet another feature on the *Hunley* when dispatch signaled one of its units. A patrol car from Team Four was to respond to a Peeping Tom in West Ashley. The Tom's description: white male, tall, slender build, wearing dark clothing and a hood. Handle Code Two.

Less than twenty minutes later, the unit reported they had a suspect in custody and were returning to "seventy-five," code for the Greenberg Center, and that the suspect had asked for a lawyer, tonight's code for "all clear" for those working the Slasher case.

The editor hopped on the phone and asked the watch commander for the particulars. The watch commander reported that the peeper had been caught at the home of an Ann Chapman who lived off the Savannah Highway and furnished an address.

"We believe he's been there before. That's why we were able to apprehend him. Give me a call later and I'll have the particulars, that is, unless the damn lawyer doesn't screw things up." And the watch commander left for dinner.

When the call came in, the one pertaining to the peeper apprehended off the Savannah Highway, the information was relayed to the office of the captain of detectives who put the watch commander on the speaker phone. Others around the desk looked at each other, smiled, and let out a sigh. It was always good to plan well and have a plan go well.

McPherson shook his head. "Hard to believe, but Darryl Diamond was not the guy."

"But," said Eugenia Burnside with satisfaction, "we were prepared and that's what counts."

"Yeah, Mac," said Tobias, closing his computer. "Kind of belies the old saw that cops are only good for solving crimes, not preventing them."

"Most important," said Burnside, gesturing with her pencil at the clock on the wall that read 11:45, "there are no dead Ann Chapmans, which means we've brought this so-called game to a halt." Taking her pad and pencil with her, Burnside got to her feet. "I want to thank all of you for staying late and especially for breaking this cycle of terror."

McPherson looked around the desk. "Don't forget, you're still sworn to secrecy regarding this case."

"But," started the SWAT lieutenant, "I thought . . ."

"Not a word." McPherson looked through the glass where the shift was changing and a new set of detectives in the bullpen stared at them. "If anyone asks, tonight was a total misfire. Wrong guy and the lid is still on."

"A lid twisted down real tight, gentlemen," said Burnside from the door.

The SWAT lieutenant frowned. It was hard enough to keep a secret in this building, and he had to go home and face his wife. At this hour. And still keep a secret?

Minutes later, another unit reported a burglar had been apprehended on Daniel Island. He, too, wanted a lawyer, and when Mary Kate's editor called to ask whose home had been burglarized, the officer filling in for the watch commander gave the newspaperman all the particulars.

When the editor got off the phone, he realized both victims had the same name, Ann Chapman, and made a mental note to clarify this. Obviously, the guy subbing for the watch commander had made a mistake.

When the call came in about the attack on Daniel Island and Ann Chapman's attacker being subdued by TASER, McPherson didn't know what to make of it.

Fenwick did. "I'll get the chief." And he was out the door and racing for the elevator. The chief had said something about stopping by her office before leaving the building. He hoped she was still there.

By the time Burnside returned to McPherson's office, Jerry Tobias was puffing away on a new cigarette, pushing his sports car up the interstate toward Columbia, and eager to report to the party that Eugenia Burnside was ready for bigger and better things.

Once her captain of detectives confirmed that another copycat had been TASERed on Daniel Island, the chief of police shook her head and took a seat in one of the visitor's chairs. And they all sat there, trying to sort this thing out. They were still trying to sort things out when gunfire erupted on the East Side. An hour later, James Stuart strolled into the room, looking none too pleased and holding an ice pack to a brand new shiner.

CHAPTER FOURTEEN

After expressing concern for James Stuart's black eye, the chief of police led the former officer out of McPherson's office and downstairs to her own office.

Watching them go, the lieutenant from SWAT said, "Well, I thought she let him down rather gently."

Both McPherson and Fenwick laughed. They remembered Burnside stepping out of McPherson's office to make a phone call immediately after it had been confirmed that Stuart had blown the head off a third copycat.

"My boy," said Fenwick, "that was for public consumption. You don't embarrass a military hero in front of mere mortals."

"Yep," said McPherson. "Dirty Harry don't work here, and that's what the colonel is about to learn." He pulled his own pad over in front of him. "Okay, we need background on the two guys brought in tonight, along with some paper on the one Dirty Harry shot. They all should've been printed by now."

"Yeah," said the guy from SWAT, "but how we going to explain this to the media?"

McPherson glanced through the glass wall in the direction of the elevator. "That's the chief's problem—once she's finished chewing Stuart's butt."

"But how can she chew another chief? Aren't they sort of equals?"

Fenwick chuckled. "Not when Burnside gets through with him, they won't be."

In Burnside's office the mayor waited. A single fellow, the mayor was tanned, trim, and had made Charleston his bride and his heir. Tonight he did not smile or extend his hand, only motioned his former Citadel classmate to take the other visitor's chair.

"Injured badly?" he asked, inquiring about the black eye.

Stuart dropped the ice pack to the floor. "Hardly at all."

Stuart looked hard at Burnside, who had taken a seat on the other side of her expensive-looking desk, certainly not something furnished by the city. Photographs of various luminaries and politicians, all shaking hands or standing beside the chief, filled the walls, and on the credenza behind her sat a computer screen, keyboard, mouse, and a single black-and-white photograph. The photo was of a ten-year-old Eugenia Burnside, dressed in her Sunday best, shaking hands with Dr. Martin Luther King.

Once seated, the chief of police took out a fingernail file, leaned back in her chair, and went to work on her nails. Her policy was to fully support James Stuart, thus giving him enough rope to hang himself. And now he had.

The mayor asked his former classmate, "Would you care to explain what you were doing tonight, James?"

"Saving the life of some little girl, it would appear."

Without looking up from her nails, Burnside said, "Don't you mean saving the life of some little *black* girl, Colonel, perhaps thinking you might gain some leverage in this little tête-à-tête?"

To the mayor, Stuart said, "I don't see that I had any other choice."

"That's a drastic measure you took, James, and you couldn't take the time to inform the chief of your plans? If you're unwilling to coordinate with Eugenia, it means we have a conflict between our Department of Homeland Security and the Charleston Police Department." When Stuart said nothing, the mayor added, "Which means you should consider resigning."

From the other side of the desk, Eugenia Burnside put down her fingernail file, took a sheet of paper from the center drawer, and pushed it across the desk. That was followed by an ink pen, one of the old-fashioned types, its fountain full of ink. That done, the chief returned to her nails.

"What you did tonight may work overseas," continued the mayor, "but in Charleston, *any* civilian casualties are unacceptable. That's why Eugenia set up this task force, and from what I've heard, it's worked like a charm."

"If you ignore the fact that a little black girl may have died at the hands of a Jack the Ripper copycat earlier tonight."

The mayor hesitated, then leaned forward and tapped his friend on the knee. "Look, James, I know you went down to the harbor and established your credibility with the longshoremen, and I don't want to know how many butts you had to kick, but as much as the city of Charleston reveres its military heroes, this city also has a much higher level of expectation from those same heroes."

When Stuart said nothing, the mayor straightened up in his seat. "You can't go off the reservation here, James."

Stuart glanced at the pen and paper. "You really want my resignation?"

"Of course not, and neither does Eugenia. Both of us agree our jobs would be much more difficult if you weren't heading up Homeland Security for the city."

Burnside looked up from her nails. "Actually, Colonel, I feel exceptionally blessed that you're on our side in this war against terror. You bring instant credibility to anything we do."

Stuart looked at her but didn't believe a word.

"I don't care if you believe us or not," said the mayor, reading his friend's mind. "All we're interested in is the safety of the citizens of Charleston, and both Eugenia and I feel the harbor is a much safer place with you on the job."

The mayor gestured at the paper and pen. "That's to let you know how serious we are about squashing any potential terror threat. But what you did tonight was nothing more than an extension of the same terror those people on the East Side have suffered ever since they were led down gangways in chains, put on the auction block, and sold off to plantations in the Low Country."

The mayor got to his feet, clapped his friend on the shoulder, and headed for the door. "Keep up the good work, James."

"You mean if I don't turn in my resignation."

At the door, the mayor faced him. "We'd miss you, James, but I'm sure we can find someone else in the retired military community, perhaps not as highly decorated but certainly not so reckless." To the chief, he said, "Good job tonight, Eugenia."

"She doesn't listen to my suggestions," complained Stuart.

The mayor looked at him. "And what suggestion would that be?"

"Bring in Susan Chase. She knows the streets of Charleston. She was born here, played on the streets as a child, and practically lives on these streets. And she's tracked serial killers before, when she lived at Myrtle Beach."

The mayor glanced at his chief of police. "I thought Eugenia had debriefed Chase about what she knew about Jack the Ripper."

"That may be so, but you had the Ripper in the morgue and three more Rippers popped up. What does that tell you?"

To his chief of police, the mayor said, "He has a point."

"But we broke the cycle," said Burnside, putting down her fingernail file. "Even the colonel was part of that. No Ann Chapman was killed tonight, and tonight, according to the legend, was the night she had to die."

"All I know," said Stuart, "is three more Rippers popped up, which means we don't have a handle on the situation. In this I speak to you as your person in charge of homeland security."

The mayor considered this, then said to Burnside, "Bring Chase on board. It may be for a day or a week, but we need to put this matter behind us."

"But where will the money come from?" asked Burnside, her hands opening in a helpless gesture.

"Don't worry about the money. I'll take care of that." The mayor was in his umpteenth term in office and had plenty of friends on the city council, many who would approve the occasional odd appropriation, if such a request was made behind closed doors.

"Okay," said Burnside, "but we may get press. We've been lucky so far, especially with the families of the two dead women, whom I briefed personally."

The mayor shrugged. "With these nuts coming out of the woodwork, maybe that's not such a bad thing."

"Okay. First thing tomorrow I'll ask SLED to send over Chase."

Stuart cleared his throat. "Actually, Chase isn't going to be available tomorrow. She had quite a shock tonight, and I lent her my schooner for the day." Stuart touched his new shiner. "That girl whose life I saved . . ." Stuart glanced at Burnside. "The black girl I saved tonight, that was Chase in disguise, staked out and waiting for the Ripper to show up."

CHAPTER FIFTEEN

I staggered out of the bathroom, and Chad took my arm, guided me over to the bed, and made me lie down. He thought I was all shook up over having some guy's brains splattered all over me. That wasn't it. It was the other thing.

Oh, I'm not saying that having someone's brain pan sprayed all over you isn't a bother. It is. But it's what the emergency room doc told me that fed my hysteria. And at that thought I stopped shaking and became very angry. At James Stuart.

Thankfully, someone at One West, the main trauma center at the Medical University of South Carolina, knew me, well, knew me under my spray-on tan and after losing the dreadlocks, and she called Chad. It would be an understatement to say I occasionally visited One West.

Before Chad arrived, the doc tried to lighten the mood, commenting on all the body armor he'd had to peel off me, along with the collar protecting my neck. Once my clothing was removed, the nurses went to work, cleaning my face, neck, and arms, and asking if I wanted to keep the dreadlocks wig. I did not, and it went into the trash.

Since I couldn't stop shaking, someone asked if I needed a psych evaluation, and that was enough to cause me to slip into a hospital gown, straighten my shoulders, and focus my anger on James Stuart. That might've been why they allowed Chad to see me. Or perhaps he walked in on his own.

"Is he a member of your family?" asked the prick involved in my cleanup.

She couldn't get over the number of weapons and the extent of the body armor piling up on the metal cart wheeled into the examination area. My jeans appeared to be clean, but I'd messed in my panties so they were tossed, and each time I glanced at those jeans on the metal table, I began to shake all over again.

"Susan doesn't have a next-of-kin," explained one of the nurses. "Chad's all she's got."

The curtains were pulled back, and there he was, looking worried and holding a grocery sack. "Suze, are you all right?"

I nodded, put my hands between my thighs, and curled my shoulders in on top of me. I'd screwed up pretty badly, and I wasn't talking about anything having to do with police procedure. Police procedure could go jump.

"Sir," said the prick to Chad, "you can't come back here without authorized permission. You must return to the lobby."

Chad handed off the paper sack to one of the nurses and took my arms, examining what remained of the spray-on tan.

I was too ashamed to look him in the eye.

"Is she okay?" he asked.

"Oh, she'll be fine," said the nurse, pulling clothing from the paper bag. "She just needs a good night's sleep."

Once they finished dressing me, I felt better, but the prick was still going full steam.

"Sir," she said to Chad, who had stood with his back to us while I was being dressed, "you can't take your girlfriend out of here. A doctor has to sign the release."

Chad turned around. "Susan will sign herself out. Where's James Stuart?" Evidently, Chad had heard about the debacle on the East Side.

"Colonel Stuart's not here," said a nurse who had just returned with two black plastic garbage bags. "I heard he's been held up at the crime scene."

Chad took the bags and started stuffing my gear into one of them.

"Look," said the prick, changing her tactics, "you can't have all these weapons in the examination area."

From the other side of the curtain, a male voice called out, "Coming in."

And the doctor did, making nice with the prick, something neither Chad nor I was capable of at that moment, maybe in my lifetime. Chad helped me down from the examination table and put his arm around my waist. A nurse held out a clipboard. From past experience I knew just where to sign.

Snatching a prescription bottle from the doctor's hand, Chad led me out of the curtained-off area, one arm around me, his free hand holding the black plastic bags. Over his shoulder, he said, "For whoever called me, thanks. You know how hard it is to keep up with this girl."

A couple of the nurses laughed, but it was enough to set me off on another crying jag, that is, until we reached the lobby—where we ran into James Stuart.

I wiped away my tears, straightened my shoulders, and looked right past him. Stuart walked over, a concerned look on his face, and Chad put down the bags, and using his free hand, punched out James Stuart. Sorry, but I don't take credit where credit's not due.

Even so, I couldn't calm down, and that's why Chad had been trying to get me to take a sedative. I fought him on that because I had to make him understand. "You know what that damned James Stuart did?"

"Susan, by continuing to talk about it you're keeping yourself all worked up. You'll never get any sleep." He forced me to lie down, and he climbed into bed beside me. We spooned, always a safe place I can go.

Moments later, the doorbell rang, and I begged Chad to stay with me, clutching his arm to keep him in bed.

He peeled my hands off. "If I don't, Suze, they'll just come back, or worse, they'll call."

When I heard it was James Stuart, I bolted upright in the bed and fumbled around on the nightstand, searching for my weapons. Any weapon.

Nothing but a couple of pieces of coat hanger, which I promptly knocked to the floor, along with the Kleenex.

I went searching for something, anything that could be turned into a weapon. You know, if I ever do have children, I've really got to do something about the way I leave my weapons lying around. And with that thought, the pain hit me again, and I bent over, holding onto the dresser.

It was a moment before I could straighten up, but I still couldn't find any weapons. All my weapons had been put away, actually hidden from me, with the exception of the pieces of coat hanger. I snatched up one of them and hurried down the hall. I would make do.

Not only did Stuart wear a shiner, but he appeared ill-at-ease as I moved in his direction. His expression turned to one of alarm just before I slammed into him and knocked him against the door. But when I swung at him with the piece of coat hanger, Chad grabbed me around the waist and pulled me off.

Still, I drew blood.

Stuart brought down his hands and saw where the sleeve of his expensive suit coat had been ripped, as was his shirt. Blood leaked from a long red wound on his arm. "Damn. I could've used more of your kind in Afghanistan."

"Get out!" I shouted. "Get out of my house!"

"Susan, stop it!" Chad pulled me across the room. "Stop it right now."

My grip weakened, the coat hanger dropped to the

floor, and I fell into Chad's arms. I was crying, but I didn't want to cry. Not in front of this man. Still, I wanted to let it all out. I wanted to cry my heart out. My God, how could this have happened to me?

"Susan, Colonel Stuart's here to offer us his boat. I'll take the day off—"

"I don't want anything from the bastard!" I threw off Chad's hands, rushed across the living room, and plopped down on the sofa.

Stuart was talking.

I couldn't hear him or Chad. I had wrapped my arms around my knees and begun to bawl.

Finally, I heard Stuart say, ". . . to give you the good news and this is how you repay me?" And without me exhibiting the least bit of interest, Stuart told us how the two copycats had been caught and that the mayor had approved my coming aboard to work the case. "We really don't know how many more of these wackos are out there."

"Make him leave," I pleaded.

"It's good news, Suze." Chad stood beside the sofa and stroked my head. "A schooner is what you've always wanted."

What I always wanted was to have Chad's baby. But Chad didn't know anything about my losing the baby. He didn't even know I'd been pregnant. I hadn't known myself, figuring I was a bit late because of all the crap that had been happening in my life.

"I don't want him here!"

"Then I'm gone," said Stuart, opening the door. "I'm through doing you favors, Chase. You're on your own from now on."

But that wasn't how I wanted it to end.

I climbed off the sofa, stumbled across the room, and charged out on the porch. Who says a girl doesn't have a right to change her mind?

Stuart must've heard me coming because he stepped off the sidewalk and his hand went inside his coat, the coat I had so enthusiastically ripped.

At the edge of the porch, I jabbed a finger at him. "You think . . . you think you're so smart." I leaned into the railing. "You think . . . you think . . ." I couldn't get my breath. My voice quivered.

"Come on, Suze," said Chad softly. He put a hand on my shoulder. "Come back inside."

"Chase," said Stuart from the sidewalk, "you need a rest. Take my boat out tomorrow. I told the chief you won't be available for a day or two."

You told who what? Stuart had no right to speak for me. "Screw you, too!"

"Susan," said Chad, "watch your language."

Up and down the street, lights were coming on, or maybe they'd always been on. Maybe I'd just noticed.

"Where . . . where did you catch those Rippers?"

Stuart had reached his double-parked Mustang.

"In Ann Chapman's yard, right?"

He stared at me.

I laughed. "You caught a couple of copycats but the real Ripper is still out there."

Chad pulled me off the railing. "That's enough, Suze. You're going to bed and this time you're going to take that sedative."

"Where . . . where'd you blow off that guy's head?"

I caught the jamb when Chad opened the screened

door to drag me inside. "Whose yard?" I screamed. "Whose yard?"

Stuart only stood there and watched as Chad dragged me into the house. Chad said I was still ranting and raving about whose damned yard I'd been in when the sedative finally took effect.

CHAPTER SIXTEEN

Abel Waring walked into Homicide the following morning and was barely given enough time to pour a cup of coffee before Sam Gadsden hustled the heavy man into their boss's office. McPherson handed each of them a sheet of paper. Waring blanched, and for a moment thought he was being written up. The sheet turned out to be a list of addresses in Charleston County.

Waring looked up from the sheet. "What's this?"

"What does it look like?" asked McPherson from behind his desk. "A list of properties, and the chief wants to know who lives in each one. Hugh Fenwick has someone checking the property records at the courthouse, but the chief wants a physical check, especially the backyards. I've split up the list and pretty much kept you in the same area, so I expect you to interview someone at these locations, or the house next door, or by phone in the event both the occupants and the neighbors are at work."

Waring shook his head. "But why?"

"Just do the job, Abel, and keep your mouth shut." McPherson glanced at Gadsden. "I don't have to tell your partner that. Remember, both of you were sworn to secrecy on the Slasher case so continue to keep your counsel, check these properties, and report back to me before lunch. And make sure you check the backyards of every single house on your list."

"Has this got something to do with the Ripper?"

"Abel, how many times do I have to tell you not to call this the Ripper case. It's the Slasher case, just as the media calls it."

"But I thought that was all over."

McPherson sighed. "Abel, just because we've known each other for longer than I care to remember, doesn't mean I'm going to take the time to explain everything I ask you to do. You're a detective, so go detect. Suffice it to say, this came from the chief. Or do you need to know the mayor's involved, too?"

"The mayor, too?"

"I swear, Abel," said McPherson, standing, "if you don't do as I say, I'm going to take you to church with me tonight so we can work on that attitude of yours."

Waring backed away, hands coming up. "No call for that." Waring didn't want anything to do with handling snakes or speaking in tongues.

Gadsden took that opportunity to grab his partner's upraised arm and pull him out of the office.

As they left, the captain of detectives shouted after them: "And keep your mouths shut!"

Waring did not. He whined all the way down in the elevator, and even more so when separated from

Gadsden in the parking lot, an area where vehicles were secured inside a twelve-foot fence.

"I don't see why we can't work together," complained Waring. "You know, two heads are better than one."

Gadsden smiled. "And why would you think that would create two heads?" The skinny man wandered off to find his own vehicle.

After Waring stopped by a Waffle House for breakfast, read the sports section of the newspaper—the Braves were going to win again but not often enough—and enjoyed a second cup of coffee, he set off to check his list.

It wasn't a very long list, so Waring believed he'd finish it before lunch. His problem was McPherson, who not long ago had been one of the guys. All three of them, including Sam Gadsden, had joined the force about the same time. But lately McPherson had let that damned church go to his head. Hard to believe McPherson attended church every night, and the nights he worked late, his wife and children went without him. And two of McPherson's kids were teenagers. How did you get teenagers to attend church regularly?

It must be the snake handling or a chance to hear some weirdo speak in tongues. Anyway, Waring didn't think a superior could threaten a subordinate with church attendance, but he wasn't going to push it. Charleston wasn't called the Holy City for nothing.

The first property on the list was a vacant lot, so Waring pulled over, leaned out the window, and spoke to an elderly gent walking his dog.

The old man reined in his poodle and looked across the street. "Been nothing there, not since I've lived here, Sonny, and that's been over twenty years."

"Have any idea who owns the lot?"

"Nope."

Waring thanked the old guy and asked his name. He wrote down the name and phone number next to the address and moved on. Fenwick's man would've already checked the lot through the property records in the county courthouse, and they could compare notes before turning in their lists.

The next house was empty, or the people had left for work. No cars in the driveway, no sound coming from inside, and when Waring walked around to the rear, he found a yard full of Johnson grass, a swing set with broken swings, and a sandbox whose seams had burst at the corners, spilling sand into the yard.

By the time he'd returned to the front, an elderly woman was waiting for him, asking from the porch of the house next door just exactly what he was up to. Waring had counted on such neighborly curiosity, that people would come outside without him having to climb a bunch of stairs to knock and wait, then move on to the next-door neighbor's house where he would have to knock and wait again. The houses were all the same: shingled slate exterior, single floor, and a concrete porch with steps. Waring asked her to sign off on who owned the property next door. The woman was happy to oblige and said the house was owned by the Long family.

"They must've lived there thirty years or more. I'm not exactly sure, but I lived in my house not long before the

Longs moved in and I've been here almost thirty years."

And where were the Longs, asked and answered the woman. Gone to see the grandkids up in Wisconsin. Left a few days ago, pulling a pop-up trailer behind their pickup, and they'd be gone a whole month. She always kept an eye on the place when the Longs were gone. The Longs were good people and always brought her a bunch of cheese when they came home. Cheeseheads is what they called their relatives who lived up north.

At the next house, the owner wanted to know what the hell Waring was doing in his backyard, but by the time the owner called from his door, the detective already knew a chain-link fence enclosed a low-cut yard containing two metal shelters protecting an old Mercury coupe, a shallow-draft boat, and a stack of wood. The old guy said he'd been tempted to haul out his shotgun, but thought he'd do Waring the courtesy of asking what he wanted before shooting him. For some reason, the old fart was also named Long.

The next house appeared to be empty, so Waring walked around to the fenced-in backyard—where a large grey and white dog leaped at his throat!

Waring stumbled back, the dog leaping and snarling from behind a chain-link fence. During the moments it took to calm his nerves, Waring realized that it was more than one dog—more than one greyhound leaping and bounding at him, and the damned things had the run of a fenced-in backyard.

Damn! How do you check this backyard?

The neighbor's backyard also had a fence but one

made of wood, so there would be no peeking from their side. Matter of fact, both neighbors had wooden fences running alongside this yard's chain-link one.

Ignoring the dogs, Waring stepped within a couple of feet of the fence and peered over it. He saw nothing more than a dilapidated dog house and chain-link fencing running across the backyard. While standing there, another old bird spoke to him from her front porch. Was there no one home this time of day but a bunch of old people?

"What do you want, young man? Why are you on my property?" The elderly woman used a cane and maneuvered her way around the swing at this end of the porch.

Waring left the fence and asked if the dogs had been in the backyard last night.

"What dogs?"

"Why, those dogs in your backyard." Waring looked again. The animals were still there, clamoring for his attention.

"Oh, no, that's not my dog. The dog you hear is down the street."

Waring looked from the dogs to the woman leaning on the cane. True, she couldn't see her backyard from where she stood, but—oh, what the hell. Couldn't be much more to see in a backyard that full of dogs. Busy dogs, too. Certainly too many for some old lady to handle.

"Your name, ma'am?"

The woman considered the question, then said, "You didn't answer my question, young man. Tell me why you are here."

"She comes and goes," said a male voice behind him.

That came from a young bearded man sitting in a wheelchair on the porch next door. The bearded guy wore a white T-shirt, plaid shorts, a Charleston Battery baseball cap, and was missing both legs. Waring walked over, and behind him, the old woman said she just might have to call the police if she found him trespassing on her property again.

The man in the wheelchair gestured at his missing legs. "Pardon my laziness, but I seem to have misplaced my legs."

"Iraq?" asked Waring. A good number of amputees lived in the Charleston area, and Waring had a cousin who'd lost an eye in that war.

"Afghanistan," said the guy in the wheelchair. "What can we do for you, sport?"

"Just need to know her name." Waring gestured with his pen at the woman on the porch behind him. The old woman seemed deep in thought, as if puzzling something out. Maybe whether she had any damn dogs in her backyard or not.

"Why's that?" asked the bearded fellow.

"Sorry, but that's a police matter."

"Sure you're not from social services?"

"What? No. I'm with the CPD." He flashed his badge.

"No sweat, fellow. Reason I ask is her kids have a social worker come round every once in a while. Her kids, at least the sister, want to put the old lady in a home, but first they have to prove she's senile. Me, I can't see the point. We keep an eye on her, and it's only a matter of time before she trips over one of those dogs and breaks something. Then she'll have to move, whether she likes it or not."

"What's the name of the family?"

"Long."

"Long? Are you putting me on?"

The wheelchair-bound man reached down to scratch one of his legs, realized the leg was no longer there, and then rested his hand on the stump. "Yep, they're Longs, and just the old lady and her dogs live there. Been running that rescue mission forever, least that's what my sister says. I moved in last year and Sis told me to keep an eye out for old lady Long."

Waring took the man's name, address, and how his sister's phone would be listed, thanked him, and moved on. It didn't take long before Waring learned that everyone on his list, except for the vacant lot, went by the same last name. Long.

Was McPherson pulling his leg?

An hour later he returned to the Greenberg Center with some very fine barbecue in a takeout bag. Running the route the way he'd laid it out, he was able to stop by Bessinger's on the return trip to the Greenberg Center.

McPherson appeared to be relieved. Still, he asked, "Just for the record, did both of you check all those backyards?"

"Of course." Waring glanced at Gadsden, who only nodded. "I can give you a house-by-house report, but it's just a bunch of old people living in those houses."

"Okay," said McPherson, waving them out of his office. As they left, McPherson reminded them to keep their mouths shut and complete their paperwork from last night's adventures.

CHAPTER SEVENTEEN

Chad called me in sick, and I slept until the middle of the day, so I was still groggy from the pill he'd forced me to take, but alert enough to remember to enter through the rear of the Greenberg Center. Contrary to what is shown on TV, people who work undercover do not walk in the front door of police stations or law enforcement centers, nor do they want their pictures taken. To be fair, some cops believe "mopes don't watch TV," but that sounds as reliable as something a guy might tell you when he's got you in the backseat of his car.

I passed through a sally port where a guard sits behind bulletproof glass and controls the space between doors, checking the credentials of anyone entering or leaving. In the days of moats and drawbridges, sally ports were small, easily secured doors in castle walls through which small groups of defenders could "sally forth" and attack the besiegers. These days they are used for the transportation of high-risk prisoners.

The chief's secretary looked up and smiled at my SLED ID. "Oh, Ms. Chase, we weren't expecting you, but go right in. Colonel Stuart is with the chief."

I took a breath and steeled myself for what was to come, then opened the door, walked in, and took a seat in the empty visitor's chair. James Stuart sat in the other.

The former officer stood as I entered the room. "Miss Chase." He still wore his shiner.

"Be at ease, Colonel."

Once Stuart returned to his seat, Burnside smiled and said, "Funny, Ms. Chase, but this is how I remember you, fair-skinned and blond, but evidently you weren't last night. How do you feel?" Burnside seemed genuinely concerned, but I'd heard she could turn nasty if things didn't go her way.

"I'm fine."

Burnside glanced at Stuart. "I thought you were going sailing today."

That reminded me to reach inside my pocket and toss a key to Stuart. He fielded the key and put it away.

A black-and-white photograph sat beside a monitor and keyboard on the credenza behind the chief. The desk was huge, but all that lay on it was a yellow pad, several #2 pencils, and a manila file with "Slasher" written on it. The walls were covered with photos of Burnside with politicians, sports figures, and movie stars.

I cleared my throat. "I spoke with my boss in Columbia and they gave me the okay to work for you, though they believe it's about a funny money case. May I ask what you've learned since last night about the Ripper?"

Burnside stared at me for a long moment, then sat up in her tilt-back chair. "One, we call it the Slasher case, not the Ripper case. Two, yes, you're cleared to work with us, but that was to begin tomorrow. And three, I'd rather discuss the two men taken into custody last night, and the one shot by Colonel Stuart."

"I—I need to know what's happened while I was . . . out of touch." I shuddered and couldn't help checking my hair to make sure it wasn't covered with some guy's brains.

"You okay?" asked Stuart.

"Yes," I snapped without looking at him.

Burnside pulled a sheet of paper over and read off the results of the backyard searches of any and all property owned by someone with the surname "Long" in Charleston County. Her detectives had found nothing, and she said so.

I sat there thinking. The game couldn't go forward without a dead Ann Chapman. A "Dark Annie," as the woman was called by her friends in Whitechapel, would fit the bill, but no Ann Chapman had died last night. And someone should've—

"Ms. Chase?" asked the chief.

"Er—yes."

"Sure you're all right?"

"Just thinking . . ."

Burnside took me at my word. She said, "It didn't take long for Colonel Stuart to return to where he killed the copycat and check the ownership of the property where you were almost assaulted."

I focused my attention on the sheet of paper in front of Burnside. In my lap my hands trembled.

"Sure you're all right?"

I looked up at her. "I'm good. I'm good, and please call me Susan."

"Very well, Susan. I can't imagine what you went through last night"—she glanced at Stuart—"but I can tell you no one will act independently like that again, will they, Colonel?"

"No. They will not."

Burnside leaned back in her tilt-back chair. "Tell her what you learned last night, Colonel."

He faced me. "When I left your house I returned to the East Side and asked who owned the house where you'd been attacked, exactly what name was on the deed. From the owners I learned you were dragged off the sidewalk in front of a house owned by a Mrs. Owen P. Long. From there I went home and pulled out my book about Jack the Ripper and reread the section pertaining to the death of Ann Chapman. According to my book, a Mrs. Long found the body of Ann Chapman in 1888, and she found the body in *her* backyard."

The chief nodded in agreement. "Perhaps my detectives need to study the case file from 1888. That way we would've known Ann Chapman would be found in Mrs. Long's backyard. That's why you staked out Owen P. Long's house, isn't it?"

I nodded.

"But why didn't you come to us with this information?"

I only stared into my lap, one hand holding the other so they wouldn't tremble. There were no rings on those fingers. I was waiting for that special ring.

Stuart filled the void. "My guess is because of how Susan's contribution was dismissed at the previous meeting at my house."

Burnside stared at him for a long moment. It had to be tough knowing, if you were a black woman, that you'd almost caused the death of a black girl, and that saving the aforementioned black girl had to be left to a pair of white renegades.

"Fair enough," said the chief, "but in the future any tip, lead, or clues you come across, you bring to me or my captain of detectives. Immediately. Are we clear on that point, Susan?"

"Yes, ma'am."

The chief tapped the list. "That doesn't change the fact that my detectives failed to find a body in these backyards, or that no one by the name of Long has reported a body in their backyard, or no missing person's report has been filed for an Ann Chapman."

"And," added Stuart, "according to the Scotland Yard case files from 1888, Mrs. Long was the first person to see Jack the Ripper. I was really looking forward to meeting Mrs. Long."

"Still," said the chief, "we're done, aren't we? No Ann Chapman killed, no Ann Chapman found in Mrs. Long's backyard, and no Mrs. Long reported seeing the Ripper."

"But three other copycats popped up," argued Stuart, "like skeletons or zombies in a video game."

Burnside let out a long sigh. "Colonel, I've heard the phrase 'popped up' so often that I'm sick and tired of hearing it. I'm not saying we won't provide the proper protection for the next two women scheduled to die: Elizabeth Stride and Catherine Eddowes, but I'm tired of hearing the phrase 'popped up.'"

"He has to pull off a double homicide?" Stuart asked of me, and I realized Stuart was the renegade I'd just dubbed him. Like me, he did not want this case closed.

"Tough enough for one guy," he went on, "and probably why our Jack brought in reinforcements."

I cleared my throat. "We need to communicate with Jack."

The chief wasn't so sure. "Jack is waiting for us to communicate with him?"

I nodded. "He knows where the body of Ann Chapman is, and he knows this information must be made public, if not by the CPD or the media, then on someone's blog or a message board, and if we don't make such information public, he might be forced to call *John Boy & Billy* and discuss, in the most casual fashion, the details of the last murder."

"Meaning Ann Chapman's?" asked James Stuart.

I nodded again.

Burnside made a note on her pad. "But you agree that we have three weeks to prepare for the next attack."

"Yes, but that much time might lull us into not playing out our role in this game."

Looking annoyed, Burnside said, "There's that game element again."

"So," said Stuart, "if we found Ann Chapman and listed her under Jane Doe—"

"Sorry," I said, shaking my head. "That would be tampering with the rules and might force Jack to go public in a manner the CPD can't control. Playing along is the best way we have of controlling the end game, and catching Jack."

"Thankfully," said Burnside, putting down her pencil, "there is only one Elizabeth Stride in Charleston County, a woman who works for a property and casualty company. There are no Catherine Eddowes, the other victim who died the night of September 30, 1888."

"No Catherine Eddowes that we know of."

Burnside's eyes narrowed. "What do you know that we don't, Susan?"

"I know that Charleston was chosen because the population closely mirrors the population of 1888 Whitechapel—"

"Sorry," said a voice behind me, "but that's—"

I jumped completely out of my chair, spun around, and faced Jerry Tobias, hands going behind my back, reaching under my jacket for my weapons.

Tobias stepped back. "Sorry, Ms. Chase. I forgot about last night."

"I haven't," I said, returning to my seat, shaken.

"Susan," asked the chief, "would you care to take a break? Perhaps a cup of green tea."

It was a moment before I could reply. "No, no, I can do this."

Stuart reached over and put a hand on my shoulder, and for some reason I didn't mind. God, if I forgive this bastard for what he's done to me, it must mean I'll make an awful mother—if I'm ever able to get pregnant again. It wasn't supposed to happen. I was that rare girl who didn't need foams, jellies, diaphragms, or sponges, or even the pill. Supposedly, my reproductive wiring had been fried when my boat was blown up a couple of years ago.

"You know," said Burnside, glancing at Tobias, who had taken a seat across the room, "SLED doesn't think you're coming on board until tomorrow. Perhaps if you took the Slasher file home you might work your way through it, come in early tomorrow, and we could discuss what you've learned."

"No." I squared my shoulders and held my head high. "Ann Chapman's out there, waiting for us to find her." Gesturing at the list of names and properties, I asked, "May I have that?"

Burnside hesitated before she pushed the sheet across the desk. It was beginning to dawn on me that the chief had not fully bought into my theory of a copycat Jack.

Tobias opened his laptop. "I was told Diamond was to film his Ripper story in New Orleans, that is, before Katrina hit."

"Not possible," I said, shaking my head. "Too many Creoles."

Their puzzled looks caused me to explain. "Because of the ethnic stock that settled South Carolina, it follows that Charleston County would have the names to put the Ripper's game into play, and if he was missing a girl, he could simply haul one in from out of town."

"Oh, my God," said Burnside, "don't say that. Don't even think it."

"But I was told New Orleans was to be the original location for the film."

"You were told wrong."

"Now, Miss Chase—"

"Call me Susan, even if you disagree with me."

Tobias smiled. "Okay, Susan, but I have friends in the movie business who've helped me raise money—"

I shot a look at Burnside. "But no one called the LAPD and asked if there was a file on Darryl Diamond, did they?"

"I hardly think we want any additional exposure," said the chief, glancing at the political fixer.

"Because when Mr. Tobias called L.A.—"

"Call me Jerry," he said, smiling over the raised lid of his laptop, "even when you're disagreeing with me."

"Touché. Because when you called your friends in the movie community, they told you they were shocked by what Diamond had confessed to, the brutal murder of three women, right?"

"Well, that's right."

"They believed Diamond could make movies about serial killers, but there was no way he could kill anyone, and if you'd probed a bit deeper, I imagine you would've learned that a modern-day Jack the Ripper project was something Diamond had tried to have green-lighted in the past."

Tobias shook his head. "But I never would've asked that question."

"Because it would've led to more questions," said Stuart.

"Exactly," said the chief with a sense of finality, "and we want this case over and done with."

Still, I pushed: "Except, three more Jacks popped up. If you have a tech guy handy, you might ask him to search the web for any recent comments about serial killers, or check any trail left by the screen names on the computer seized at Diamond's house on Rainbow Row. You may learn Diamond was in contact with several serial killers, or those professing to be such killers, and since serial killers like to demonstrate their cleverness, one of them may have lured Diamond to Charleston to show him what he was capable of."

"So," asked Tobias, "there's an unlimited supply of these guys?"

"Not unlimited, but enough to make a small number of women's lives miserable, especially if you unfortunately have the wrong name. And if this game concludes, or is interrupted, what's to keep the game from resetting April eighth next year? May I ask where the three men were from who attacked Ann Chapman last night?"

Burnside appeared stunned. Probably considering the possibility of the Ripper game resetting every April eighth. That had to be every cop's nightmare, and it was a moment before she pulled another sheet from the Slasher file.

Very quickly she ran down the list. "One was a juvenile from Boulder, Colorado, with his prints in the system; the other taken into custody was a Dean Kline from San Jose, California, who works in the healthcare industry; and the one killed by Colonel Stuart was Henry Lee Tingle from Miami, Florida, though it appears that Tingle has no permanent address."

I nodded. "All joined in a common cause to play out the game created by Jack. I'll bet Jack is someone who knew Diamond in L.A., maybe even hung around his movie sets."

Burnside appeared to consider this, but said, "What concerns me is that I have no idea how we're to check the background of these three suspects or gain access to their computers without giving away what they were up to. The modern-day police department works on information and cooperation from other jurisdictions, and right now we don't have either, nor do we want to supply anything ourselves."

"You could always go to the media," suggested Stuart, again playing the devil's advocate.

"That's being considered," said the chief, "but since there are no murders scheduled until the end of the month, the mayor has agreed that we have some flexibility."

Stuart asked me, "So you believe Diamond actually felt remorse and threw himself off that hotel roof?"

"I don't think so . . . Serial killers come from different backgrounds, but what they all share in common is a feeling of superiority and a sense of inadequacy. You might think these feelings are mutually exclusive, but if Diamond *had* been the killer, he would've believed he could talk his way out of anything. Instead, he left behind a note and leaped off that roof." Looking at the chief, I added, "I'm sure you're having the handwriting analyzed."

Burnside nodded.

"So you don't think Diamond was the Ripper?" asked Stuart.

"I believe Diamond was involved, though to what extent I don't know." I got to my feet. "I really need to get going. Jack is waiting for us to find Annie Chapman and he wants little or no media involvement until the conclusion of the game."

"He doesn't want the media to know?" asked Tobias from the other side of the room. "But I would've thought—"

"Media involvement would be like having a parent looking over your shoulder while you were playing a violent video game. How much fun could that be, and how effective could you be as a player?"

Burnside asked, "So Jack is working as hard as we are to keep this hush-hush?"

"I believe so . . . With authenticators, such as peritonitis and the fire in the harbor, this has become a contest between Jack and the CPD, and you can assume Jack doesn't believe the cops are up to the challenge." I held up the sheet of paper. Now that my nerves had calmed down, the adrenaline had begun to flow. "So it's okay to check these backyards?"

"Of course, and take Stuart with you. I want someone other than one of my detectives double-checking those properties."

I glanced at Stuart. "I usually work alone."

"Not this time you don't. To be blunt, Susan, after last night I want you partnered with someone."

"He'll need a disguise."

"Disguise?" asked more than one of them.

"Well, I'm not going out there looking like me." I held up the list of properties. "You've already had your detectives knocking on these doors, haven't you?"

Burnside nodded.

"What kind of disguise?" asked Tobias.

"What? Oh, I'll probably borrow a pickup from SCE&G, along with a pair of coveralls, an ID, and a flashlight."

"Sounds reasonable," said Tobias, nodding.

"And if we find the body of Ann Chapman, you know what that means?"

"Yes, yes," said Burnside rather gloomily. "It means the game continues."

"Actually," I said, feeling more like myself, "in the words of a famous detective from that era: The game is afoot!"

CHAPTER EIGHTEEN

Jerry Tobias put down his computer and followed Chase and Stuart out of Burnside's office. There he took the young woman aside, into a waiting room, commonly called the docks.

A proprietary look from Tobias sent Stuart on his way down the hall. "A question for you, Ms. Chase."

"Yes?"

"About this boat that blew up a couple of years ago in Murrells Inlet . . ."

"*Daddy's Girl.* I wasn't aboard. My mother was. I was blown off the pier and into the Waterway."

"Sorry to hear that. Did they ever catch the guy who did it?"

She shook her head. "Never did. Still hiding out in Francis Marion, as far as anyone knows."

Tobias stared at the young woman for a long moment, and then gestured toward the chief's office door. "Eugenia has good reason to be worried about any aftereffects from your escapade last night, but I'm more concerned that you suffer residual effects from the blast that blew up your boat, though it happened years ago."

The young woman flashed a reassuring smile. "I understand your concern. But happily, it appears that I have fully recovered."

"That may be true," said Tobias, "but if you're such a hotshot investigator, why did SLED stick you in cold cases? All due respect to cold cases, but that makes you about the lowest investigator on the SLED totem pole."

Tobias returned to Burnside's office but continued to stare at the office door. Even once he closed it.

"She has a boyfriend, Jerry."

Tobias continued to stare at the door.

"Please, Jerry," said Burnside with some degree of irritation, "as young as she appears, I don't think Susan Chase is the type of woman to be rescued, by you, by anyone."

Tobias left the door, picked up his laptop, and took a seat in front of Burnside's desk. In the vacant visitor's chair he placed his laptop, then pulled out his cigarettes.

After lighting up, he said, "I've been told that you can drop Chase in the middle of Francis Marion National Forest and that you'd never find her, but she could find you."

"And this is relevant how?"

"Because the guy who blew up Chase's boat and killed her mother hid out in Francis Marion, and he's never been found."

"So?"

"So, on the way back down here, I contacted a former diplomat by the name of Harry Poinsett, who put me in touch with a guy named J.D. Warden, now retired, who supervised Chase in Myrtle Beach. Warden says you underestimate Chase at your own peril. Nothing brings out the huntress in Chase like a woman in jeopardy, and Charleston will have more than one woman in jeopardy by the end of this month."

Next up were McPherson and Fenwick, who took seats in Burnside's visitors' chairs and spent considerable time waving away the heavy odor of cigarette smoke.

The chief used her pencil to check off an item on her yellow pad and add yet another item. When she raised her head, she found the two men staring at her. Burnside almost smiled, but that was one of the habits she'd had to break in her climb up the ladder. Now she masked her face with what she called her professional expression.

"Anything I should know?" It was her favorite preemptory question and always put the ball in the opposition's court.

McPherson knew how to play the game and returned the ball with vigor. "Well, Chief, something like this doesn't happen in a vacuum and it's taxing our resources. Sam Gadsden flew up to Columbus and spent the day learning nothing more than Mary Ann Nichols' family were regular folks, not to mention their trip to Charleston had been planned for months. It was their sixteenth wedding anniversary, so the killer had to know they were coming and where they were staying.

They had reservations all over town."

"Handwriting analysis of the suicide note?"

"Not Diamond's, and there was no usable trace or serology evidence recovered at the Nichols' crime scene. Anyway, when Sam returned from Columbus, he re-interviewed everyone at the crime scenes and came up with zip. Everyone's accounted for at that hotel." McPherson shook his head. "This is becoming a regular whodunit, and that's not good for anyone's budget."

"The mayor said he'd cover the overtime. And while you're being taxed to the limit, has anyone found Catherine Eddowes?"

"I have one of my people working on that," said Fenwick. "John Patrick said he could handle it, working an extra hour or so into his schedule each day. In the event anything slips out, it's being referred to as Operation Slasher."

"An after-action report," said Burnside to McPherson, "as to what the city of Charleston could've done to better protect the victims of Darryl Diamond."

"Nothing from what I can see," said McPherson.

"Of course not, but this is what the mayor wants."

"The mayor's just covering his butt."

"Covering everyone's butt. Continue, Hugh."

"John Patrick will report directly to me, and, of course to you, if you should want to know anything."

"Only after you've sorted through his information. Even with a wild man running around the streets of Charleston, I don't have time for more meetings. Your man knows all this is hush-hush?"

"Chief, everything we do is hush-hush. The people picked for the Intel Squad undergo a vigorous background check. There are no men with a wandering eye, no gays still in the closet, no women who're party animals."

"Very well then," said Burnside, and she related the high points of her conversation with Chase.

McPherson was not pleased.

"I know you think she's too young, Mac. Hell, I think she's too young, but Chase believes she knows something—what that is I have no clue, but we should have some idea by this afternoon. Besides, her hours don't come out of your budget." She gestured at Fenwick with her pencil. "Tell him, Hugh."

Turning to McPherson, Fenwick said, "Chief Burnside asked me to do two things: first was to set in motion the protection for both Stride and Eddowes—"

"The next victims of the Slasher," explained Burnside, "aka, the Ripper."

"I know who they are," said McPherson, nodding. "I have one of the books."

"I just hope you didn't purchase it at a local bookstore or borrow a copy from the library."

"I bought it on the web. I don't have time for shopping, or reading, but I'm going to read this one cover-to-cover, just as I did the Good Book."

Burnside nodded and looked at her Intel chief.

"Regarding your second request, I have someone working out of the office and checking every . . . Chief, it's really clumsy talking about the Slasher when it's all these Jack the Ripper sites being checked."

"That's just what I want to hear. Look," she said, shaking her pencil at them, "you want to call the UNSUB the Ripper when we're discussing the case, so be it, but when it comes to the file, its name is the

Slasher file, a handy way to remind you to watch what you say because you never know who may be listening or feeding information to the media."

"Makes sense," said Fenwick, and he went on to explain that one of his detectives would be working at home. "Isaac Henry actually has better computers than we have in our own department, and he's sorting through the Jack the Ripper web sites, message boards, blogs, et cetera. He's also working with the servers who handled the e-mail for the two men taken into custody and the one killed by Colonel Stuart. Since they haven't been booked, we can't begin negotiating for access to their computers."

"And if either of them asks for a lawyer," said McPherson, "the request has to come through me." The captain of detectives set his jaw. "There'll be no lawyers for these two birds unless they understand it'd go a lot easier on them if they give us complete access to their computers."

Fenwick looked up from his yellow pad. "We can get warrants for all three if you'd like. They're just hanging fire."

"Not yet." Burnside pondered something on her list, then looked up. "You do realize there may be someone who knows where the body of Ann Chapman is."

Both men frowned, not getting her drift.

"It's the reason Chase insists on double-checking behind Waring and Gadsden. She believes there's a dead Ann Chapman out there and the Ripper wants us to find her."

"I don't like someone from SLED checking behind us," groused McPherson.

"No one does, but they do it all the time. Chase says a Mrs. Long should've seen the Ripper last night, and if we don't make such information public, it will be published on the web, on a message board, or in a blog, so the players know the game can proceed."

McPherson grinned. "I thought you didn't want the Ripper case referred to as a game."

"I still don't. It trivializes the women this maniac kills."

McPherson continued to smile. "How did you handle the story of Dirty Harry striking fear into the hearts of evildoers? The dealers on Nassau Street have never been lonelier."

"The mayor did it for me. But I did ask Stuart to call Mary Kate Belle and explain that he was at a friend's house when he heard a girl scream. He charged out the door, shot the bad guy, and ended up on desk duty. I tried to impress on Stuart that if he was really good, he'd make sure Mary Kate Belle never approaches anyone at the hospital where the injured girl was taken. Personally, I don't think Mary Kate is all that smart, but just in case, the mayor called the hospital administrator and told him that what happened in his ER last night was the result of a sting being run by the CPD and asked that no one in the ER speak to the media."

"Might work," said McPherson.

"Mary Kate Belle is James Stuart's cousin, for any of you who don't know—"

"I didn't know that," said Fenwick, "but I do know Mary Kate Belle is tight with Chase."

"I wouldn't be surprised if Chase was feeding information to Belle," predicted McPherson.

"Is this something you know for sure, Mac, or is this your innate sexism raising its ugly head?"

Fenwick stared at his pad while McPherson sputtered about how evenhandedly he treated the personnel under his command.

"Yeah, yeah. I'm just happy I don't work for you."

"If you remember, Chief, you did work for me."

"I also remember I had difficulty improving my efficiency ratings while under your command."

"Now, Chief, don't make this personal—"

Fenwick jumped in to get the conversation back on track. "This investigation Stuart and Chase are conducting, double-checking the Longs' backyards, is this make-work or do you really think Chase is on to something?"

"Chase insisted on it," said Burnside, leaning back in her chair, "and since she had someone's brains splattered all over her last night, I gave her the benefit of the doubt."

"What she did last night was just plain stupid, Eugenia. She could've been killed."

"Oh, yeah, like this department has ever done anything to encourage this girl to share her ideas. Chase also predicted that the guy who murdered Ann Chapman might drop the information during a conversation on *John Boy & Billy,* unless the CPD finds the body first."

"What's that?" asked McPherson.

"A morning radio show."

"And how are we supposed to cover talk radio?" asked McPherson, becoming more exasperated.

"Sadly, the media will bring the matter to our attention when and if it happens."

"Which," said Fenwick, "is not something we want, right?"

"Like I told James Stuart, if the story comes out, it comes out. I'd rather it didn't because we'd have a feeding frenzy on our hands; CNN, Fox, the whole freak show would be here."

"And," said McPherson, "you put the two people who have the most contact with the media searching for this supposedly dead Ann Chapman. If they don't find her, Chase or Stuart might let it slip what they're up to, just to compensate for the lack of a body."

Burnside regarded him. "Mac, I don't think I'd want it known that I'd called James Stuart a liar. Dueling may have been outlawed years ago, but you know how jealously reputations are guarded in this city. Still," she said, sitting up, "I think Chase can pull this off. For one thing, she told Stuart he'd have to wear a disguise to accompany her today."

"What kind of disguise?" asked Fenwick.

Burnside told them. The information irritated McPherson but seemed to intrigue Fenwick.

"That might work," said the Intel chief, nodding in agreement. "People of discretion are hard to come by."

McPherson frowned at Fenwick.

"Hey," said the Intel chief, "I'm just saying—"

"Mac," said the chief, looking up from her notes again, "if you're running short of personnel, request help from burglary, stolen vehicles, or white collar crime. Tell them I asked you to ask, and like Hugh said, seek out those who can be discreet."

McPherson seemed to be considering how discreet

he should be. He looked everywhere but at the chief.

"Mac, if you've got something on your mind, spit it out."

"All right, I will. You know that Mary Kate Belle was with Chase when they found Diamond's body."

Burnside and Fenwick only stared at him.

McPherson shrugged. "Belle was taking pictures with her cell phone, the ones that showed up in the newspaper. In the ensuing investigation Waring and Gadsden found Chase and Belle in Diamond's hotel room. Chase and Belle may be lesbians, Chief."

Burnside sighed. "Since Chase has to work with you, I certainly hope she's not."

"I'm not making this up. When Waring and Gadsden arrived at Diamond's room, the women didn't have all their clothes on."

"Uh-huh, and where are Waring and Gadsden now?"

"Working on their paperwork from last night."

"Have them come see me."

"I will."

Burnside pointed at her phone with her pencil. "Call them now, Mac. I want to clarify what you've just said."

McPherson made the call and told the two detectives to immediately report to Burnside's office. "Really, Chief, I'm not making this up. I checked the hotel tapes. The camera on the fourth floor had been tinkered with—"

"Probably shoved upwards by a mop handle or a broomstick," said Fenwick. "The hotel doesn't pay much attention to camera maintenance unless there's a complaint."

McPherson wasn't finished. "That doesn't change the fact that lobby cameras filmed Chase with a high-priced call girl and later that night with Mary Kate Belle."

"Which may mean," said Burnside, speaking to her Intel chief, "that Darryl Diamond did not commit suicide."

McPherson looked from Fenwick to his boss. He didn't know what they were talking about. He was busy chasing other rabbits.

"So what are you saying?" Fenwick asked the chief.

"That Darryl Diamond never was the Ripper but knew Jack. That's why I sent Jerry Tobias to L.A. to dig into Diamond's past."

CHAPTER NINETEEN

I was chatting up the guard in the sally port when I heard the honk of the Mustang. I smiled, said good-bye, and was buzzed through the back door. Still, I remained mute all the way over to South Carolina Electric and Gas. At SCE&G we struggled into our coveralls, were shown a vehicle I had to sign for, and hit the road, Stuart driving once again.

On the way to the first house, he asked, "So, that guy you're living with, are you planning on marrying him or what?"

My head snapped around. "I really don't think that's any of your business."

Stuart went silent; right through our examination of the empty lot and the backyard of the first house.

Back in the pickup, I shifted around to get comfortable, not only in my seat but because of the tight fit of my coveralls. And maybe that wasn't it at all. Stuart had apologized more than once, offered Chad and me the use of his schooner for the day, and nobody even knew I'd been pregnant. Probably never would.

Except Jacqueline. Jackie could keep a secret. I couldn't tell Mary Kate without having it broadcast all over Charleston. And I did have to confide in someone. I wasn't living in guy country. Well, actually, I was, which made it even more important for me to talk this out with someone.

"Had lunch yet?" asked Stuart, breaking into my thoughts.

"I never had breakfast."

"Oh, one of those women."

"No. I like to eat. I just didn't take time this morning."

Stuart raised a finger off the steering wheel and pointed in the direction of Bessinger's up ahead on the Savannah Highway. "Would you eat barbecue?"

"Right now, I'd eat just about anything."

While we waited for our meal, and because of our coveralls, we fielded complaints about the power company. To back off these jokers, I leaned toward Stuart and asked him if he knew the first serial killer in America hailed from Charleston, and that *he* was a *she.*

"One of the first women to be hung in the colonies, that is, after spending a year in the Old Jail on Magazine Street."

"I know the place. It houses the American College of the Building Arts."

"Exactly, and two hundred years ago, a fur trader by the name of John Peeples was traveling into the backcountry when he stopped to water his horses at Six

Mile House on the Old Dorchester Road. Several men lounging around Six Mile House threatened Peeples when he and his traveling companion wouldn't give up some of their gear, and this gang included a woman. A fight broke out, and it was said that one of the most savage fighters was the woman. When Peeples moved on, some of the gang followed them and relieved them of their money.

"Now John Peeples could stand being threatened, harassed, and even being kicked around, but he wasn't going home and tell his wife that he'd lost all his money. He returned to Charleston and alerted the authorities, and Peeples was willing to name names. At the time, highway robbery was a hanging offense in the colonies."

"Lavinia Fisher, right?"

"Exactly. She and her husband, John, spent a year in the Old Jail, and tried to escape when they were moved upstairs to the debtors' quarters. Unfortunately, their rope made of blankets broke, and John, being the stand-up guy that he was, left Lavinia holding the rope, so to speak. Later, he was captured and returned to the jail."

Stuart laughed. "I wouldn't have wanted to be Lavinia's husband, and here I'm not talking about the hanging."

"You've got that right. Lavinia's spirit's so strong it's tough to get anyone to spend the night with you in the Unitarian cemetery. That's where she's buried."

Stuart had been looking toward the kitchen. Now he looked at me. "Sounds like you've tried."

"Well, I was much younger then."

Again he laughed. "Well, don't tell anyone you were ever younger. Everyone thinks you're too young as it is."

"Gee, thanks for sharing."

"Maybe it's in your genes. When all your girlfriends have lost their looks, you'll look ten years younger."

"Sorry, I'd rather be taken seriously now."

One of the jokers I could not back off had continued to stare at me as I told my tale. He dressed like a used car salesman and spoke with the same authority.

"That ain't the way it was."

I gave him a frosty smile. "You mean the legend."

He got up from his table and came over. "It's no legend that Lavinia was a real beauty and men come from all over to see her. That's why John Fisher was able to trick them into staying the night."

"That might've been rather unhealthy," said Stuart, "considering the guys Lavinia hung out with."

The guy laughed. "Well, you know women. They're going to get us one way or another." And he left, leaving his tray on the table instead of dumping it into the trash.

I watched him go. "Some people can't handle reality."

"Personally, I've always preferred the legend myself."

"Hey, you want legend I can give you legend." I drank from my lemonade before beginning again. "One dark and stormy night John Peeples was traveling on the Dorchester Road when he stopped at Six Mile House. But there were no rooms at the inn. There was, however, a beautiful innkeeper and she charmed Peeples into having a draft of ale before pressing on. It was really raining out there, and while Peeples talked, he never wondered why such a beautiful woman would take an interest in him. But what made Peeples nervous wasn't Lavinia but her husband and a couple of his guy pals. They'd welcomed Peeples in out of the rain, even gone out into the storm and stabled Peeples' horse. They fed the animal, then fed Peeples.

"There was little Peeples could do without being rude, so he accepted the meal and more conversation with this gorgeous gal. Anyway, to make a long story short, over dinner and several tankards of ale, Peeples told Lavinia how much money he carried and that no one would miss him if he failed to return home. Then, when Lavinia returned with a hot cup of tea, she had good news. A room had just become available.

"Now, this is where Peeples got lucky, or finally wised up. Alone in his room with that hot cup of tea, which Peeples didn't drink, an oddity for an American at that time in the colonies, he remembered the stories about men rumored to have disappeared at Six Mile House. So instead of sleeping in the bed, he took a seat in a chair in the corner. If Lavinia's husband and his friends planned on sneaking in and emptying his pockets, he'd be ready for them. And in the middle of the night, just as expected, Peeples heard someone coming through the door. But when he lit his lantern, he saw the noise wasn't coming from the door but the bed. The bed had disappeared!"

Our food had arrived, and the waiter stood, rapt, listening. "Taking the lamp over to the opening, Peeples found a contraption that John Fisher had rigged up, where, with one jerk of a lever from behind a false wall, the bed turned upside down and dumped the occupant into a pit where the victim either died from the fall or was left to starve to death.

"That was enough for Peeples, and despite the storm, he jumped out the window, threw back the doors of the barn, leaped on his horse, and raced into Charleston. When the sheriff arrived to investigate, he wasn't swayed by Lavinia's charms but went straight upstairs, dismantled the bed, and sent his men down into the hole, where they found more than one set of bones. While his deputies investigated the hole, the sheriff searched the pantry and found herbs that, if mixed in tea, would be enough to knock out a grown man."

The waiter shoved our trays on the table and beat a hasty retreat to the kitchen.

Stuart watched the kid go. "Like I said, all in all, I like the legend better."

"Well, we gals certainly hope so," I said, squirting ketchup on my fries. "It certainly enhances our feminine mystique."

CHAPTER TWENTY

As we got out of the pickup at the next address, a pack of greyhounds appeared to take no more than a few steps, racing from the rear of the backyard to the chain-link fencing near the front of the house. There appeared to be five of them in all colors from grays to fawn, one of them brindle.

I said, "No way anyone checked out this backyard."

"The dogs might not've been back here when the body was dumped, if the body was dumped here."

I pointed at the fresh droppings on the rear side of the fence. "I don't know about that . . ."

Stuart stood on tiptoes, stared for the longest time, and then pointed at the rear fence. The pack instantly leaped for his hand, though he held that hand a good yard from the rusty chain-link fence.

"What?" I asked, stepping back involuntarily. The chain-link fence of the backyard was flanked by wooden fences, courtesy of both neighbors, and both neighbors' homes were similar: slate shingle homes with long front porches but no railings.

"I think there's another fence back there."

"Sure. The one running across the backyard."

"No, no," said Stuart, coming down off his toes. "I think there's another chain-link fence even taller than the Longs'." He studied the pack. "Perhaps the neighbor has children and the mother won't let them play in the backyard without the security of a secondary fence between her yard and the Longs'."

Gosh, I'd never thought of that. God, but I was going to be the worst mother ever.

"On the other side of the second fence appears to be a swing set, sandbox, and concrete pad with an inflatable swimming pool."

"You have good eyes."

"Well, you have to in . . ." His voice drifted off.

"People?" called a female voice from the front of the house. "Who are you people?"

An elderly woman wearing a housecoat and leaning on a cane peered at us from her front porch. There was a swing at her end, and as we approached her, a bearded man rolled his wheelchair over to the edge of the neighbor's porch.

"May I help you?" asked the elderly woman wearing the housecoat.

"Mrs. Long," said Stuart, "would you call your dogs inside so we can enter your backyard?"

"Why certainly. Anything for the power company." She turned to go.

The bearded neighbor eyed us and our coveralls. "Mrs. Long, make these people show you some ID. They may be from Social Services."

The elderly woman returned to our end of the porch. "That's certainly reasonable."

We held up the phony IDs from SCE&G clipped to our coveralls, and Mrs. Long went inside for the key to the car gate located on the other side of the house. While she was inside, Stuart began chatting up the legless vet, and it was only minutes before the two of them were laughing and joking, which, if you thought about it, was the only way to handle what had happened in that hellhole halfway around the world.

I busied myself by spraying the gate lock with a can of WD-40 found in the pickup. It'd been a long time since anyone had stuck a key in this lock. The roll-away trash containers sat nose-in against the fence, street side. After unlocking the wide gate of the chain-link fence and swinging it back, the two of us strolled into the backyard. I glanced at the back door of the house but mainly concentrated on where I was putting my feet. We passed a doghouse in need of repair and a shelter where the dogs could feed out of the rain.

"We're just lucky they weren't guard dogs."

"I've been trained to handle guard dogs," said Stuart in all seriousness.

"Yeah, right. Reminds me of the old joke about the two hikers running for their lives from a bear. One hiker turned to the other and asked why they were running since neither of them could possibly outrun a bear. His fellow hiker said, 'I don't have to outrun the bear. I only have to outrun you.'"

A rusty chain-link fence ran across the rear of the Longs' property, and as I've mentioned, both neighbors had wooden fencing flanking the Longs' yard, making it perfectly clear that both neighbors knew if the greyhounds saw someone, anyone, they would instantly be at that section of the fence. Which, if you understood the psychology of the breed, didn't make much sense, unless, of course, you had small children who might startle easily.

Stuart was right. Another chain-link fence had been built behind Mrs. Long's, perhaps a foot taller than hers, and set off from the Longs' fence by about six feet. And in this narrow area between the old and new fences, despite some crazed digging by the greyhounds, lay the body of a woman.

CHAPTER TWENTY-ONE

Each of us placed a hand on the top rail and vaulted the fence, landing in the six-foot area between the two fences. Stuart caught me and steadied me when I came over, and together we approached the dead woman. One of her feet had been gotten at by the dogs, but with everything else wrong with her, that was easy to ignore as we knelt beside the body.

The woman was much older than the other three victims, and she lay on her back, legs drawn up, small intestines and abdomen cut away. Above her right shoulder lay the intestines that had been removed from her abdomen, and the upper part of the body was covered in dried blood, as was the ground around her upper torso. Her throat had been cut in a ragged manner—she'd probably been murdered here, and all she wore was a nightgown, ripped open. At her head lay two new potatoes.

"Potatoes," grunted Stuart. "In eighteen-eighty-eight, the prostitute Ann Chapman was eating potatoes in the kitchen of the house where she'd been living."

"She only slept there. She didn't have a room."

Stuart shook his head. "Hard to believe people paid for a chair to sleep in and called it lodging."

"Maybe that's why so many people came to America. Even an indentured servant would have a bed of his own."

From where he knelt, Stuart looked beyond the rusty fence and the dilapidated doghouse to the house. "You figure Mrs. Long had anything to do with this?"

"No, but we'd better treat the backyard, and parts of the adjoining backyards, as the crime scene, perhaps her whole yard."

There was something under the woman, and using my pen, I lifted her elbow.

"Oh, this guy is good." I pointed at the coins and the rings under the woman's elbow.

"Right out of the legend." Stuart stood up and pulled me to my feet. "The prostitute Annie Chapman told the landlord not to worry about the money for the night's lodging, that she'd be right back."

"And the next time she was seen," I gestured at the body, "was when she was found dissected like this in Mrs. Long's backyard."

Both of us needed a break from being this close to such slaughter—the woman had literally been gutted—so we walked to the opposite end of the narrowly enclosed area.

The neighborhood appeared quiet and desolate, everyone at work. No trees, few bushes, and the wooden fences on both sides of the Longs' backyard making it impossible to see into the next-door neighbor's yard.

I looked from one wooden fence to the other. There

was something different about the fences. I wandered back in the direction of the body.

"Strange the body wasn't noticed," said Stuart, trailing along.

"Maybe the neighbors are on vacation. No," I said, shaking my head. "Children have to return to school by the third week of . . . " My voice drifted off. I looked from one set of fencing to the other, then I slapped my forehead. "What a dummy I've been."

I pointed to the wooden fence on the other side of the Longs' yard, then back to the wooden fence near where we stood. "The fences are different but the same wood was used. The fence over there is on the neighbor's side of the chain-link fence and faces the neighbor's yard, meaning the strips or railings holding the fencing together can be seen from our side. But the fence near us—this fence was built by someone in the Long family and built inside the chain-link because it faces the Longs' backyard."

Stuart looked from one fence to the other. "And the significance of that is?"

"You have a perfect storm of a dump site. I could've caught the SOB. No," I said, shaking my head once again. "I *should've* caught the SOB."

"You could . . . should've caught . . . ?" asked Stuart. He was being left way behind.

I straightened up to my full height and scanned the neighborhood. The world continued to turn on its axis, but it appeared to swirl around me: the houses in their rows, the lack of bushes or trees, the streets I could see from this yard, the miscellaneous stuff in backyards, and the damn fences! I should have been ready . . . I should've been prepared!

"Susan . . .?"

I became aware that he was speaking to me. Stuart's face came into focus but only after I gripped the chain-link fence.

"Are you all right?" he asked.

"No, no, no. I botched this." I looked to where Ann Chapman's body lay. "I screwed up just as I did when Mary Ann Nichols flew into town. Of course she would've been the better prospect for the game. She was a tourist, not some massage therapist."

"Better prospect? What the hell are you talking about? What was it you were supposed to know?"

"I was lurking that night . . ."—my voice drifted off and I smiled at him, "just as you were lurking across the street from Ann Chapman's when you shot that copycat."

Stuart became rather stiff. "I think I've apologized quite enough for that."

I took my hand off the chain-link fence and put it on his arm. "No, no, it wasn't anything you did. It was what *I* didn't do." I gestured at the neighborhood. "I should've anticipated this dump site as I did the murder of Mary Ann Nichols."

Stuart looked around, trying to understand. "And how would you have known Ann Chapman would be dumped here?"

My hand fell away from his arm. "I could've had the cops on Ann Chapman. Hell, you were already there." I pointed at the ground at my feet. "I should've been here." I felt like stamping my foot.

"I don't follow . . ."

"Because Jack would've been here. Ann Chapman

might have died—maybe not, since I think she was murdered here. But I was caught up in catching Jack somewhere else. I should've known about this place. I should've known he would be here."

It was a moment before Stuart processed all this, or wanted to move onto something more sensible. Sometimes I babble when my mind begins to race.

"Okay, then," he asked. "What's next?"

"Why don't you start by interviewing anyone you can find at home, and start with the house behind the Longs'." While Stuart unzipped his coveralls and fought to pull them over his feet, I stared at the house directly behind us. "None of the other neighbors have chain-link or wooden fences. I wonder what their story is, and if they got a look at Jack."

We didn't have to wait long to find out. A young woman came out of the house, slid the glass door shut behind her, and stepped off the concrete slab serving as a patio. She had a child on her hip.

Oh, thanks. Just what I needed. Another reminder of my aborted motherhood.

"Start with her," I said. "But you may want to make a quick call to the chief and tell her what we've found."

"Thanks," said Stuart, smiling. By the time the mother reached us, Stuart had finished his call and reported that Burnside had not sounded pleased.

"Of course not. Not only did one of her detectives blow it, but it means the game continues."

The baby was a handsome blond boy with a tentative smile, and the mother a slender blonde with more than adequate hips.

"You're with the power company?" she asked. "I don't blame you for wearing those . . ." Her voice trailed off as she realized there was a body lying between the two fences, technically on her property.

"Oh, my Lord!" She turned away, shielding the child's eyes.

Stuart thrust his coveralls into my hands, then vaulted the taller fence, caught up with the woman, and put an arm around her. When she tried to look again, Stuart wouldn't allow it, walking her back to her house.

"See if she needs to call a family member or if she has other children," I called after him. "Find out where they are, at day care or at a neighbor's."

Without turning around, Stuart waved his acknowledgment.

I opened a line to the captain of detectives and explained what we'd found. "How do you want to handle this?" I asked, using as neutral a tone as possible.

"You're sure the woman's dead?" asked McPherson.

"Well, some of her intestines have been removed and are lying on her shoulder. Yeah. I'd say she's pretty much gone."

"You don't have to be a smart aleck, Chase."

There was a pause at the end of the line; McPherson considering who he had left to send to another crime scene. The pickings had to be slim.

"Isn't Stuart with you?" he asked.

"Interviewing the neighbors."

"He's not qualified to do that."

"Well, whoever searched this backyard wasn't qualified to search backyards."

"Secure the crime scene, Chase, and keep your opinions to yourself, especially until we ID the victim."

"Don't worry. It's Ann Chapman."

"And how do you know that?"

"She has two new potatoes above her shoulder, along with some coins and rings under her arm."

"Can you identify the coins and rings?"

"The rings appear to be cheap costume jewelry, but the two coins are farthings."

"What's a farthing?"

"A discontinued English coin."

"Rare?"

"Not at all. The farthing was last issued in 1956."

"Chase, how do you know all this?"

"It's part of the Ripper legend."

"Anything else?"

"Yes. I believe the crime-scene unit will find an envelope bearing the crest of the Citadel under the body, probably placed there to keep it from blowing away."

"What's the Citadel's connection with Jack the Ripper?"

"None that I know of, but a torn envelope was found near the body of Ann Chapman in Whitechapel, an envelope containing a couple of pills. The envelope had the regimental crest of the First Battalion, Surrey Regiment, North Camp, Farborough, England. Any decent copycat could come up with a farthing, but the Surrey regiment no longer exists as a separate entity, so an envelope from the Citadel would fill the bill."

"And you know this how?"

"I googled it."

CHAPTER TWENTY-TWO

I was handing the pairs of coveralls through the window of the SCE&G pickup when sirens filled the air. The guy from the power company dropped both pairs on the seat and tossed me the keys to Stuart's Mustang, parked across the street.

"Tell the colonel he has a fine ride."

He drove down the street, whipped around the corner, and was gone before two patrol cars, light bars flashing and sirens wailing, pulled to a stop near the curb. Correction: Make that one patrol car with lights and siren. The other ran silent.

One of the patrolmen I knew, the other I did not, and the cop I did not know got out of his car, stood on the far side, and called for me to identify myself. I did, and he came around his patrol car and asked to see my ID, light bar still flashing.

I glanced at my SLED ID hanging outside my blouse and saw that he could read the information if he cared to. "Please turn off your light bar. You're drawing unnecessary attention to a crime scene, Officer Gibbes," reading *his* nametag.

Up and down the street, people wandered out on their porches. The other patrolman, McKelvey, an older guy who still worked the streets, greeted me as he always does.

"Well, well, little Miss Susan Chase, and what sort of trouble have you gotten yourself into this time?"

"We have a body in the backyard, actually between two chain-link fences between the two backyards."

He frowned.

"You'd have to see it to understand, but I don't think you want to go back there until the crime-scene unit clears the area."

McKelvey glanced at the house. Mrs. Long stood at the storm door, leaning on her cane, the disabled guy in the wheelchair was making a phone call on his cell, and the greyhounds were at every window, excited by the growing crowd. More friends to play with.

By the time I'd finished explaining where the crime-scene tape should be unfurled, the coroner arrived, followed by the mobile crime-scene truck with Jacqueline Marion at the wheel. Officer Gibbes joined us after extinguishing his light bar, and I noticed he'd eaten more than his share of donuts since joining the force.

To Gibbes I said, "The wooden fencing is high enough on the neighbors' sides that someone would need a ladder to throw a body over, so I'd concentrate on Mrs. Long's yard, the yard behind hers, and an area of at least ten feet inside the adjoining yards. You'll need permission to enter the adjoining yards."

Gibbes looked at McKelvey for the okay before heading to his car to dig out the crime-scene tape.

Across the street, a guy on a walker shouted from his porch, "You going to get rid of those damn dogs?"

Everyone looked at the man, but essentially ignored him.

When the coroner climbed out of his sedan, we could see he no longer wore white. Of course not. It was past Labor Day. "Where's the body?" he asked.

"In the backyard."

He peered at the dogs staring at us from the windows and the storm door. "Crime scene secured?"

"We're working on it."

"You do that." He returned to his car, leaned against it, and took some paperwork from a coat pocket.

Jacqueline Marion walked over, leaning to one side from the weight of carrying her crime-scene kit. "Public information officer is right behind me. They're trying to keep everything off the radio. Use your cell if you have to. What you got?" Jacqueline appeared rather pale for someone with so many freckles, and I wondered if she was ill.

"We believe it to be the body of Ann Chapman."

"You have a definite ID?" asked Gibbes, returning with the yellow tape dug out of his trunk.

I only stared at him.

"Did the neighbors know the deceased?" he pressed.

McKelvey broke in, "Why don't we give Susan a chance to finish and then you can make a proper ass out of yourself, Gibbes."

To McKelvey and Marion, I said, "There's staging around the body so treat the whole yard as a crime scene, and watch where you put your feet."

Jacqueline was staring toward the Longs' backyard. "I never believed . . ." She looked at me. "I thought Ann Chapman was a figment of someone's overheated imagination."

"Don't I wish." I told her where the body could be found, explained the situation with the double fence, and where James Stuart was at the moment.

"Sheesh," said McKelvey, shaking his head. "That guy always gets the girl."

As if hearing us, my phone rang.

"Woman's calmed down," said Stuart. "Her mother's coming over to pick up the children, but she wants animal control to take the dogs away or no one enters her property." He added, "She's locking the sliding glass door and pulling the curtains as I speak. I've called Chief Burnside for a warrant."

"What kind of dogs are these?" asked the coroner, looking up from his paperwork.

"Greyhounds."

He laughed. "Then we'll be mauled to death by love."

To the younger patrolman, McKelvey said, "Get started with the tape, Gibbes."

"Run tape everywhere she said—why?"

Before he could answer, a loud screech came from the far end of the street, and one of those new Buick sedans raced around the corner and headed toward us, pulling to a stop in Mrs. Long's driveway.

"That's why," said McKelvey to Gibbes.

A middle-aged man climbed out of the car, slammed the door behind him, and strode in our direction.

"What's going on here?" He was a thin guy with a stomach that made him look as if he was hiding a watermelon under his pullover.

"Sir," said McKelvey, stepping forward to meet him, "you must move your vehicle from that property."

"Why? Is there something wrong with my mother?" The man looked from one of us to the other and then headed for the house.

"The dogs must remain in the house," I said to his back.

The guy stopped and returned to where we stood. During his return trip, he waved at the man in the wheelchair. "Thanks for the call, Eddie."

The man in the wheelchair acknowledged him by holding high his cell phone.

"Mr. Long," I asked, "are you going to comply with the request of this police officer?"

"Do I know you?" He peered at my lanyard ID, then looked at the other two men. "What's going on here?"

Sergeant McKelvey, who knew better than to mess around with an active crime scene, got in the man's face. "Well, sir, in about thirty seconds I'm going to have Officer Gibbes put the cuffs on you and your mother's neighbors will see him do it."

Long stepped back. "But why?"

To Gibbes, McKelvey said, "Cuff him!"

Of course, the younger cop had not rolled out an inch of crime-scene tape, but remained where the action was. Gibbes did, however, unhook a pair of cuffs from his utility belt.

"You are now under arrest for trespass," said Sergeant McKelvey.

"But this is my mother's house!" objected the watermelon man.

"Yes, sir, I understand, and I want to make it perfectly clear that if you don't move your car, you will be handcuffed and taken downtown. Think of how that will affect your mother."

"But I need to talk with her."

"First move the car."

"Is she—is she okay?" he asked, looking at me for sympathy.

I ignored him and headed for the house.

He followed me. "You have to tell me what's going on." When he saw that I wouldn't, he added, "Really, greyhounds are no threat."

"I know that."

I climbed the steps to the porch, and when Mrs. Long tried to open her storm door, I put a foot against it. The greyhounds slammed into the door, cracking the glass. When the animals realized they couldn't get to me, sad looks appeared on all their faces.

"Mrs. Long, could you secure the animals in a bedroom and come out here so I can explain what we need to do?"

But she was watching her son climb into his car. "Why is Ronald leaving?"

"He's moving his car to the street."

"I want to see Ronald." She looked me over, as did the five dogs, one of them standing on his hind legs and resting his paws on the glass. "Why, you're not with the power company at all, are you?"

No, but soon you'll wish I was. Gesturing at my ID, I said, "I'm an investigator with the State Law

Enforcement Division, and what I need you to do is secure your animals so we can talk on your front porch."

She made no move to do anything, even with a second explanation, so, keeping my foot securely against the door, I called animal control. Raising my voice over the racket of the clamoring dogs, I told animal control that I had a problem with dogs at a crime scene and gave them the address.

"Shoot 'em," said the guy on the other end of the line. "No, no," he said, laughing, "I was only joking. I'll have someone out there in a half hour."

"Make it quick or I will shoot the dogs."

"Hey, we're changing shifts like everyone else, but I'll get someone out there as soon as possible." Before he broke the connection, I heard him hollering for someone to get his ass in gear.

Mrs. Long's face pinched with apprehension. "Please don't shoot the dogs. They have no place to go."

"Then lock them up so we can talk."

Behind me, a third patrol car arrived, and soon this cop was blocking the other end of the street.

"What's—what's going on?" asked Mrs. Long, trying to look up and down the street from behind the storm door glass.

"Mrs. Long, there's a body in your backyard and—"

"Did the man in the cape leave it?"

I have to admit that the dogs' incessant demands for attention made it impossible to think, so what she said didn't immediately register. "We need to cut through your rear fence."

"No, no, you can't cut my fence. The dogs will get out."

"Wait a minute," I asked, shaking the stuffing out of my head. "What did you say about a man wearing a cape?"

From the bottom of the steps, Jacqueline asked, "So what's the story, Susan?"

"Mrs. Long, this is Jacqueline Marion. She's one of our crime-scene techs and she and the coroner need to reach the body." By now, the coroner had joined Jacqueline at the foot of the steps.

Mrs. Long glanced at my lanyard. "But you're from SLED."

I sighed and looked over my shoulder, all the time keeping one foot firmly planted against the door. "Send the son up here."

Minutes later, the greyhounds were in a back bedroom, and Mrs. Long and I sat in the swing at the end of her porch.

"Mrs. Long, you said you saw a man in your backyard last night."

"Yes, I did. I went out to feed the animals, but they were so agitated they wouldn't eat. And greyhounds burn up enormous amounts of fuel, especially when they're active. When they remained agitated right up until the time when I usually go to bed, I turned on the light and looked outside. "

"And what did you see?"

"The strangest thing. The man in my backyard looked just like Zorro."

CHAPTER TWENTY-THREE

Once the media began to arrive, I slipped off Mrs. Long's porch and walked around to the rear of the house. There I found Jacqueline Marion, the coroner, and Officer Gibbes cutting their way through the chain-link fence. Using the links that fell to the ground, we pinned the fence back. Actually, we assigned this chore to Gibbes, who didn't appear to be all that thrilled to be working for a couple of gals. As Jacqueline and I watched, James Stuart strolled into the backyard. The appearance of Stuart seemed to impress Gibbes and he bent to his labors with renewed enthusiasm.

Once finished, which included hooking the end of the fence back so the crime-scene techs and coroner could have access to the body, Gibbes said, "There you go, Colonel."

But Stuart only watched Jacqueline carry her crime-scene processing kit through the opening and follow the coroner down to the body. "This is not my crime scene, Gibbes."

"Yes, sir."

Jacqueline and the coroner knelt beside the body, and as she opened her kit, Stuart told me that the young mother in the house behind Mrs. Long's had reported the dogs on more than one occasion.

"But there's nothing anyone can do about it," said Stuart. "The dogs are not loud, they're fenced in, and the droppings are removed once a week. Baynard, that's the guy in the wheelchair, told me there's some kind of conflict between Mrs. Long and her daughter. The daughter wants to move Mom into a retirement home and sell the house."

"For the money?"

"I don't think so. The daughter wants to be out from under the responsibility of Mom living alone, but Mom won't give up her rescue mission. The daughter seems to understand that the money from the sale of the house would go to care for her mother wherever she lives. But there's one thing I did learn. The dogs spend their nights inside the house with Mrs. Long."

I saw the old woman staring at us from the rear storm door. She and five other snouts, that is. "Kept inside at night, you say?"

"So unless they sensed someone out here, there's no way they would've barked."

"Ah," I said, smiling, "the curious incident of the dogs in the nighttime."

"But the dogs did nothing last night."

"That was the curious incident."

Stuart gave me an odd look.

When I looked directly behind the Longs' property, I saw the young mother standing at the sliding glass door and staring at us. What was up with that woman?

"Her name's Robinette," added Stuart, "and she's expecting that the dogs will be taken away, hopefully euthanized. More than one neighborhood kid . . ."

Jacqueline suddenly stood up, left the crime scene, and raced past us. Near the far wooden fence she puked. Still retching, she stood, leaning against the wooden fence. No one went to her assistance. The coroner didn't even watch her go.

Gibbes smirked. "Looks like we need some tougher women working these crime scenes."

I was about to say something, but the colonel cut me off.

"You know, Gibbes," said Stuart, punching the patrolman's paunch with his finger, "I served overseas with women who carried more weight than you do, and it was all on their backs."

When I looked again at Jackie, she was staring at me, pleadingly. I joined her in the narrow area between the two fences where she gulped down Gatorade from her crime-scene kit.

Her freckled face was pale and her smile faint. "Been a long time since I've done that."

I put a hand on her shoulder. "Anything I can do?" I looked toward the street where the media was being held at bay and another tech had arrived, parking down the street behind the crime-scene truck. "Looks like Bobby's here."

She whispered, "I'm pregnant, Susan."

I wasn't sure I'd heard her properly. "Pardon?"

"I'm—I'm pregnant."

I looked at Stuart. Now that was dumb. Stuart

couldn't possibly be the father. And I didn't know my best friend was pregnant. Didn't even know who she was hooking up with.

"It's Dewayne, Susan." Dewayne was Jacqueline's ex.

I couldn't believe what I was hearing.

A twisted smile formed on her face. "I'm sorry. The kids were asleep and we got to talking—"

"So that's why you've been so bitchy lately. Even Bobby mentioned it. How far along are you?"

"Three months."

"And you didn't tell me?" I held up my hands and stepped back. "No, no, we're not getting into this right now. We have a crime scene to process. But you'll have to tell Stuart."

Jacqueline glanced in his direction. "Why?"

"Because Dewayne is one jealous son of a bitch, and you've been out on Stuart's boat, even taken Dewayne's kids along."

"But that was early this summer."

"Yeah, about the same time you were letting Dewayne have his way with you."

"Susan!"

"No, no," I said, backing farther away. "I don't want to talk about this right now."

What could Jacqueline have been thinking? And as a woman, I knew she hadn't been thinking. A man, even a bastard, starts working on you, and you can't help yourself, especially if you're lonely.

Bobby and the guy from animal control waved from the wrong side of the house. "Hey," called Bobby, "where's the gate?"

Jacqueline cleared her throat, spit into a Kleenex, and motioned them around to the other side of the house. Once they started toward the car gate, she said, "Susan, please don't mention this to anyone. It's embarrassing."

"You think? But if you don't tell Stuart, I will. Dewayne's beat the hell out of more than one guy who's taken an interest in you. He's a freaking control freak."

"That's only because he cares about me. He said we can start all over again."

"Jeez, Louise." I turned away, not trusting my mouth. My best friend had been seduced by the rottenest bastard in town and my sweet man just wanted a family. And I'd blown it.

I was shaking my head and passing the doghouse when Mrs. Long opened the back door and screamed, "What are you people doing in my backyard?"

And as soon as she opened the storm door, the greyhounds brushed past her, leaped down the steps, and raced in the direction of Stuart and Gibbes. Both men saw the dogs coming and stepped back, Gibbes struggling to pull his weapon and James Stuart setting his feet. Me, I ducked around the corner of the doghouse and out of the way. Everyone froze as the greyhounds leaped and bounded—and hurled themselves at Gibbes and Stuart.

CHAPTER TWENTY-FOUR

Mary Kate Belle was leaving *The Post and Courier* to cover the story about a dead woman found in a backyard over in West Ashley when someone called the tip line about a man waving a knife around at the Charleston Museum. Suddenly, the police frequency exploded with activity.

Everyone in the newsroom stared at the police scanner. It appeared the body in West Ashley was that of an unidentified homeless woman and that the police were having difficulty extracting the body because of a pack of dogs. That was quickly followed by the report of a man with a knife, or knives, taking up a defensive posture near the replica of *CSA Hunley* at the Charleston Museum.

Mary Kate opted for the guy with the knives, and so did TV, following the mantra of local reporting: If it bleeds, it leads. That meant the members of the CPD assigned to Mrs. Long's house were left with a skeleton crew of reporters, actually some rather disgruntled second-stringers from both print and TV. They milled around and cursed their fate while reporters in the historical district responded to a call from mounted patrol officers returning to their stables.

The mounted cops had called for backup because if they took action, they'd have to dismount—not a good thing, not since a drunken Wofford student had stolen a tethered mount and galloped the length of Market Street until the horse realized it was about to run into a car. The horse came to an abrupt halt, and the college student landed in the middle of East Bay with more than broken pride.

When Mary Kate and her photographer arrived at the museum, she was excited to find a guy waving more than one knife and screaming for everyone to stay back. It was a few moments before Mary Kate realized the guy with the knives was a prominent Charlestonian she'd grown up with, someone she had actually played with on these same streets.

CHAPTER TWENTY-FIVE

Under assault by the greyhounds, Stuart stumbled back and Gibbes became very busy trying to unholster his weapon. From where I stood on the other side of the doghouse, I wasn't immune to the pack's affection. Gibbes was knocked down and I was pushed against the doghouse where one of the dogs began licking my face. It was only Stuart who caught the paws of the brindled-colored greyhound and held the dog upright.

"Grab them! Grab them all!" screamed Ronald Long as he hurried down the back steps and lumbered into the backyard. Ronald knew he was in for a long day if the greyhounds found a way out. One of them did, and in a flash, which is the only way you can describe how these dogs move, the grey-colored animal was at the car gate, through it, and down the street.

"No, no! Close the gate, close the gate!" screamed Ronald, his watermelon stomach bouncing ahead of him as he ran for the gate.

More dogs bolted for the gate, and one of them was mine. I tried to put my arms around my dog, but it was like catching smoke. He left, following the dog that had knocked Gibbes to the ground. Snaking their way through the closing gate, the greyhounds broke for the street before the animal control officer could completely close it.

Brushing off my jacket, blouse, and pants, I walked toward Stuart, who still held the paws of his greyhound. The greyhound did not look pleased. His friends had discovered a new game and he wasn't being allowed to play.

Stuart lowered the dog to all fours and took him by the collar. "One day I'll have to demonstrate how to handle an attacking guard dog."

"Yeah, right." To Gibbes, I said, "Holster your weapon, Gibbes, or you'll spend the rest of the day filling out paperwork."

Gibbes holstered his weapon and got to his feet, brushing off dog poop. Stuart turned his animal over to Ronald Long, and Ronald looked really miserable as he walked the animal toward the house. Outside the fence, the animal control officer was running to his van in a vain attempt to follow the dogs.

"Take your patrol car and go with him, Gibbes."

Instead of looking me, the young officer looked at Stuart once again.

"Gibbes," said Stuart, "get your butt in gear and do as Agent Chase says."

Gibbes left at a waddle.

When Ronald returned from the house, he policed up the dog that had tried to reach the body of Ann

Chapman and now ran around the backyard. Both crime-scene investigators had looked up at the sound of Mrs. Long's shouts and saw the dogs racing across the backyard, one of them headed their way.

Jacqueline and the coroner leaped to their feet and waved their arms. This caused the last greyhound to return to the larger backyard and bolt for the open car gate—where the gate was slammed shut by the animal control officer. Members of the media trailed the dogs down the street, but the greyhounds were long gone, even before their cameras could be focused.

Jacqueline called to me from the other side of the chain-link fence. "You okay?"

"Yeah. I'm okay."

Mrs. Long came down the back steps and clomped across the backyard on her cane. "What are you people doing in my backyard? Speak up, speak up."

I identified myself again, holding up my lanyard, and, taking the elderly woman by the arm, walked her over to the rear fence where she could see the opening.

"Someone will have to repair that," snapped the old woman.

"Someone will."

"Well, I certainly hope so."

Mrs. Long saw the dead woman. "You're going to have to clean that up, too."

She was right about that, but all in all, I'd had enough public relations for one day. "I'll see you back to your house, Mrs. Long."

As we headed for her house, she said, "If you've noticed, there's nothing on the ground either you or your friends have to be afraid of stepping into. I have a young man who comes by every week and he keeps the yard immaculate. His name is Stephen."

I wasn't going to contradict her, but I did want to find a stick to scrape the dog droppings off the bottom of my shoes.

Ronald Long stuck his head out the back door and hollered to his mother. "Are you all right?"

The elderly lady pulled me up short and asked, "Who's that?"

"He's here to help you with your rescue project."

"Oh," said Mrs. Long. "Well, I don't think it's appropriate for strangers to be in my house without my knowledge."

And with that, I turned the woman over to her son.

Through all of this, Stuart had tagged along. "You know, Susan, I really meant it. I've been trained to take down guard dogs."

"Well, Colonel, next time this happens, I'll let you demonstrate a little of your technique."

The public information officer called from the car gate, and we walked over. "There's a man downtown with a knife and I need to be there, you know, if they have to take him down in front of all the tourists." The PIO was a loose-jointed, shambling man who went to work for the CPD when his contract hadn't been renewed by one of the local television stations. Maybe because he'd lost all his hair. They don't really care about how you walk when you read the news on TV.

"Is the guy wearing an apron?" I asked.

"Don't know. You or Colonel Stuart will have to take the media. Got to go."

"Call and ask about the apron," I insisted.

The PIO wasn't so sure.

"No sweat," said Stuart, taking out his cell. "I'll have the chief do it for you."

"No, no, I've got it." The PIO opened his phone again.

"What's the status of the press out front?" I asked.

As his phone ran through its digits, the shambling man said, "Most of them left to cover the guy at the museum, so I've got to get down there."

"The museum?" asked Stuart.

"That's where the guy with the knife is. LuAnn's on vacation. I'm all they've got."

Stuart looked at me. "So the press bought the story about the homeless woman?"

My head snapped around. "Stuart!"

The PIO clicked his phone closed. "What's this?"

"Hey," I said, gesturing at the phone, "you want to take off, okay, but we need to know if the guy's wearing an apron or not."

The PIO bit his lip. "There's something you're not telling me."

"Sure, there is, but isn't that always what happens to the guy who meets the press?"

The PIO tried to pry more information out of me, but I walked away, in the direction of the crime scene.

From the other side of the rear fence, Bobby smiled. "I've got it all on tape."

"You filmed us being attacked by the greyhounds?"

"Sure," he said, grinning. "I was thinking of sending it to *America's Funniest Home Videos.*"

"Give me the tape." I held out my hand.

He backed away. "I don't know about that."

I looked over at where Jackie worked on Annie Chapman. "I want this tape, Jackie."

"Give her the tape, Bobby," said my friend, "and put in a new one."

"I'm not so sure . . ."

"I'm sure," said Stuart. "You can follow me around with your video cam for the rest of my life, but that particular tape is going to be destroyed."

From where she bent over Chapman, Jacqueline said, "Just film the corrupted crime scene, Bobby, just as you did at Martha Turner's. That's your job."

Bobby frowned, popped out the tape, and handed it over. Crossing the yard to return to the street, he stepped into something and hopped the rest of the way to the gate.

I said, "And close the car gate after you."

The coroner left the narrow area between the two fences and came through the cut in the chain link. "The woman's been dead for over twenty-four hours, Miss Chase, and you, young lady, need to learn a thing or two about protecting the integrity of a crime scene."

Stuart started to speak again, but I raised a hand.

The coroner continued. "The reason I say this is that control of the crime scene is part of any coroner's report."

"Actually, it's not, but it can be if you want to be difficult."

The coroner stiffened. Mechanically, he added, "Portions of the woman's body not covered by clothing were discolored from the sun. That's all there is to that, Miss Chase, nothing more." And the coroner was out of there, stopping only long enough to update the burly guys leaning against the meat wagon parked in the street.

Stuart watched him go. "I guess you get a lot of that—you know, people talking down to you."

"Yes. I even get it from you."

CHAPTER TWENTY-SIX

The public information officer reported that the knife-wielding man was indeed wearing an apron and it was covered with blood. Moments later he headed for the Charleston Museum and left James Stuart to face the press. Turned out there were few questions. Everyone wanted to go downtown and see the wacko waving the knife.

"No ID, no jewelry, no wedding band," Stuart told the remaining media. "Can't tell who the woman is or even if she's homeless, and she appears to be too clean to be a homeless person. Nor do we know how she came to be found in the yard behind Mrs. Long's."

Stuart described the woman's features, sans the intestines mounted on the woman's right shoulder. Neither did he mention the new potatoes, jewelry, or farthings.

"The dogs had to be removed from the backyard for the safety of the personnel working the crime scene. We cut a pretty good hole in that fence."

Uh-oh. Too much information, Stuart.

"But why'd you cut the fence? Why not go in from the backyard of the neighbor's?"

Stuart regrouped nicely. I guess he'd briefed the press more than once while serving overseas. "Remember, people, there's a double fence in the backyard. These two fences are not flush. The neighbor has children and was afraid of the dogs, though I don't know why. They're greyhounds."

Nice recovery. But he did look down and examine his shoes.

Once the coroner, the dead woman, and all the techs took off, and the fence had been pieced together, I vaulted the neighbor's taller fence and headed toward Robinette's patio. On the way I used my phone to call a friend of Stuart's who owns a fencing company. Once I finished my call, Mrs. Robinette opened the glass door and allowed me inside, only, it would appear, to question me.

"What about the dogs?" she asked.

The family room had a sofa, a recliner, and a wall-mounted plasma TV, along with several large toys for tots. There were few photographs on the wall, leaving huge vacant areas. No rugs on the floor.

"Mrs. Long's animals will remain in house until the fence is repaired."

"And the fence?"

"There should be someone out to replace the fence by tomorrow, certainly before the end of the week."

"Well, my kids aren't going out there before that fence is repaired, I can tell you that much. Those dogs have attacked people before."

That sounded a bit odd. Still, I took out my pad and pen. "Did they lodge a complaint?"

Robinette shrugged. "Neighborhood boys."

"Oh," I said, smiling and putting away my pad and pen, "boys taunting the dogs from your backyard."

The young mother shrugged again.

"So you could get a little payback."

Robinette glanced through the sliding glass door. "The children won't go outside when those dogs are out there, and it's not good for children to stay inside so much."

"It's my understanding that the dogs were taken in at night."

She glanced at the sliding glass door again.

"Were they out last night?"

"You'd have to ask my husband. He was up late watching a ball game. The Braves were playing on the West Coast."

I asked where he worked.

When she told me, I said, "Call your husband and tell him I'll be there shortly, that an agent from SLED wants to interview him."

"He has nothing to do with those animals."

I smiled as I went out the door. "No one does, but still the dogs remain in a highly agitated state."

Once I was seated in the Mustang, Stuart wheeled away from the Longs' curb and started down the street. While I'd wasted my time with Robinette, Stuart had checked on those in the neighborhood he may've missed during the first go-round.

He asked, "What'd you learn from the neighbor, or were you just checking on me?"

"I'll always be checking on you. As far as I'm concerned, you're a rookie."

An edge came to his voice. "What'd you learn that I didn't?"

"That Mrs. Long is the only one who saw the man dressed like Zorro, unless you've come up with someone in your interviews."

Stuart shook his head. "Nothing."

"No one saw anything, and that would be because of the wooden fences, so it would be a good idea if we stopped by the husband's place of employment and spoke with him." I told Stuart where that was.

"And we need to talk to him—why?"

"Because after dark, men look out windows. Women check their locks."

We rode along in silence until Stuart couldn't contain himself any longer. "What's this with the coat hangers holding your weapons at the rear of your pants?"

"Something I learned from a cop who buys handguns off the street in New York. They don't want anyone to know they're carrying, so they hook their weapons into their pants and use a very flat weapon, the Walther PPK or something like it."

"And it's that important to appear attractive with no unsightly bumps or humps in your apparel?"

"I won't dignify that with an answer. You've obviously spent too much time in the desert."

"You're a girl, Susan. The bad guys need to know you're armed and dangerous. But two weapons? No cop would ever need two weapons, unless she was going to give up her primary weapon to the bad guys." He glanced at me. "It's way too much firepower."

"Maybe," I said, smiling sweetly, "but how would you know? You're not a girl."

Crossing the Ashley, I connected with Burnside, and the chief told me that the man with the knives had been disarmed and returned to his home. He'd been off his meds. Well, okay.

In the Jack the Ripper legend, an unemployed butcher, wearing a bloody apron and selling meat door-to-door, had been detained by the Whitechapel police as a possible suspect. While checking out the butcher's alibi, the authorities learned the butcher was a certified lunatic. I kid you not. It's in the Scotland Yard files.

I asked the chief. "What about our Jane Doe?"

"The medical examiner will call once he knows something."

"I'm thinking it's up to us to learn who this woman is." I leaned back in Stuart's bucket seat. "I can't think of an Ann Chapman you didn't have covered last night, so that leaves the possibility I mentioned before."

"That this particular Ann Chapman is an out-of-town girl."

"Well, yes, but now that we have a victim much older than anyone killed so far, and she was found in the remnants of her nightgown. Maybe she's a patient from an assisted living facility."

"So," said the chief, "you think our Jack kidnapped this woman and the institution has failed to report her missing?"

"Well, it hasn't been twenty-four hours so they may believe their patient was counted as someone else, or is wandering around the grounds, or is locked in a building where she can't get out. They probably believe they'll eventually find her. She may have wandered away before."

"I can't say it hasn't happened, institutions not reporting people wandering away, so why not in Charleston?"

"So it follows—"

"That Jack knew this particular Ann Chapman."

"Better yet. He may have a relative in the same institution."

That caused a silence that lasted several blocks of Market Street. Maybe Burnside was scribbling a note on her legal pad with one of her #2 pencils.

Finally, she came back to me. "I just received a phone call from the coroner. He said there was some trouble with security at the crime scene."

"Mrs. Long's backyard is used as a rescue mission for retired greyhounds."

"And?"

"They got out of the house where they'd been locked up."

"Perhaps you needed more backup."

"Only from you."

Dead silence on the other end of the line, and it went on long enough that Stuart even glanced at me.

Without preamble she came back. "What about the envelope with the Citadel crest found under the body? What was inside the envelope?"

"Appeared to be a couple of ibuprofen. I sent it along to the lab, but it's practically impossible to get partials off medication."

"I just didn't want to forget that point. But now, we have our first clue, don't we?"

"I believe so, and tomorrow morning, I'd have a detective start knocking on doors of assisted living facilities and make those facilities physically produce any Ann Chapman registered with them. But he'll need search warrants, not only for the rooms but for the medical records, and perhaps, fingerprints."

"Stuart still with you?" she asked.

I glanced at the colonel, who was looking both ways before crossing Meeting Street. "He is."

"Tell him everyone's to be in my office tomorrow morning at eight. I've cleared my calendar and we're going to do some brainstorming."

Of course, at that time, I had no idea I'd be spending another night at the hospital.

CHAPTER TWENTY-SEVEN

Robinette worked in a bank across the street from the public market, so Stuart left the Mustang in a lot where the attendant seemed to know him—doesn't everyone?—and the kid said he'd watch the car. No charge.

Because of the phone call from his wife, we were ushered right in to see Robinette. On the banker's wall hung all sorts of paraphernalia for the South Carolina baseball team, a team that occasionally goes to the college world series.

"What's going on?" asked Robinette, standing. He was one of those self-absorbed people with a miniature phone stuck in his ear. "My wife called and said the cops wanted to talk to me."

In the middle of my explaining what the investigation was all about, Robinette took a call.

Stuart didn't hesitate. He stepped around the desk— Robinette stepped back—and Stuart reached over and plucked the phone from the banker's ear. "This is police business, sir."

Stuart put the ear phone on Robinette's desk and returned to stand next to me.

Flustered, all Robinette could ask was, "Are you making Mrs. Long get rid of all those dogs?"

When Stuart saw me sit down, lean back in my chair, and allow him to become the lead investigator, he took a seat himself, as did Robinette. "What we want to know, sir, is did you see the dogs out last night—after dark?"

"Of course not," said the man, a pallid fellow who needed to lose a good deal of weight before I or any other woman would give him a second glance. "Mrs. Long always takes the dogs in at dark." He glanced at the phone lying on his desktop. It may have buzzed, but, at the moment, we were the center of his attention.

"On the night in question," insisted Stuart, "did you see anyone in your backyard?"

"Last night? What was on TV last night?"

Stuart told him, and they did some male bonding over the baseball game played last night.

"Now I remember," said the husband, shifting around in his chair, "you played for the Citadel, didn't you?"

"Not baseball."

"Yeah, but you won all those Southern Conference championships."

I cleared my throat.

Both men looked at me.

Stuart asked, "Did anything happen during the game that you remember?"

Robinette straightened up in his chair. He was a very excitable guy. "Now, I remember! It took forever for Mrs. Long to get the dogs inside. I almost went out there myself."

"You saw who?" I asked. "A man or woman?"

"It was Mrs. Long."

"You could make her out," I asked, leaning forward again, "a woman using a cane?"

"Who else would've been out there?"

"Perhaps someone wearing a cape and looking like Zorro?" Well, what the hell, I was the dumb blonde in this act.

The banker stared at me.

Stuart asked, "Sir, you do realize we're investigating a homicide and the body was found on your property."

"Whose body?"

"Older woman, at least seventy, five feet and a couple of inches tall, a hundred and thirty pounds, with gray hair, green eyes, and a pale complexion."

"But what was she doing in my backyard?" he asked, looking from one of us to the other.

"We were hoping you could tell us."

"Well, it wasn't my mother-in-law," he said with a chuckle. "I can tell you that."

"How long did the disturbance with the dogs go on?" asked Stuart.

"Oh, at least a half hour."

Robinette noticed that both of us were staring at him intently.

He corrected himself. "Well, maybe fifteen minutes. Anyway, those dogs are a menace."

"Greyhounds?" I asked.

"Absolutely, and I hope you can do something about them before my children forget what it's like to play in their own backyard."

Outside the bank, I cursed.

This amused Stuart. "You're just unhappy that you don't have a more reliable witness than Mrs. Long."

"I'm surprised Mrs. Long hasn't been taken to the livability court." A livability court focuses on cases involving noncompliance with codes and standards regarding noise and animal control. The first livability court was established in Charleston, and not many years ago.

"With those fences flanking her property," said Stuart, "there's no way anyone saw anything. I checked with everyone, even called some of Long's neighbors at work. They saw nothing, heard nothing. Most of them were asleep."

"The dogs didn't keep them awake?"

"I don't think the dogs are that much of a problem. The problem appears to be with the Robinettes."

"Actually, Mrs. Robinette, and a guy living directly across the street from Mrs. Long's house."

"The guy on the walker who kept yelling about taking the dogs away?"

"Yep."

"That's Mrs. Robinette's father."

"Oh, boy, a double team."

"So the Ripper used the Robinettes' yard to dump the body over the fence. That's why you asked Jackie to check their backyard for footprints. What's wrong with Jackie? She hardly spoke to me today."

"She didn't tell you?"

"Tell me what?"

We moved to the curb, and I looked down Meeting Street toward St. Michael's. "Hell if I know. I thought she might've told you."

"Maybe she was embarrassed about throwing up."

"Probably." Damn you, Jackie, you have to warn this man about your ex. "I'll call later and see how she's feeling."

We were both quiet as we watched the tourists head for the restaurants flanking the public market. The tourists were an orderly bunch, waiting their turns at the signal. In Charleston, even the tourists are polite.

Stuart looked down Meeting in the direction of the museum. "Did you notice that the man with the knives and wearing the bloody apron didn't appear on our radar until after we'd found Chapman?"

"Which confirms that Jack is holding himself accountable for every single item of the Ripper legend."

"Holding himself accountable . . . ?"

We stood on the curb through another light change. "It won't be his fault if the rules are not strictly observed."

"How do you suppose he did it, knowing when to release the guy with the knives?"

"Probably used a podcast." Podcasting is feeding files, such as a view of Mrs. Long's backyard, to a device willing to receive it, such as a cell phone or home computer. "But to find his camera you'd have to take all those backyards apart, and it might tip off the media what we were up to. But even if you found the camera, what does that prove? Jack only used it to know when to turn the lunatic loose with his knives."

"So we don't need to go to the museum?"

"Nope," I said. "I'm sure the CPD is working that particular angle."

The light changed again, and we crossed the street.

"Jack probably spiked some poor guy's food or drink, someone who's really paranoid. It didn't matter where the guy was, or who he was. The poor bastard just had to be seen wearing that bloody apron and holding those knives."

"So, you don't think Darryl Diamond had anything to do with these murders."

"Doubt it." My mind was elsewhere as I watched the five o'clock rush join the tourists. It had just occurred to me that I wasn't finishing a long commute from Columbia, and Chad and I could go dancing. Anything to get my mind off this case for a few hours.

By the time we'd reached the car, I'd checked with Chad, surprising him by my early call. He said he'd head home right away, and I asked Stuart to drop me off at the house.

"Then that's it for the night?" he asked, resting his arms on top of the Mustang.

"Yes, but in the morning there are three things: One is whether there were any other nine-one-one calls reporting any sort of prowler. Not the guys snared by the CPD, but whether dispatch responded to Mrs. Long's neighborhood for any reason."

"Like someone parking a car where it didn't belong or crossing a backyard to drop off a body."

I nodded. "Second would be to try to learn who spiked that apron-guy's food or drink, but I imagine the CPD's on that. If Jack knew what this guy's reaction would be, he had to know something about this guy, and maybe it's another clue to the identity of our Jack. Perhaps he hung around homeless shelters."

"And the third?"

"One of us needs to talk to Mary Kate. While you were driving in, I checked *The Post and Courier's* web site. It appears Mary Kate filed the story about the guy waving the knives at the museum. If Mary Kate isn't curious about the homeless woman that we found, then we know the information dam is holding. Can you think of a reason to call her?"

Stuart smiled. "I think so." He flipped opened his phone, dialed MK at the paper, and asked if she'd like to go dancing.

I just had to laugh.

Mary Kate heard me, and when Stuart put his cell on speaker and held it across the top of his car, I leaned into the Mustang and said I had the prettiest outfit picked out.

"I'll be ready in an hour, James, and I'll dance Susan's ass off. What are you wearing, Susan?" Then very quickly that was followed by, "Oh, what the hell. Why would I care?"

CHAPTER TWENTY-EIGHT

I wore my little black dress with spaghetti straps, an item I truly believe is a bit too small for a gal my size, but when you're competing with Mary Kate Belle, you'd best bring your A game. Mary Kate wore a ruffled gray-green silk slip dress, and she just about burst out of the top.

This did not please James Stuart. "Mary Kate, I should call your mother. You look like a trollop."

MK glanced at her chest. "Hey, can I help it if cleavage is back in style?"

We were at Trio Club & Lounge, where the trendy crowd meets across from Marion Square, and soon MK and I had danced our dates off the floor. We faced off doing whatever the music called for: rock, jitterbug, or the shag. Our dresses became thoroughly soaked, our bangs flattened against our foreheads, and our grins more maniacal as the band tested our mettle by playing the Charleston, created, where else but in Charleston; the Big Apple developed in New Orleans with the Black Bottom originating in Columbia. And for those who wonder what the fuss was all about, flappers dancing in speakeasies would dance alone or dance together as a way of mocking the "drys," or those who supported Prohibition. That led to the Lindy Hop and other variations, including swing and jazz, all wiped out by rock 'n' roll.

Once MK and I stopped and caught our breath, plus taking congrats from many of the patrons, we retired to the restroom and tried to do something about our hair and makeup. One of the women, a blonde with rather harsh features under the unforgiving mirror lights, wanted to know which of us was with Colonel Stuart.

Mary Kate turned away from the mirror and leaned her butt against the counter. Putting her hands beside her and gripping the counter, she casually blew back a hank of hair that had fallen across her face. "You're looking at her."

"Is the relationship serious?"

"Is it any of your business?" I asked.

"I wasn't talking to you, child." The blonde gave me the once-over more than once. "They probably carded you at the door."

"Mary Kate," I asked, "I'm really a mess after all that dancing. Think it'd be okay if I knocked this woman on her ass?"

The blonde stiffened.

Mary Kate told the woman to hit the door.

She did. Totally miffed.

Once the door closed, a toilet flushed and another gal popped out of a stall, smiled nervously, and without pausing to wash her hands, scurried out the door.

Mary Kate returned her attention to her image in the mirror: black hair, pale skin, and blue eyes, all the signs of a Belle of Charleston, along with a touch of pink in the cheeks from all that dancing.

She said to herself in the mirror, "I do believe it's time I married James Stuart."

"Mary Kate Jane Belle, you can't marry your cousin."

Speaking to my image in the mirror, she frowned. "What gave you the idea Stuart and I are cousins?"

"But I always thought . . ."

"Uh-huh. You've heard me call James 'cousin,' right?"

"Er—yes."

"That was just a way to make the Stuart brothers back off when I visited their sister on Pawleys Island."

"Well, you've got your work cut out for you . . ." I'd been looking at her. Now I faced my image in the mirror instead of finishing the thought. It was not my place to reveal that James Stuart could not father children.

My reddish-blond hair was a total loss. The multidimensional shape of the 'do gives my hair an illusion of movement created by short lengths underneath and on top; longer lengths at the side and the middle give depth to the cut. But there was no depth or movement anywhere, and the best I could do was work on my face, touching up spots with eyeliner and a press pad.

"Me—I'm moving out until Chad pops the question."

"Really? How did Chad take it?"

"Haven't told him. I'll probably tell him when we get home tonight."

Mary Kate said, "You could move in with me."

"Not possible. You don't have the closet space."

"Sure I do. I had the smaller bedroom converted into a walk-in closet."

"Nah. I've already got a place picked out." I didn't tell her that the flat was listed under the name of Catherine Eddowes, one of the two women slated to die at the end of the month.

Mary Kate laughed. "I'll bet it's not far from Chad."

"Hey, I'm not stupid."

"That's still a long commute to Columbia."

"That commute is probably why I moved in with Chad when we first moved down from Myrtle. There are just too damn many good-looking women in this burg."

MK grinned. "That's the College of Charleston for you. Well, Chad's a great guy and I wish y'all the very best, but why don't you think I can land James Stuart?"

"I didn't say you couldn't." I brushed down my little black dress and turned to leave.

"Oh, yes, you did," she said to my image in the mirror. "You said I'd have my work cut out for me."

At the restroom door, I faced her. "I'm not saying you can't, MK, but you heard what Stuart said earlier tonight. As far as he's concerned, you're a trollop."

And I left her standing there, both hands palm down on the counter, leaning forward and staring at her image in the mirror.

CHAPTER TWENTY-NINE

The four of us were leaving Trios, and Stuart was drunk enough to think we wanted to see how he would've handled a guard dog earlier today. When I say Stuart was drunk, that also meant he was too drunk to realize he was in dangerous territory—a reporter was present—and Chad flashed me a warning glance.

"What's this about a dog?" Mary Kate had taken Stuart's arm to return to the car. If you haven't experienced it, Charleston has sidewalks you can break an ankle on. "I didn't hear anything about a dog," she said.

"Check with Mike Rutledge," I said hastily. "He had the story. We were in the middle of a greyhound rescue mission and couldn't reach the body."

"I could've done it!" said Stuart, nodding vigorously. "I could've done it!"

"What bull," I said, snorting and looking away.

Stuart unhooked himself from MK, turned around and faced us, walking backwards.

"Guard dogs come at you hard, knock you down, and once they have you on the ground, that's when they get serious."

"So," I said, swinging my purse, practically skipping along, "you have to take them down before they take you, right?"

"Oh, come on, Suze," said Chad, "give the colonel a break. This ought to be good for a laugh. Demonstration, sir, if you don't mind."

"Yeah," said MK. "I want to see this. It's making me hot."

Stuart frowned, and I explained MK was hot from dancing, not anything any military hero had done.

Stuart grinned. He and Chad had shared a couple of pitchers of beer while MK and I faced off on the dance floor. Chad said watching us dance made him tired; Stuart said it made him thirsty.

"Anyway," said Stuart, walking backwards to face us, four or five feet separating us, "there's one time when any guard dog is vulnerable and that's when he commits to the leap."

"Yeah, yeah." I had never heard such nonsense.

Stuart raised a finger to make a point. "Now, since I have no dogs . . . Susan, stop twirling your purse and toss it at me. Not fast, but like a dog launching himself at me."

"Okay, okay, I get the idea. Here comes, Rover."

Stuart set himself in a crouch and brought up his hands. At that very moment, Dewayne Marion stepped out of an alleyway, set his feet, and took a swing at Stuart. Dewayne used an aluminum bat from slow-pitch softball, which is where the ball comes across the plate at an arch and the batter has time to judge how to hit the ball.

Dewayne's target was Stuart's head, and when Dewayne swung, Stuart had already gone into his crouch and was explaining that you must catch the dog's paws when he presents them to you. Then you use the leaping power of the animal to throw yourself and the dog backwards, head over heels, and toss the dog a good distance away. If done properly, the dog's lucky if it doesn't break its neck.

If Stuart had grabbed one of the greyhounds in his demo, he would've thrown the damned dog right into Dewayne's chest. As it was, Stuart caught my purse as he fell back, and the bat clipped him across the top of his head. There was a "bonk," Stuart's head snapped forward, and the bat continuing into Stuart's hands, held higher than his head. Stuart went down, Mary Kate screamed, and Chad rushed to Stuart's assistance.

"No, no, Dewayne!" Chad was on one knee, throwing out his hand to protect Stuart from being hit again. "Stop, stop!"

Stuart lay limp on the ground, and Mary Kate totally flipped out, crying, "Call nine-one-one! Call nine-one-one!" forgetting all about her cell phone in her purse.

I felt as if I'd taken the blow myself. My chest ached and I swallowed hard. I'd failed to warn Stuart about this jerk, and when Dewayne grinned and swung again—ignoring Chad's pleas to put down the bat—I launched myself, somewhat like a guard dog.

I hit Dewayne under his swing, with my left shoulder at his beltline. The blow knocked him back and twisted him around. Both of us went down, and Dewayne landed on his belly. I landed on top of him, and the bat bounced away.

When the cops arrived, they say—because I sure as hell don't remember—that I was sitting astride Dewayne's back, knees locked into the bastard's sides, and had the strap of my purse around Dewayne's neck, pulling it tight. What I do remember is when they finally pried me off, I still managed to fit my foot between his legs, landing a good solid kick to his balls.

CHAPTER THIRTY

Before the next Ripper attack, a couple of things happened:

I met Mary Kate coming down the hallway of the hospital at the Medical University of South Carolina and she was mad. I guess that was a good sign. At least she wasn't in tears. Her outfit was rather subdued for such a clotheshorse: a white silk jacquard Raj coat and pegged pants, matching flat bag, and heels with open toes. She'd pulled her black hair back into a bun.

"James is asking for Jackie," she said angrily. "Dammit, Susan, knocked out like that and who does he ask for? Jacqueline Marion." Her eyes welled up and she hurried away. "God, what did I ever see in that man?"

I watched her rush to the elevator, punch the button, and while waiting, pinch her nose to stop the tears. When the doors opened, she almost fell in the lap of an old guy in a wheelchair. MK backed off long enough for the passengers to disembark, and then stepped inside, head bowed, and disappeared behind the closing doors.

Stuart's grandmother, mother, sister, brother, and his sister-in-law sat in a tight little circle with tight little smiles. There were other hangers-on, but those were the ones I recognized, particularly Lizzie Stuart, a young woman who had run with Mary Kate and her crowd; all graduates of Ashley Hall and the College of Charleston, now married and repopulating Charleston with only the best and the brightest. When I asked how Stuart was doing, Lizzie took me aside.

"They still have him sedated," she said, lowering her voice, not because anyone but the family would overhear, but because that was the way bluebloods conduct family business. "More tests will be run later today, including x-rays of his spine to rule out any potential problems. They're more worried about his spinal column than his head, which was only grazed by the baseball bat. Hopefully, if the tests are negative, he can go home in a couple of days, but they'll keep him in a collar, and he's got weeks and weeks of rehab ahead of him."

"I heard it was a severe case of whiplash."

"Cervical whiplash, but there's also swelling to the back of his head and several of his fingers were fractured."

I glanced at the floor. "I'm sorry I couldn't do more."

Lizzie put a hand on my shoulder. "Susan, from what I've heard, you did more than could be expected."

"May I see him?"

She nodded and escorted me over to a door she pushed open. Lowering her voice again, she said, "Now don't expect too much. He won't even know you're here."

Stuart lay in a hospital bed and flowers filled the room. Stuart's head was in a soft cervical collar, and he was completely out of it. Both hands lay at his sides with several fingers in metal splints. An IV was plugged into his arm and he hadn't shaved in several days.

"He has a great deal of swelling in the soft tissue at the back of his neck, literally a knot on the back of his head, and he was in a great deal of pain. That's why they have him sedated. Still, all things considered, my brother was very, very lucky."

"He was demonstrating how to survive a guard dog attack, that's what saved him."

Lizzie stared at me blankly, then said, "Mary Kate told me you subdued the man."

"Yeah, well, it was Mary Kate who got EMS moving faster than they've ever moved before."

Lizzie looked at her brother. "Strange how a man survives tours in Iraq, Afghanistan, and even one in the Philippines, only to have this happen at home. I once asked why he kept returning to the war zone and he said he had buddies over there who were depending on him." She faced me. "I told him I felt like those stateside weren't making the proper sacrifice, you know, going without. James said ever since the Indian Wars there've been dragoons operating on the fringes of the American Empire, and that if I wanted to go to the mall while he was overseas, none of the soldiers would object. It was their job to keep America safe."

"I know, I know," I said, nodding. "I once asked him how we could end all these stupid wars and you know what he said?"

"Oh, yes," said Lizzie, her face brightening. "It was his mantra: Find a way to drive the price of oil down to forty dollars a barrel and every country in the Middle East will line up for Washington's help, actually financial assistance, the good guys, the bad ones, all of them. Imagine, forty dollars a barrel . . ."

Stuart was stirring, calling for someone. But Stuart wasn't calling for Jacqueline Marion, as Mary Kate had thought. There were other images running through his unconscious mind.

"Jack," he moaned. "Got to find Jack . . ."

Jerry Tobias called from the West Coast with information later relayed to me.

"What you got, Jerry?" asked Burnside.

"If you can spare someone who's into computers and can keep their mouth shut, I'd send them out here to L.A."

"Can you tell me more?"

"Let's just say because of other articles I've written for *Rolling Stone* and *Vanity Fair,* I have unlimited access to our friend's house. His girlfriend's returned from location and wants something more positive written about her boyfriend's career, and she's calling in markers to make sure someone, somewhere, prints something. Anyway, from what I've read on our friend's computer, he did have a special friend, perhaps the one we're looking for."

Burnside nodded, though there was no way Tobias could see. "I have just the man. I'll send Isaac Henry out. What's his job?" Meaning his cover.

"He'll do the scut work any journalist finds tedious, you know, searching through records and data bases."

"How long will he be there?"

"As long as it takes for him to trace any thread found on our friend's computer leading to *his* friend's identity."

"Meaning Jack, right?"

"That would be correct."

"Okay," said Burnside, reaching for her pad. "I'll give him your cell phone number, find out what kind of equipment he needs, and stuff him on a plane tonight."

And I had to answer questions about my enthusiasm in restraining Dewayne Marion.

"Ms. Chase," said the chairwoman of the three-person panel conducting my grilling. She was a prim little woman who looked as if her greatest accomplishment in life had been to become a civilian interrogator. "Mr. Marion is suing the city of Charleston and SLED for excessive force, and we must have something to pass along to the county solicitor to determine whether charges will be brought or not."

I looked at all three of them, but particularly held the eyes of the two men. "Then what's a girl to do?"

"Are you mocking us, Ms. Chase?" asked the woman, frowning.

"Not at all. I just don't understand the complaint. Dewayne Marion outweighed me by a hundred pounds and carried a baseball bat."

"An aluminum baseball bat."

"It was still a baseball bat."

"Your boyfriend was there . . ." offered the woman.

"Yes, but as a member of the South Carolina law enforcement community, it was my responsibility to subdue Dewayne, not some civilian's."

"Dewayne? You knew Mr. Marion personally?" asked the woman.

"I knew he had a reputation for jealousy, and Jackie told me that's why she divorced him. She couldn't make a move without his okay. When Jackie moved to Charleston I thought he was out of the picture. No one could've been more surprised when Dewayne stepped out of that alley and pasted Colonel Stuart with that baseball bat."

"And how would you characterize your relationship with Colonel Stuart?" asked the woman, leaning forward, eager.

"He was paired with me for the day." I shrugged. "I hardly know the man."

"You went dancing with him later that night."

"I went dancing with my boyfriend. Mary Kate Belle brought along Colonel Stuart."

"I don't know what the other panel members think," said the woman, glancing left and right, "but Colonel Stuart seems to be a bit too old to go dancing with such young women."

"I'd have to agree," I said, laughing. "I've seen him on the dance floor."

Now it was the older of the two men who had to get this charade back on track. "But you do admit you have a relationship with Jacqueline Marion, one that could influence your technique of subduing Mr. Marion?"

"I don't know what kind of relationship you mean, but, yeah, I know Jackie. She and I worked a couple of cases along the Grand Strand."

"So you are . . . ?"

"Professional friends. Someone I respect."

"But in Myrtle Beach you were more than professional friends," stated the woman.

"We had a beer on occasion, but Jackie is married with two small kids." I smiled at the men flanking this little twit. "She would've cramped my style."

Both men nodded as if they knew what a hot chick like me might do if let loose on the bar scene in Charleston, and the way I know this is both men checked out my legs. The younger guy looked as if he might even ask for my digits. I'd worn a skirt for the occasion but would change into pants once I was out the door.

The eager young man had to clear his throat to speak. "You must understand, Ms. Chase, we're just clarifying your relationship with the Marions."

"Of course, but like I said, when he stepped out of the alleyway with that bat, Dewayne Marion was just another bad guy to me."

"With an aluminum softball bat," clarified the woman.

"Yes," I said, "bats which have been outlawed by the city of New York as too dangerous for high school play." To the two guys, I said, "I was damned lucky when Dewayne double-clutched before taking his second swing at Colonel Stuart."

"Double-clutched?" asked the woman, puzzled.

"Yes," said the eager young man, nodding, "it could've been much worse."

I flashed him a thousand-watt smile. "Yes, sir, it certainly could've."

"And Dewayne Marion?" asked the other man.

I shrugged. "He didn't regard me as a threat. That's why I was able to catch him off guard, put him down, and then go to Colonel Stuart's assistance, you know, calling EMS and such."

"But," said the woman, "when the patrolmen arrived, they said you were trying to strangle Mr. Marion with the strap of your purse."

"Nah," I said, shaking my head. "They've got that all wrong. I was just trying to tie his hands behind his back."

The chief of police met with me alone, either to protect me from her captain of detectives or vice versa.

After taking a seat, I asked, "What's the story on the homeless woman Stuart and I found?"

"Someone stuck a needle in Ann Chapman's arm, threw her over his shoulder, and walked out a back door of an assisted living facility in the middle of the night. You know, most assisted living homes have an open door policy."

"Because grown children know that if Mom suffers from dementia, they'll never be missed if they don't stop by. That's why the assisted living facility encourages visits, even at odd hours."

"That's a rather cold assessment, but an accurate description of the relationship some of the elderly have with their children. We believe the abductor to have disguised himself as a Baptist minister, since that particular minister hasn't returned to the facility since

Mrs. Chapman's disappearance."

"Nobody missed her?"

"You've heard of those inflatable dolls that Japanese sailors become overly friendly with on long sea voyages? One was put in her bed as a substitute—wearing a wig— so Mrs. Chapman wasn't missed until the following day. Unfortunately, no one from the family missed her either. Her sons haven't visited Mrs. Chapman since Mother's Day."

I was silent for a long moment. "You know, some parts of our society are broken."

"Tell me about it," said Burnside, seemingly to reflect on my comment. "Do you have anything to add, Susan, before I send you back to cold cases?"

"Oh, I ran into Mary Kate and I can tell you that the information dam is holding. There is no interest whatever in what Colonel Stuart and I were doing in West Ashley. What'd you learn about the guy running around with the knives?"

"Oh, that's George Huddleston. He suffers from paranoid schizophrenia, and feeding his fears is the fact that he's a member of *the* Huddleston family. People *have* been after his family for generations, during the Civil War, the Revolution, all the way back to his family's disputes with the proprietors who originally founded South Carolina."

The family Burnside spoke of had arrived from Barbados before 1700 with the single-minded purpose of making a buck. The experience of the Barbadians arriving in Charleston and the Pilgrims landing at Plymouth Rock could not have been more striking, and is much more representative of this country's history.

While the Pilgrims devoted themselves to piety and the simple life, the Barbadians brought Old World chic and frontier rowdiness.

Ostentatious in clothing, city houses, and plantation "big houses," they liked their guns, hunting dogs, and a huge midday meal. After a light supper, they would decamp to the local tavern, turning over the running of the household to their wives and servants. Of course, the modern-day George Huddleston was generations removed from all that, but the paranoia was still there, and in many homes south of Broad you could find families who spoke of Yankee transgressions as if they had occurred only yesterday.

"The Huddleston family has worked very hard to keep George from being institutionalized," said Burnside, "so when he wanders out into public, the uniforms pick him up and take him home. George is a common enough presence in the historical district, talking to himself but essentially harmless."

"Unless someone gives him a pair of knives," I said.

"True, and when George woke up near the museum, he was wearing that bloody leather apron and had knives tied to his hands. It wasn't difficult for him to think he had to defend himself."

"I've seen leather aprons before at Home Depot, but the knives?"

Burnside glanced at her pad. "Sam Gadsden traced them to a shop in the historical district. The owner remembered the buyer and gave us a description: six feet tall, fat, wearing a beard and a Hawaiian shirt."

"Oh," I said with a laugh, "that has to be a disguise.

I doubt this guy gave the shopkeeper his name for the mailing list."

"But he did," said Burnside.

"Oh, let me guess. Diamond's address."

"But not on Rainbow Row—the one in L.A."

"So, he's toying with us."

"And, I would imagine, very pleased to have us participating in this game he's created, as there were no prints on either knife or the bloody apron. Even after being back on his medication, George has no idea what happened. One moment he was talking with"—Burnside shook her head in disgust—"a fat guy with a beard who wore a Hawaiian shirt, the next, he woke up with those knives tied to his hands—knives, and a bloody apron, he could not rid himself of." Burnside leaned back in her chair and took her pencil along. "And that's why no one is pressing charges against George, not because his family is a member of the Charleston elite."

Well, maybe.

"Jerry Tobias and Isaac Henry just returned from L.A. where they were given complete access to Diamond's computer. Isaac combed through all the contacts Diamond had on the web, including the Undernet. You know what that is, Susan?"

"Oh, yeah. The dark side of the web."

"Anyway," said Burnside, still leaning back, "while Isaac had access to Diamond's computer, he downloaded all the user names, passwords, games, and access codes, web sites, message boards, blogs, the whole nine yards, and burned them onto CDs and brought them back to Charleston. Now he uses the computer seized in Diamond's house on Rainbow Row to phish for contacts until someone wants to chat about serial killings. Anyway, Isaac's up half the night talking with these nuts, hoping he'll come across someone, anyone. And I regret to say, quite a few people know about our game."

She tapped the eraser of her pencil against her teeth. "But we have found one person Diamond held serious conversations with. The reason we know this is that Diamond copied the chats to disk."

"Did it lead to someone specific?" I asked, holding my breath.

"That's a yes and a no. This guy always used an Internet café and paid cash."

"Uh-huh. Sounds more and more as if we're looking for someone living off the grid."

"Yes, a real ghost, and this guy, Jack, always contacted Diamond at the same time of day. You could see that from the time stamp on Diamond's disks."

"Which reinforces the impression that Jack is a highly organized killer determined to see the game through."

"Yes, and if you believe what Jack says, the number of women he's killed in the past, even discounting that number, you'd still have two or three murders he could be credited with." She sat up and put down her pencil. "By the time you become chief of police, you've developed contacts with other jurisdictions across the country. I checked what Jack bragged about. Two of the cases are just as he wrote on his blog, including information never released to the media, and both are unsolved murders."

"So, this is no kid fooling around on the web."

"Absolutely not, and all these contacts between Jack

and Darryl Diamond originated on a server in Southern California until the messages began to come from Savannah once Diamond moved here. And while Tobias was in L.A., he learned there was one guy who showed up at various movie shoots, had freedom to roam the set, and spoke as an authority on serial killers. Some of the people who worked on Diamond's movies referred to him as the Fed, though Jerry was unable to come up with a name and the name of this 'Fed' never appeared in the credits. Everyone else was accounted for."

"So our guy was in Savannah, and if he chatted with Diamond regularly, there's the possibility you could track him."

"That's already been done. We asked every police and sheriff's department between here and Savannah for any speeding tickets issued to vehicles passing through their jurisdiction."

"And?"

"We came up with two guys, one we cleared who was servicing restaurant equipment from here to Savannah. The other we've yet to find."

"Let me guess. It's not some fat guy with a beard wearing an aloha shirt."

"Not even close." Burnside took a sheet from the Slasher file and slid it across the desk. "He favors the Baptist minister who visited residents at Ann Chapman's assisted living facility. Their receptionist worked with our sketch artist and gave us this."

The sketch was of a lean young man with a trendy beard and a burr haircut. He had dark eyes, pale skin, and was described as warm and friendly, always wearing a suit and tie, in other words, someone who could establish instant rapport. Not only was he not fat, but he was quite small, according to the stats.

I'd seen that face before . . . I tapped the sheet. "This is the Baptist minister?"

Burnside nodded, and I realized she was watching me, watching me very closely.

"Recognize him from somewhere, Susan?"

"It seems like I've seen this guy before . . ."

Burnside said nothing.

I said nothing but continued to lean forward.

Then I understood! Burnside knew I'd been in the hotel with the hooker the night of Diamond's death and later with Mary Kate. She'd seen the tapes. But did the chief really want to question me about what had happened that night? Or simply want a quid pro quo.

I tapped the sheet again and slid back in my chair. "This guy was working room service the night Diamond leaped to his death."

Again, Burnside nodded. "Perhaps then, as Hugh Fenwick and I have long suspected, Darryl Diamond was pushed off that roof."

"I'd have to agree with that assessment."

"Anything else you want to tell me about that night, Susan?"

"Well, it's nothing you want to hear about."

And Chad and I fought over my moving out.

He said, "You didn't make such a big deal about living together when we first moved to Charleston."

"Because I was headed to cold cases in Columbia and we'd have little or no time together."

"With the Slasher case all wrapped up, you're still

going back to cold cases." Chad gestured at our sparsely furnished living room. "Both of us are pouring money into this place so one day we'll own it free and clear."

"I'm all for that, but I have to move out."

"But why?"

"To see if this relationship is going anywhere."

"Of course it's going somewhere, and you don't have to move out to learn that."

"Really?" I held out my left hand, palm down. "So where's the proof?"

So I moved into my new place under the name of Catherine Eddowes, and Chad was really ticked off when he learned I took a sick day and moved my stuff while he was still at work.

"Are you trying to keep where you live a secret from me?"

"Not at all."

I walked him down the street to my new digs, fully equipped with a mattress on the floor and a couple of ubiquitous white plastic chairs purchased at Home Depot. A crate served as a table, and several plastic cups in a variety of colors sat on a kitchen counter. An old color TV provided what entertainment there would be, that is, until my new friend, Jack, arrived. He'd liven up the place considerably, one would think.

"This is nuts," said Chad, shaking his head. "People live together all the time."

"We didn't when we lived at Myrtle Beach."

"That was different. My mother lived there."

"Well," I began, escorting him out of my side of the duplex and back down the street, where the bed was much more comfortable, "you have relatives in Charleston, don't you?"

"Not that I pay any attention to."

Behind us, the guy in the unit next door called out, "Catherine, I have a package for you."

I ignored him, instead proposing marriage, a pretty good distraction, if I have to say so myself. "If we're ever going to get married, you're going to have to court those relatives. They know people we should know."

"We're getting married?"

"You did say you wanted children, didn't you?" I pulled away to the length of my arm. "I certainly hope you don't have some other gal in mind."

Chad pulled me to a stop. "When did you find out?"

I took his arm again and swung him down the street, away from the neighbor holding the package for Catherine Eddowes. "I've been taking tests."

"You're pregnant, aren't you? So you can't move out. We need to go see a justice of the peace."

"I'm not pregnant. Yet."

"Then when do you want to get married?"

I snuggled against him as we strolled along. Two coeds from the College of Charleston passed by and my look told them my sweet guy was already taken. "Since I've always lived along the coast, I've looked forward to what little change of seasons we have each fall and I'd like to have a fall wedding." I dropped his arm. "But this is all speculation on my part. I haven't even been asked."

Mary Kate helped me fix up the place, as, everyone knows, she has an eye for color. Still, that didn't temper her initial reaction.

"God, what a rat hole."

"I'm not a Belle of Charleston."

Mary Kate walked into the bedroom where the mattress lay. "Now I know how the other half lives."

"Good. Because I need to borrow some furniture, and you bluebloods always have more stuff than you can properly display."

"Are you sure Chad is okay with this?"

"Last I heard he was out shopping for a diamond."

"Sheesh. I wish I had a guy like him."

"You do. James Stuart."

"He had a setback when he returned to work, some kind of problem with the longshoremen. I only go by to make sure he's doing his physical therapy. "

"Of course."

We returned to the living room.

"He doesn't remember asking me to go dancing. James has never done that before, and it about blew me away when he called."

"It's temporary amnesia—so induce him to ask you to go dancing again."

"He's not even that good of a dancer." Mary Kate stood at the window. Outside the street was warm and quiet. "You know, if I didn't know better, I'd think someone was watching your place."

I joined her at the window. "I certainly hope so. Otherwise, why do us gals put in all this effort?"

And Isaac Henry became so engrossed in digging through the data on Darryl Diamond's L.A. computer that he forgot all about the victims scheduled to die in Charleston, so it took awhile for him to get around to checking on the September victims: Stride and Eddowes. When he did, he immediately called his boss, who reported the information to the chief of police.

Burnside's secretary had orders to put Hugh Fenwick through whenever the Intel chief called, because the only reason Fenwick would call would be about Charleston's own Jack the Ripper. Burnside sat in a meeting with Operation Midnight, the CPD's program to keep children and young teens off the streets between the hours of midnight and 6 a.m.

"Chief," said Fenwick, "you're not going to believe this, but a Catherine Eddowes just appeared on our radar."

Burnside glanced at those sitting across the desk from her. "Would you repeat that?"

Fenwick did.

"Why don't you schedule something with my secretary for later today?" Which was code for: you and McPherson had better get your butts down here and fast.

Fenwick told the chief he would do just that.

"And put someone on Eddowes' place. We need to talk to that woman."

CHAPTER THIRTY-ONE

The modern-day Jack the Ripper, the one who had been responsible for all the gruesome killings in Charleston, was, on this Wednesday afternoon, dressed as a tourist and looking from his map to the houses along the street where Elizabeth Stride lived. He appeared to be trying to figure out just where in the world he was.

At this point, Jack could view his life as a kid growing up in the Midwest rather dispassionately. He was in control now, ever since watching that History Channel program about Jack the Ripper, a clever fellow whom no one ever caught, and who made his life's work killing prostitutes.

Watching that program, Jack accepted the call to kill prostitutes, or his mother, over and over again, and as he delved deeper into the legend, he eventually crossed paths with the very malleable and desperate Darryl Diamond, a producer who specialized in serial killer movies, that is, until television stole the genre and put it on TV every night.

As a child, and because of his small stature, Jack had been at the mercy of adults until the day he captured and tortured the neighborhood cat. After several more animals met a similar fate, and an attempt to kidnap the kid next door failed (the boy thought they were playing hide and seek and had hidden too well), Jack moved on to adults, and in this he had plenty of training.

That training came from his mom, a lonely woman screwing her way through as many men as possible to find her one true love. And it didn't hurt that each of these men, if they failed to hang around, left money on the dresser going out the door. The few who stayed longer and gave Jack's mother the illusion of having finally found her true love, beat hell out of her only child, some literally throwing the small boy across the room. But teenaged Jack finally fought back.

That particular boyfriend, drunk beyond reason, staggered back and examined the blood coming from the side of his head. Son of a bitch! The little punk had hit him with one of his own beer bottles!

In a rage, the guy broke the bottom off another bottle and came at Jack, who, backing away, fell out a first-floor window, through the screening, and onto the ground below. Shaken, Jack scrambled to his feet, dodged the remains of the beer bottle thrown at him, and ran away from the monsters inhabiting his home.

Jack became a street kid, and the gang he fell in with played out their roles in an abandoned warehouse, called "squats" by its inhabitants. But soon the local cops swept through, busting heads and the kids attached to them. In court Jack's luck held when a judge could find no record for this kid who cleaned up well, was small for his age, and smiled up at the judge while the other kids remained sullen and angry, just waiting for a chance to smart off.

You didn't turn over a boy of such size to the prison system to become someone's butt buddy. So Jack was returned home, and lucky again, the police had just arrested the latest love of his mother's life. Now, whenever Jack looked back on his life, because he'd never done a day inside, he understood the saying: "I'd rather be lucky than good."

Jack and his mother, living on money left behind by her latest "husband," established a semblance of a normal life, and Jack returned to school, where he was befriended by a teacher. Other young men on the bubble of life had gone on to make something of themselves under the tutelage of this woman: one young man attending the military academy at West Point, another gathering the courage to send off his illustrations to Marvel Comics.

Still, because of his mom's rocky relationship with men, Jack was unable to grasp the concept that this teacher, who had recently divorced an abusive husband, did not want another man in her life. She was starting all over again, this time focusing her attention on young males, in hopes she could prevent them from becoming the kind of man she'd recently divorced.

Jack heard the schoolteacher say she believed in him, but he paid scant attention to the fact that she complimented other young men in the same class. To Jack, every touch of her hand, every clasp of his shoulder, and every word of encouragement became a secret signal between the two of them. And when she smiled at her pet in this particular class, her eyes more often than not came to rest on Jack, a young man who displayed an incredible sense of how to diagram a sentence, synopsize a book, or summarize a lecture in several sentences.

But the Friday night she rebuffed him, even laughed at him when he showed up on her doorstep, Jack fell back on the only way he knew to treat a woman, having learned well from all those men passing through his mother's life. The schoolteacher was found in her bathtub the following Monday after failing to report to work, the ME ruling that she had been raped, sodomized, and beaten to death.

And Jack's luck held. He wasn't even a suspect.

Since the neighbors hadn't seen or heard anything, the police figured the teacher had gone looking for Mr. Goodbar and invited him to sleep over, though the authorities never found the man or the bar where she might've met him. And when Jack drifted to the West Coast, and eventually into the orbit of Darryl Diamond, the movie producer became enthralled with the idea of actually knowing a real, live serial killer.

Diamond didn't take Jack's word for it but had the murders checked out. After all, there was no way Darryl could be suspect; he produced movies about serial killers, and because the young fools running the studios didn't understand how to mine this genre, it wasn't long before Darryl was drawn into Jack's fantasy of recreating a story of a modern-day Jack the Ripper. They just had to find the right city.

Jack said the original victims would lead them to the right city, and when Darryl objected to the lack of prostitutes in Charleston, Jack said all women were whores. Besides, he was inventing a new role-playing game, similar to the ones played by the street kids he'd met in that abandoned warehouse. And when Diamond hesitated, and finally faltered, Jack shoved him off the roof of that downtown hotel.

Jack had actually been in Diamond's home on Rainbow Row when Detective Sam Gadsden opened the front door with Diamond's keys and announced that the CPD were on the premises and anyone on said premises must show himself. As the lights came on in Diamond's house, Jack folded up his laptop, turned the light off over the producer's desk, and was "in the wind" before the cops reached that part of the house. It was the following day before Jack learned everyone had bit on the suicide note and believed his benefactor, overwhelmed by guilt, had thrown himself off that hotel in the historic district.

Jack had scoped out Catherine Eddowes's duplex in Radcliffeborough and had moved on to reconnoitering Elizabeth Stride's fourplex in Wraggborough. Charleston, one of the richest cities in the American colonies, had been built behind a wall to keep out the French and Spanish, Indians and pirates, but once these dangers subsided and the British had been sent packing, Charleston spilled outside its wall into Wraggborough and Radcliffeborough. And there was no one on the street today but Jack, a couple of college students, and the Avon lady.

The Avon lady pulled her Cadillac to the curb in front of Stride's fourplex, checked her makeup in the rearview mirror, and went to the door of a middle-aged woman, who, for some reason, had Wednesday afternoons off from one of the largest property and casualty operations in Charleston.

From where he stood, there was no way Jack could hear what was being said, or know the woman he believed to be an Avon sales rep was Danielle Motte, the vice cop who had helped subdue one of the attackers of Ann Chapman.

Danielle smiled and told Elizabeth Stride that she had been referred to her by someone in Elizabeth's Bible study group. This was true. The Intel Squad had been sending people through Stride's life for the last few weeks, and they knew enough about Stride to know she would allow a sales rep into her house, if only for a polite turndown.

Once Danielle made the customary compliments about Stride's apartment and seated herself on the living room couch, she began to cough and was unable to stop. When Stride disappeared into the kitchen for a glass of water, Danielle quickly assessed what magazines Stride subscribed to, so that, three days later, Elizabeth was cornered at her office with balloons and celebratory people who told her that she'd won an all-expense trip to Paradise Island from *Sandlapper: The Magazine of South Carolina*. Faced with the overwhelming enthusiasm of her fellow coworkers, Stride was hooked, as was her employer, who gave her the week off.

Elizabeth Stride had been an easy mark for the CPD. Catherine Eddowes, however, was proving a bit more elusive, that is, until Sam Gadsden realized who he was tracking.

CHAPTER THIRTY-TWO

Early one morning, when I was approaching the gate of the Charleston Naval Weapons Station, my cell phone chirped. It was Burnside asking me to report to her office, telling me that she had cleared the meeting with SLED. I wasn't to drive to Columbia today.

The weapons station is located on the west bank of the Cooper and encompasses seventeen thousand acres of land, including ten thousand acres of forest and wetlands. It has more than one entrance, and each day I drove through because the sticker on my rental car allowed me to pass through, and because anyone tailing me would have to possess the same sticker. I didn't think our Jack could qualify for one of those stickers. The security for nuclear weapons, as you can imagine, is very tight.

But now the jig was up.

"Close the door behind you, Susan," said Burnside, rising to her feet and spreading a series of photos across her desk.

The photo array was of me coming and going from my new apartment, and passing through the Naval Weapons Station.

"Do you have an explanation for these?" she demanded, hands going to her hips. Today the chief's business attire included a skirted suit.

I'd half expected this. After all, only criminals think cops are stupid. Still, I stalled by taking a seat in one of the visitors' chairs. "We needed a Catherine Eddowes and I furnished one. There was no reason for anyone to know about what I was doing until we got closer to September thirtieth. I didn't need to be slammed with attention."

Burnside's hands came off her hips. "I don't know about this . . ."

I looked her in the eye from where I sat in the visitor's chair. "I want this bastard as much as you do, and I'm pretty sure he knows where Eddowes lives and where she works."

"You've been followed?" The chief took a seat behind her desk, worried.

"Probably, but I haven't really been looking."

"Then what's this about passing through the gate of the Naval Weapons Station each morning?"

"To rub off Jack. Catherine Eddowes has to have a job, and I gave her one, a job where she has to go in early so I can continue out the other side of the weapons station on my way to Columbia."

Burnside shook her head. "This is a dangerous game you're playing, Susan."

"Not until September thirtieth."

"Did you ever consider that this guy could've put a

GPS tracking device on your car and track you over the web, hell, even on his cell phone. This is not a fool we're dealing with."

I shook my head. "Something like that would've been detected by the personnel at the gate. They run mirrors under my car when I drive through and stick monitors through my windows. No GPS locator has been found. If they'd found one, I'd probably be in the brig. And I have a handheld device that I sweep the interior of the car with twice a day."

I crossed my legs. "Ever since I've been involved in this case, from the night you sent James Stuart to tell me that I'd failed to protect Mary Ann Nichols—the one from Ohio—I was aware that there was no Catherine Eddowes in the greater metro area. For this very reason I've been building an ID for Eddowes: rental car, driver's license, charge accounts at Citadel Mall, the whole nine yards. If the Ripper's as sharp as we think, he knows Eddowes arrived in Charleston a few weeks ago, after living overseas."

The chief shook her head. "I don't even want to know how you obtained a military ID." She leaned back in her swivel chair. "I assume there is a Catherine Eddowes?"

"At Ramstein Air Base in Germany. Catherine is of Canadian birth, a civilian employee of NATO, and married to a GI. Her husband's a navigator on a C-17."

"He's still overseas?"

"Yes, but if you checked, you'd find there's a paper trail from Miami to Charleston for his wife, who appears to be moving to Charleston ahead of him for his next assignment."

Burnside's eyes widened. She sat up. "Making it appear that Catherine Eddowes caught a ride on an Air Force plane to Miami, where she connected commercially? So, the same system Jack uses to track his victims, you're using against him?"

"Exactly. Besides leasing an apartment in her name, renting a car, and staying at the Holiday Inn several nights, Catherine Eddowes was arrested for speeding entering South Carolina."

"In what county?"

"Jasper."

"But we wouldn't know anything about that, would we?"

I didn't answer that question but said, "And now you don't have to worry that Jack will bring in an out-of-town victim you couldn't control, nor will he be in such a hurry to use his private tracking system to see if a Catherine Eddowes will arrive by boat, plane, or rental before September thirtieth. All he has to do is focus on me."

Burnside shook her head. "People warned me that you were a loose cannon."

"Well then," I said, standing, "let's do this. I'll move out of Eddowes' apartment and the CPD can pick it up. It'll also have the additional benefit of making my boyfriend happy, and, in that way, you can cover both Eddowes' apartments."

"Both apartments?" asked Burnside, looking up at me.

"Surely the CPD has created a bogus Catherine Eddowes of its own and has laid all the preliminary groundwork just as I have." I smiled at the chief. "It's your call."

The following day Mary Kate's editor, Keith Fraser, took Mary Kate to lunch at 82 Queen, where Low Country cuisine is served in private dining rooms and an open-air courtyard. Fraser and Mary Kate opted for the courtyard, and in a breeze off the harbor, the waiter took their drink order.

Once the waiter left, Fraser asked, "What's your friend Susan Chase up to these days?"

"What?" asked Mary Kate, looking up from her purse. "Oh, some sort of currency scam. Lots of fake twenties showing up on the street and the merchants were beginning to complain. But that's all over. She's headed back to cold cases."

"Is there a story there?"

"You could ask the crime beat guy to check it out, but then you've got to ask yourself if the Chamber of Commerce would let us run the story."

Fraser glanced at the door leading to the courtyard. "Any idea why Chase showed up the night Darryl Diamond leaped to his death from that hotel roof?"

Mary Kate had taken the mirror from her purse. Now she flipped it open. She was not looking at Fraser when she said, "It had to do with some hooker."

"So," asked her editor, "what's your friend working on: busting escort services or chasing funny money?"

Mary Kate clicked the compact shut and looked across the table. "What are you trying to say, Keith?"

"You were at the museum when George Huddleston came off his meds—"

"I still think we should've run the story."

"No, you don't. Your family and the Huddlestons go all the way back to the founding of Charleston."

To this Mary Kate said nothing, only smiled across the courtyard at someone who had nodded to her. What was that woman's name?

The waiter returned with two sweet teas, and once he'd left with their orders, Fraser glanced at the doorway again, and then shook out his napkin and laid it across his lap. "You know, the Feds always use local cops for funny money busts in the hopes that one of the locals will take the bait and run with the money."

"You'd think the Feds would have enough to do dealing with the War on Terror."

"Which brings me to my point: Did you ever ask yourself why an elderly woman who wandered away from an assisted living facility would be important to Charleston's Department of Homeland Security and James Stuart?"

Mary Kate only stared at him.

Fraser chuckled. "You've really got it bad, haven't you?"

Mary Kate picked up her napkin and snapped it open. "I used to hang with his sister. He's practically family."

"Uh-huh, and how's his recuperation coming along?"

"He's coming along just fine, Keith, and he's not part of my love life."

"You haven't had a love life since James Stuart was hospitalized, and the people at the newspaper have noticed."

"I might point out that my love life is none of their business. Or yours."

"But if you miss a story happening right under your nose, now, that *is* my business." He motioned to someone standing at the entrance of the courtyard.

Mary Kate turned to see a guy weaving his way toward their table, and the guy could've worked for the Geek Squad with his white shirt, black tie and pants, and horn-rimmed glasses. His black hair was parted down the middle and pulled to each side, and his pale face covered with pimples. Several guests openly stared as the young man crossed the courtyard.

Fraser gestured to one of the chairs. "Have a seat, Gerald."

Without acknowledging Mary Kate, the geeky-looking guy sat, then picked up the chair by its seat once his bottom was in it, and with both hands, lifted the chair and moved it several inches away from Mary Kate, canting the chair toward Keith Fraser.

"This is Gerald Wooten," said her boss. "His cousin is Spenser Wooten—"

"That's Spenser with an 's,'" said Gerald, still not looking at Mary Kate. "Like the poet."

"Er—yes," said Fraser. "Anyway, Gerald's cousin operates the press for the paper, and Gerald is a Ripperologist."

Not used to being ignored by any man, Mary Kate asked, "And just what the hell's that?"

Now the geek looked at her. "Someone who knows everything there is to know about Jack the Ripper."

CHAPTER THIRTY-THREE

The captain of detectives assigned Abel Waring to make sure Elizabeth Stride got on her plane for Paradise Island. When McPherson made this assignment, he did not take into consideration that there was a Waffle House on Aviation Avenue, and many other restaurants, especially on Ashley Phosphate Road, where a former phosphate mine, cleared and graded in 1928, provided landing strips for aircraft. In one of those coincidences of history that usually make conspiracy buffs salivate, the Charleston airport opened the same week as the Grace Memorial Bridge was dedicated, otherwise known as the first Cooper River Bridge.

Paradise Island! Just the name of her destination sounded exotic, and Elizabeth Stride left home early on September 29th, the day before she was to die at the hands of the Ripper. Leaving early gave her well over two hours to catch her flight and the people confirming her room, the flight, and the meals had really meant it. Everything was paid for, including one week's free valet parking at the Charleston airport.

Except that driving down Aviation Avenue, Elizabeth realized she'd left her . . . stuff at home and she wasn't going to any paradise without her . . . stuff. Not since she'd driven all the way out to Summerville and purchased that stuff at a CVS.

Paradise Island! The name alone lifted her spirits from the tedium of keeping records for the largest property and casualty company in Charleston. So what if they'd brought in computers to make her job easy. Every morning before she left for work, every day when she stared in the mirror, Elizabeth saw the face of a woman about to turn forty and realized Paradise Island might be her last chance to meet her Prince Charming. Or at least to become one of those girls gone wild she'd seen on cable TV.

But she had to have her . . . stuff. She didn't have the nerve to purchase it at the airport, or once she arrived in the Bahamas, though by the name of the place, Paradise Island, they should have every birth control product imaginable. So Elizabeth made a u-turn in front of the airport terminal and headed home.

Abel Waring saw none of this. He was already seated at the counter of the Waffle House, his back to Aviation Avenue—as Elizabeth's car raced by, then down the ramp, and back on I-26 to return to Charleston, and a chance meeting with Jack the Ripper.

Disguised as a green-card Hispanic, and the day before Elizabeth Stride was to die, the modern-day Jack trimmed bushes in Stride's backyard and smiled up at the lady on the porch of the second floor. Once the woman disappeared from her balcony, Jack wandered over to Stride's ground floor apartment, trimmed a few more bushes, here and there, and then removed a pane of glass with a glass cutter. He used a piece of stickum to prevent the glass from falling inside and possibly shattering. Reaching through the opening in the glass, he turned the lock, raised the window, and crawled inside.

Piece of cake, thought Jack, relishing Charleston's long history of servants, black, white, or brown, who blended into the woodwork. Really, you hardly ever noticed them.

Sitting on the floor and leaning against the bed, Jack waited to be found out, but nothing happened. Stride was at work and wouldn't return for several hours, so Jack made himself comfortable, as comfortable as a guy could be crawling from one room to the other to check out the situation.

In the kitchen Jack found the back door closed but unlocked. Startled, he whipped around, saw no one, heard no one, and then peered through the door glass. Overhead, the woman came out on her porch, sang a few lines of "Rocket Man," hung out her wash, and returned to her unit.

Telling himself to calm down, Jack locked the back door, returned to the bedroom, and finally the bathroom where he took a seat on the toilet and stared at the birth control products on the counter. Still, it was several minutes before his hands, clad in workman's gloves, stopped shaking.

At the Greenberg Center, Chief Burnside dropped by the office of her captain of detectives and found Michael McPherson and Hugh Fenwick eating a late lunch at McPherson's desk.

"How's it shaping up?" she asked, closing the door.

McPherson finished half of his sandwich and brushed off his hands. "I'm worried about the equipment Chase checked out."

Hugh Fenwick knew to keep on eating.

"What equipment?" asked Burnside.

McPherson told her.

"Sounds like Chase is trying to bring Jack in alive."

"Actually, it sounds stupid. A girl can't do that, and she sure as hell can't do it alone."

Burnside looked at Fenwick, busily gobbling down the rest of his sandwich. "What do you think, Hugh?"

Fenwick swallowed and cleared his throat. "I believe we're all set for tomorrow night and have all the monitoring gear in place, especially in the apartment adjoining Chase's."

Burnside nodded, then said to her captain of detectives, "I think Chase is just being overly cautious. It never would've dawned on me to requisition such a weapon."

"I don't care, Eugenia," said McPherson. "She's too damn young to be making these decisions."

With the use of her first name, Burnside realized this was one of those times when her captain of detectives was determined to make his point. Well, there was nothing to be gained by further discussion. McPherson had teenage daughters. She had all boys.

"So," she asked, "would you mind telling me what you have planned?"

McPherson pushed the other half of his ham and cheese aside and pulled a pad over in front of him. "We have the houses across the street from Stride's and Eddowes', and around six tomorrow night our people will move in. They'll appear to be coming over for a party, carrying paper bags filled with equipment and enough food to last overnight. Both units have recruited girls from the secretarial pool to accompany the SWAT team members into the house, and the girls have been given the following day off, so they're happy to go along. Those who leave the party early will be the owners of the two houses. Both couples will be picked up by Checker Cab and taken to the Holiday Inn at Folly Beach, where someone will babysit them. The one child between the two couples will spend the night with her grandparents in Goose Creek."

McPherson drank from his can of Coke before continuing. "When the SWAT units move in, detectives from the drug unit will set up behind both houses, somewhere where a bum can't be seen but wouldn't appear out of the ordinary if spotted. After dark, patrols in both Wraggborough and Radcliffeborough will be reduced to a skeleton crew; before that, vans will have moved in, one after school lets out, the other shortly after dark. We have civilian cars taking up spaces on both streets so there'll be no question of finding parking."

"I assume they've been told to be discreet."

"Eugenia, everyone's been told to act like their next promotion depends on how they handle themselves tomorrow night."

Burnside looked at her Intel chief again.

"Chief," said Fenwick, "when I checked the COMMO gear, I made sure everyone believes this sting is for a couple of dealers selling drugs to the students at the College of Charleston."

McPherson snorted. "What would we do without drug dealers to blame for the woes of the world?"

"Easy," said Burnside, "we'd blame terrorism. Does either the Stride unit or the Eddowes' unit know the other is there?"

"No," said Fenwick, "but since one's in Wraggborough and the other's in Radcliffeborough, I think we'll have decent spacing. I'll be in the command center, and if someone's cover has to be blown, I'll do the blowing, shutting down either operation."

"What about Danielle?" Danielle Motte was the female vice cop who had helped subdue one of the Ripper wannabes.

McPherson had picked up the other half of his sandwich. Now he put it back down. "Danielle will go in tomorrow afternoon just after five, and she'll have a radio and a cell phone in her purse. Once Danielle's inside, she'll clear the interior and make sure the land line works, then check in with Hugh. Dispatch will send a patrol car down the street after Danielle enters the apartment. The unit will pause thirty seconds in front of the house and one of the undercovers will jog through the alley in case Danielle needs assistance when she first enters the premises."

"And Catherine Eddowes?"

McPherson shrugged. "Chase's place is a duplex, and a couple of our people will be in the next-door apartment, along with SWAT and a sniper with night glasses across the street. Both Stride's house and Chase's will have vans up and down the street and similar bums loitering in the backyard."

"But when they arrive, everyone stays put, right? Nobody moves from any house or van or wanders away to take a pee?"

"Don't worry, Chief," said her Intel chief. "We've been planning this all month. Everything's under control. Why don't you take off? You have a long day ahead of you."

"I could say the same for you."

So, when Burnside went home and found her husband passed out in front of the television, she shrugged, changed into something more comfortable, and started cooking dinner for the teenage son still living at home.

"What about Dad?" asked the teenager, coming in from football practice and seeing his father passed out on the sofa.

"What have I told you?" asked his mother from the stove.

"That he suffers from post traumatic stress syndrome from when *USS Cole* was attacked by terrorists, but life must go on."

Burnside smiled at her son, a strapping young man and a natural athlete. "I'm sure your father would want us to keep the family together. One day, he may be healthy enough to rejoin us."

"Yeah, right," said the son, plopping his schoolbooks onto the kitchen table. "And what will you do when I go off to South Carolina State? You'll have lots of free time on your hands."

"Oh, I don't know," said Burnside, raising the lid of the mashed potatoes and smiling into the pot. "If I get bored watching you score too many touchdowns, I may run for public office."

So, the chief of police, her acting chief of detectives, and the head of the Intel Squad each slept late the following day, September 30th, and came in at noon. And once the Greenberg Center emptied of office workers at the end of the workday, Burnside, Fenwick, and Jerry Tobias went upstairs and walked into McPherson's office just in time to hear Danielle Motte screaming from the speakerphone.

"Stride is dead! I repeat, Elizabeth Stride is dead! You better get some people over here and fast!"

McPherson gaped at the speakerphone, as shocked as the chief and those trailing her into his office.

"What's she talking about?" asked Tobias, closing the door behind him. "It's not even dark."

Burnside sank into one of the visitors' chairs. "No, no," she said shaking her head. "This can't be happening."

McPherson told Motte not to mess with the crime scene.

"You don't have to worry about that," blurted Danielle over the speaker. "I was checking the closets when Stride fell out. Her throat's been cut."

"Calm down, Danielle."

"Oh, yeah, right. Tell me how you would've handled a dead woman who falls out of a closet at your feet. I'm alerting dispatch. This guy might still be in the

Wraggborough neighborhood."

"No!" shouted Burnside, sliding forward in her chair and reaching for the desk. "Nobody moves."

Fenwick, who had taken the seat next to Burnside, asked, "You want Wraggborough flooded or not?"

McPherson picked up his handset, breaking the connection with the speakerphone. He put his hand over the mouthpiece so Motte couldn't hear what was said on their end. "I understand not flooding the area, but you can't leave Danielle with a body where she's expecting some guy with a knife to show up."

"He's already shown up, and yes, I can. She's as tough as you guys, just upset at finding the body."

"Sounds worse than that."

Burnside asked Jerry Tobias, "Would you contact Chase, tell her what's happened, and caution her to be on her toes?"

"Gotcha." Tobias stepped to a corner of McPherson's office and took out his cell phone.

Fenwick shook his head. "This isn't right. It's not even dark."

On the other side of the glass, detectives in the bullpen, once again, stared at them.

"I'll have Waring's head for this," growled McPherson. "He was to make sure Stride got on that plane."

"But the Ripper," said Fenwick, shaking his head, "I mean, the Slasher couldn't have killed Stride. It's not even the correct date."

Burnside pointed at a wall-mounted clock. "Of course he could've. He killed Stride the morning of the thirtieth, while we were all sleeping in, and then stuffed her in a closet for us to find later in the day."

Everyone looked at the clock, and McPherson realized the Ripper had outfoxed them again. He'd killed Stride on the correct date, doing her in the early hours of September thirtieth, instead of waiting for the evening, such as now, as the clocks neared 6 p.m.

Over the phone, Motte asked McPherson what they wanted her to do, that she had her pistol out and couldn't be responsible for whoever she might shoot.

"What'd she say?" asked Burnside.

McPherson put Motte back on the speaker and asked Danielle to repeat her question.

When she did, Burnside said, "Danielle, I want you to leave the building immediately and walk down to the corner in the direction of the harbor. Dispatch will send a black and white."

"I have my car parked around the corner."

"No, Danielle, I want you with our people." To Fenwick she said, "Hugh, could you make sure dispatch knows exactly where that cross street is?" And she told Danielle the corner where she would be picked up.

Fenwick nodded and pulled out his cell phone.

"And call SWAT. Have everyone remain in position so we don't have any excessive comings or goings, or people dragging ass since their mission's been canceled. But wherever they are, they are to stand down."

Tobias closed his cell. "Chase is already in place, and her side of the building is all clear."

"We need to get Chase out of there," said McPherson. "This is way over that girl's head."

"No," said Burnside, setting her jaw, "but I can tell you one thing, we are going to be loaded for bear when we camp out next door to Susan Chase tonight."

SEPTEMBER 30TH

I sat in one of my new plastic chairs, its back to the wall, and in a position to see both the back and front doors of my apartment. That is, until visitors came calling.

Chad was the first to drop by, probably because I wasn't answering my cell. He knocked, and when I didn't answer, he knocked several more times, probably because the light and television were on inside my apartment.

All that knocking caused the guy next door to come to his door, stick his head out, and ask what was going on, couldn't Chad tell there was no one at home?

Chad pointed at my apartment as I moved to a window to watch the show. "Susan's not answering her phone and I was worried about her."

"Susan?"

"Yes. Susan Chase."

"And you are, sir?" inquired the neighbor, a skinny guy in a business suit, stepping out on our joint front porch.

"Chad Rivers. I'm the boyfriend."

"I'll tell her you came by."

Chad gestured at my door. "But I hear the TV. Maybe we should check inside. Do you have a key?"

Oh, hell.

"For that I'd have to call the owner." Then in a voice I could barely make out, Sam Gadsden asked, "Did you ever think your girlfriend might be working tonight?"

"No," said Chad, shaking his head, "Usually she's back from . . ." Chad stepped back, almost stepping off the porch. He looked at my door and turned away. "I—I must have the wrong house."

Gadsden and I watched Chad go down the steps, stop on the sidewalk, and take out a sheet of paper.

He glanced at it and called from the street, "Sorry. My bad."

I smiled. My sweet man knew how to pull off a mistaken address, because, as I watched, I saw him look up and down the street and resolutely march off in the opposite direction. Still, that didn't stop the phone on my hip from vibrating. The text read: WOULD IT HURT TO TELL ME WHEN YOU'RE WORKING???

Mary Kate arrived a half hour later and wouldn't take no for an answer. This time, instead of a guy who came to my neighbor's door, it was a woman.

"What's the problem?" asked Danielle Motte.

"I want to know where Catherine Eddowes is."

"And you are?"

"Mary Kate Belle from *The Post and Courier.*"

"Well," said Danielle, stepping out on the porch, "I guess she's not home."

"Oh, I think she's in there, just not answering the door."

"That doesn't make sense," said Motte. "Why wouldn't Catherine answer the door if she's at home?"

"Because she's not who she says she is, and maybe you're not either."

"What's that supposed to mean?"

"A Ripperologist explained it all to me, and I've come to spend the night with Susan. Do you even have anyone in there? This guy is pretty vicious."

Danielle was good. She did not look up and down the street but only lowered her voice. "If that's true, then the apartment next door has policemen inside who've been told to shoot to kill on sight. You want to talk to Chase, you'll have to come in here." Danielle gestured toward my neighbor's door.

Mary Kate followed her but did not go inside. "Send Susan out. I want to see her."

"Sorry, Miss Belle," said Danielle from inside the door, "but your friend can't be seen in public tonight. People must believe that she's inside Catherine Eddowes' apartment."

"So Jack the Ripper believes she's inside."

"And you just said the magic phrase, and if you don't come inside this very instant, you'd best get your butt off this porch before someone calls your publisher."

"You can't threaten me."

"Of course I can, and when we take you downtown, we'll lose your paperwork, just as we did for those poor bastards who tried to kill Ann Chapman."

"Ann Chapman?"

"Don't play stupid, Miss Belle. If you know about

Jack, you damn well know about his last victim."

That was enough for Mary Kate, and after glancing up and down the street, she crossed the porch and disappeared inside the next-door apartment.

Which was about the same time someone put an arm around my waist and a knife to my throat.

"Not a sound, Catherine," said the male voice over my shoulder. "Now step away from the window."

I did and felt his erection against my butt. When he had me away from the window, a cell phone was held out in front of me, in the palm of the hand holding me around the waist. The guy had small, delicate hands. Women's hands.

A button on the cell was touched, the screen lit up, and America Online was dialed. Immediately after making connection, his fingers punched more buttons and lines of text began to scroll across the screen, transmitting information to the World Wide Web.

The text said Catherine Eddowes' throat had been slit tonight and that she'd been disemboweled, despite the best efforts of the Charleston police to protect her. A portion of a torn, bloody apron had been found near a wall of her apartment, and on the wall above the apron had been scrawled: "The Jewes are the men that will not be blamed for nothing."

Well, grammatically correct or not, the same stuff had been written in chalk on a wall over a piece of bloody apron found in London in the year 1888.

"You see, my dear," whispered Jack into my ear, "you're about to become famous."

With the blade at my neck, I had to clear my throat

to speak. "No sane person could've killed Catherine Eddowes. It must've been the work of a lunatic."

Jack faltered. Those were the same conclusions drawn by the police who had found Eddowes' body back in 1888. Catherine Eddowes was also the only victim of Jack the Ripper whose body was found outside the Whitechapel District, but the similarity of her murder easily linked her death to the others.

Since the guy had an arm around my waist, locking my left arm down along my leg, all I had to do was twist my wrist around and jam the hand-held TASER into his thigh, setting off the compressed nitrogen that fired two small probes into his thigh. Unfortunately, because I stood so close, each of us felt the shock. The electricity ran through us, causing us to shimmy and shake. We collapsed to the floor, the knife falling away from my throat and the TASER dropping from my hand.

Next door, Mary Kate had been escorted by Danielle Motte into a rear bedroom that had been blacked out for the occasion. Hugh Fenwick sat on one side of the bed, headphones to his ears, and Isaac Henry sat on the other side, facing a row of computers, one with thermal imaging, another seized from Darryl Diamond's home on Rainbow Row, and a third screen that duplicated the watch commander's at the Greenberg Center.

When Mary Kate appeared in the bedroom doorway, Fenwick looked up from concentrating on the sound coming from bugs planted in the apartment next door. He lifted his headphones and asked what a reporter was doing here. Isaac Henry turned away from his computers as Motte tried to explain, but Sam Gadsden, who had followed the women into the bedroom, was staring over Isaac's shoulder at the computer screens.

"What's that?" he asked.

Fenwick twisted around to better see the screens on the other side of the bed, saw the thermal imaging, and refitted his headphones over his ears. Mary Kate slipped out of her flats, got up on the bed, and walked across it on her knees for a better look. The thermal image could be interpreted as two people in the next-door apartment or one very large person.

"That can't be Chase," said Motte.

As Isaac studied the thermal imaging screen, text began to fill the screen of the computer seized at Diamond's home on Rainbow Row, the one connected to America Online, Darryl Diamond's internet connection of choice.

"What's this?" asked Mary Kate, reading the information. "Has another Catherine Eddowes been murdered tonight?" She looked from Diamond's computer screen to the cops crowded into the bedroom. "Or is this Jack with Susan? If so, you'd better get your asses over there."

Isaac glanced from Diamond's computer screen to the one duplicating the screen at the Greenberg Center.

Nothing on the watch commander's screen. Nothing at all.

Fenwick pulled off his headphones and stood up. "I can hear a struggle in Eddowes' apartment." He dropped the headphones to the bed and said, "Take the back, Sam. I've got the front."

"No, you don't," said Motte, pulling her pistol from a holster on her hip and following Gadsden out the bedroom door. "This is no job for a paper pusher." And Motte went down the hall toward the front of the house, followed by Mary Kate, who was pushing into her shoes as she trailed along.

As Fenwick alerted SWAT and members of the CPD in the two vans, Gadsden raced out the back door and across the common back porch—where he tripped over Abel Waring. Even in the darkness, the skinny detective found the blood running down the fat man's head. Gadsden put two fingers against Waring's throat. As he did, he saw another form lying in the backyard, perhaps that of the narcotics detective.

Finding a pulse, he shouted into the apartment, "Hugh, call EMS. We've got a man down, maybe two."

Then the skinny detective scrambled to his feet, stepped over to Eddowes' back door, and kicked it in. "Make yourself known!" he shouted. "Charleston Police coming through."

NOVEMBER 9TH

I ran into Mary Kate at the new Piggly Wiggly on Meeting Street. To tell the truth, I'd had to plan on running into Mary Kate because she'd have nothing to do with me, not since her publisher agreed with the chief of police and the mayor that there was no reason to print anything about a Jack the Ripper copycat slaughtering women in Charleston, especially since one of the victims had been a tourist. Mary Kate could write all she wanted about police officers valiantly preventing the assault of Catherine Eddowes and working the (unconnected) murder of Elizabeth Stride, but nothing about Jack the Ripper (too inflammatory), only a simple assault and break-in—which was all we had on Jack the night I fitted my TASER against his leg. We hadn't even learned where he was staying.

Though charged as a John Doe, Jack wasn't talking to the CPD or his public defender, and between that and MK's publisher laying down the law, Mary Kate resigned from the paper and left Charleston. It was almost three weeks before she returned. Of course, no one would be fool enough to fire someone as competent as Mary Kate Belle—or Mary Jane Belle—because either grandmother's name could open doors to other bluebloods, people who really hated to be written up in the crime section of their local newspaper.

After she paid the cashier, I smiled and said, "Good morning, Mary Kate or Mary Jane. Which one is it today?"

"I'm not talking to you." She noticed me staring at her cart piled high with vegetables, fruits, and chocolates. "What?" then she asked again, "What?"

"Oh, nothing. Just odd to see you bluebloods shopping. I thought you had servants for that."

"I have to work for a living, and that's why I returned to Charleston."

With me walking beside her, MK pushed the buggy out of the store, across the pedestrian crosswalk, and right into the path of a huge red SUV.

I grabbed Mary Kate's arm and tried to pull her back. But being obstinate, Mary Kate wouldn't let go, so I brought my other hand down on her fingers, causing her to yelp and release the cart. Both of us fell back as the SUV slammed into the cart and sent groceries flying. The SUV continued to the end of the parking lot, where it made a noisy turn onto Spring Street.

Mary Kate and I ended up on our butts, and that caused the automatic doors to remain open while we watched the damaged grocery cart twirl around at the far end of the parking lot. Several black people hurried over and asked if we were okay. Strewn along the pavement were vegetables, fruits, and bottles of liquid mixed with boxes and sacks of cereal, rice, and eggs. And since Mary Kate takes paper, not plastic, everything was pretty much soaked through and through.

"Jesus, Joseph, and Mary," said Mary Kate, clutching her oversized handbag to her chest. "Who the hell was that?"

"Probably got his pedal stuck." I took out my cell and called in the tag number, along with the vehicle make and color.

"It's kids," said one the patrons of the Pig. "They race through here like that all the time."

Two black guys gave us a hand to our feet, and we thanked them, brushed off our bottoms, and checked our clothing for rips, dirt, or smears. I wore my usual business attire, but Mary Kate wore white painter's overalls with plenty of pockets, buttons, and strings. Underneath she wore a white tee and on her feet a brand new pair of running shoes.

"Those boys could've killed you," said one of the women who had walked out of the store behind us.

"You got that right," said several onlookers, nodding.

The manager hustled out and asked what happened. Once he understood how close MK had come to being killed, he promised to replace all her groceries at no charge.

"Can you remember what you bought, Mrs. Kelly?" he asked, using her married name.

Mary Kate shook her head, then remembered her grocery list in her oversized handbag. "I might . . . I might have my list . . ."

"Good," said the manager, a guy about our height

and built like a fireplug. He ushered us back inside the Pig and over to his office. Opening the door to the low wall, he said, "Take a seat, and whenever you feel like it, have someone page me and we'll do this all over again. At no charge."

Over the PA system someone laughed. "Clean up in the parking lot. Matt and Norm, clean up in the parking lot." Another laugh, then: "This is no drill."

The manager was not amused. A tight smile crossed his face. "There appears to be something that needs my attention. You ladies make yourselves right at home."

"I—I'm sorry," said Mary Kate, clutching her huge bag and staring at the floor. "I didn't mean to make a fuss." Her cheeks were pink.

"Mrs. Kelly," said the manager, once again addressing Mary Kate by her married name, "it certainly wasn't your fault."

We took a seat, but it was a few minutes before my friend's hands stopped trembling.

"Look at you, Susan, you're not even shaking."

"Well, things like this have happened to me before."

MK glanced away. "They should've let me run the story."

"To what good?"

She didn't address this point but tried to make one of her own. "I remember when you used to make headlines at Myrtle Beach, and now you're so establishment it's sickening."

"It takes a team to catch someone like Jack, and for your information, Jack's still not talking, just sitting in his cell mute, being held as an Unknown White

Male. They don't even have his prints on file: NCIC, Homeland Security, the military, nothing. It's like he never existed."

"I don't want to talk about it."

"Then let me show you my ring." I leaned over and held out my hand, as there's nothing that'll get a gal's mind off her troubles like a decent-looking rock.

She took my hand. "Gosh, Susan, that's gorgeous. It looks like an heirloom."

"It's Chad's great-great-grandmother's. She was a Rivers, and lived around these parts."

"Yes. North of Broad. When did he give it to you?"

"A week ago," I said, pulling back my hand, "but you still weren't taking my calls."

"Because you were trying to wreck my career. That Ripper story had Pulitzer written all over it."

"'Wreck' is not the word I'd use in this particular instance."

Mary Kate tried not to laugh and began to cry. She took out a tissue to keep the tears at bay. "Thank you, Susan. I appreciate what you just did. You could've been killed."

I put a hand on her shoulder, and when the manager stuck his head over the office wall, I smiled at him. "Delayed reaction."

Mary Kate snuffled and dabbed at her eyes.

The manager asked if we'd like a cup of coffee. Anything. All on the house.

"Thank you," said MK, getting to her feet, "but I think I'd better finish my shopping."

"I'll get a cart," said the manager, and he disappeared on the other side of the low wall.

"Sure you're up to this?" I asked.

"I have to be," she said, balling up the tissue and tossing it in the trashcan under the desk. "I've been gone over three weeks and I'm way behind."

We ended up hauling home twice as many groceries as Mary Kate had come for. The manager insisted on it. But Mary Kate was way too rattled to drive, so I drove her BMW convertible to her condo overlooking Waterfront Park. Along the way I tried to get her mind off her near-death experience.

"So you and Stuart . . . ?" I began.

"He's still in a collar, but he won't wear it in public so we've been spending a lot of time on his veranda."

"I don't ever remember you doing that with any man."

"I'm trying to let him know how much I care, that I'm not the skanky woman he thinks I am." She paused. "I may have to enlist his sister to put in a good word for me. You wouldn't believe the number of women who stop by to see him with the excuse of bringing food or baked goods."

"I told you that you had your work cut out for you."

Turning into the short alleyway between condominiums, I reached up and touched the remote. The walls on each side of the condominium parking—there is no underground parking in Charleston—were louvered and sat on a low concrete wall that ran along the sidewalk.

"No, no," said Mary Kate, shaking her head. "Leave the door up but park on the street. I told the paper I'd cover anything they asked me to."

So I backed out of the alleyway and into the cross street, where, lucky me, I found a parking space. Well, it was the first of November and the middle of the week.

We unloaded the car and carried as many sacks as we could into the garage. Crossing the underground parking and heading for the elevator, a lean-looking guy with a terrific tan opened the fire door and stepped into the garage.

He looked from one of us to the other. "Is either of you Mary Jane Kelly?"

Mary Kate shook her head. "I'm divorced. I don't go by that name. I go by Mary Kate Belle."

"But your legal name is Mary Jane Kelly?" asked the man, swinging a pistol from behind his leg.

"I'm changing my . . ." Mary Kate saw the pistol. "My God, what are you doing?"

The guy carried a nine millimeter with a silencer, a nasty little item that could literally blow your head off and not make much noise. All the noise was being made by MK—who screamed.

I threw my grocery bags at the guy, hitting him in the chest. His pistol discharged, but we didn't hear anything more than a small swoosh, then the round ricocheting off the concrete. It buried itself in one of the louvered walls.

By the time he brought up his weapon a second time, I'd reached behind my back and under my coat to pull out both Walthers. Shaking off the pieces of coat hanger clipping them to my waist, I stepped forward and stuck one pistol in his gut, the other in his face.

"Drop it! Drop it right now!"

He thought about it. After all, I was just a girl, and the girl I was with had been changed into a statue that could only clutch her groceries—and scream.

He smiled and dropped his weapon to the concrete floor.

"Good choice. Now face the wall and assume the position."

"How'd you know I'd be here?" he asked.

"Because I know how you guys think."

I checked the fire door, the elevator, and the garage door—but only after clubbing the guy over the back of the head. He went down in a heap, and I kicked his weapon away, then stuck one of the Walthers in my waistband.

"Sweet Jesus," said Mary Kate, trembling and clutching her groceries. "What's—what's going on, Susan?"

I rolled the unconscious guy over on his face and took out my cuffs. "MK, watch the fire door and the garage door."

"But—but . . . ?" She continued to tremble.

"I asked you to watch the fire door and the garage door."

"But, Susan . . . ?"

"Mary Kate," I said, clipping the cuffs to the unconscious guy's wrists behind his back, "do I have to scream to get your attention?"

"No, no," she said, clutching her groceries and looking around. "I'll—I'll watch the doors."

I was using the cuffs to drag the guy out of the way when the elevator bell rang. The door opened and a swarthy guy with a MAC-10 stepped out and chambered a round. He didn't ask who was who but simply leveled his weapon at Mary Kate. I doubt he even saw me.

I dropped the unconscious guy and pushed off, throwing myself between Mary Kate and the swarthy-looking guy. As I flew between them, I fired several rounds, knocking the guy back inside the elevator. His MAC-10 came up and discharged, tattooing the ceiling.

Plaster rained down on us, Mary Kate squealed, and I landed on my side, rolled over twice and came up in a sitting position, legs splayed, both Walthers extended in front of me. I scanned the garage, the fire door, and the wider door leading to the street.

Nothing—only Mary Kate, again with her hands at her face and sacks of groceries at her feet. And a pair of feet sticking out of the elevator. The door attempted to close. Repeatedly.

"Watch the garage entrance, MK."

I got to my feet, picked up the MAC-10, and threw the weapon across the garage where it slid under a Mercedes.

"Oh, my God," cried Mary Kate. "Look out!"

I whirled around and brought up my weapons. The red SUV from the Piggly Wiggly was barreling through the garage entrance.

I put several shots through the driver's-side windshield, but the SUV kept on coming—so I stepped over, and wrapping my arm around Mary Kate's waist, pulled her out of the way. She'd turned into a statue again, albeit one that was no longer screaming. The SUV plowed into the elevator, and along the way crushed Mary Kate's groceries once again.

Releasing MK, I stepped over and jerked open the

driver's-side door. A dark-skinned guy who hadn't shaved for several days was pinned upright by the airbag, and he was very much dead. Somewhere in the building a siren began to wail.

Brushing off the plaster and shaking it out of my hair, I crossed the garage to the wide door opening on the street. What plaster had fallen down my blouse, I'd have to live with.

"Stay with me, Mary Kate. There may be more of them."

"But who . . . ?"

"In a minute."

Mary Kate was blinking, wiping her face, and brushing plaster out of her hair and off her coveralls. She stumbled over to the garage door.

"You want the door lowered?" she asked, since she was the one with the code.

But I was on my cell. "Flood the area and flood it now!" I gave McPherson the skinny on what happened, beginning with the incident in the Piggly Wiggly parking lot. Actually, I gave him the Cliff Notes version.

"You two stay inside that building," ordered McPherson.

I flipped the phone shut, fitted it on my hip, and said, "Okay, MK, you can lower the door."

Mary Kate punched in the code on the keypad and the overhead door began to slowly unwind. I watched our backsides and explained, over the noise of the lowering door, that the first person who kills Mary Jane Kelly wins a hundred grand held in a bank account in the Caymans. "The game created by Jack and financed by Diamond is being played out, even if none of us wants to play along."

For the first time since I'd known her, Mary Kate was at a loss for words, and that's probably why I was able to hear the fire door open and something hit the floor. A grenade spun its way across the concrete in our direction.

"We're out of here, MK." I took her hand and pulled her under the lowering door.

We rolled onto the sidewalk, and I came up again on my butt, surveying the short street between the two sets of condos. Again my hands were filled with pistols. Up, down, left, or right.

Nobody.

"I tore the knees out of my overalls," complained Mary Kate as the door thumped down behind us. Evidently, she'd not seen the grenade.

She tried to get to her feet, but I pulled her down. "Stay here!"

"But why?"

The grenade detonated and pieces of shrapnel blew through the louvered walls on both sides of us. Small pieces of wood splintered off and flew by, some making it as far as the parking garage of the condo across the street.

"That's why." I scrambled to my feet, jammed a Walther in my belt, and pulled Mary Kate to her feet. "Now we go."

As we approached the cross street where her car was parked, a minivan turned into the alley, and I almost shot the driver.

When he threw up his hands, I shouted, "Pull to the end of the street, lock your doors, and remain inside your vehicle!"

Nodding frantically, he did.

Mary Kate had started for her car and I hustled to catch up, looking both ways, of course, before crossing the street. We were halfway across when Mary Kate's convertible exploded in a ball of flames.

We were knocked backwards and made to take another hard seat on the pavement. The blast fried the hair off our faces, burned our skin, and slightly deafened us. From where we lay on our backs, I looked up and down the street. Someone had been a little too quick on the trigger, or perhaps the guy in the minivan had just saved our lives.

Mary Kate sat up and gaped at the pile of burning metal and stinking rubber. I sat up and collected my pistols. The driver of the minivan stuck his head over the seat and peered in our direction. Soon he was on the phone to someone. Hopefully, nine-one-one.

Shaking off the blast like a dog coming out of water, I pushed myself to my feet and pulled Mary Kate along. Whether she could hear me or not, I said, "We've got to keep moving."

I forced her to hobble across the street—where we came under fire from the direction of the Battery. We tumbled to the pavement again, this time behind a yellow Hummer. Bullets slammed into the yellow vehicle.

"Okay," I said more to myself than her, "we'll take this ride."

I shot out the Hummer's rear window and the car alarm went off, sounding like it was somewhere off in the distance. Reaching up, I cleared the broken glass with the barrel of one of my Walthers and then helped

Mary Kate scramble through the opening. When I knew she was settled in the foot well, I peered around the rear of the vehicle and fired at a guy a block away. He had been aiming a rifle in our direction. As soon as his head went down, I climbed through the rear of the Hummer and made my own way forward. MK took both pistols, and I slid behind the wheel, most of me below the dash, to begin hotwiring the ignition.

My hands were feeling around, but my head was up enough to see down the street and the entrance to the parking garage. The overhead door had not moved, and the rifleman down the street appeared to have taken cover. Well, I am a snap shooter and many of my shots come much closer than even I might imagine.

"Know how to use one of those?" I asked, gesturing with my head at the Walthers held by Mary Kate.

"No problem," she said, a little grit coming into her voice. "They blew up my car, didn't they?" We were practically yelling at each other to be heard.

"Well," I said, "don't shoot unless they shoot first."

The engine roared to life, and that brought a fresh hail of bullets from the rifleman down the street, one of them penetrating the windshield. If there was only one of them, he'd have to reload soon, wouldn't he?

No matter. The garage door began to rise, and a pair of feet stood there, shifting around impatiently; occasionally a figure peered through the louvered slats.

In the direction of Waterfront Park, two bicycle policemen dismounted, took cover behind the minivan, and shouted at the guy who had been revealed by the rising garage door. They ordered him to put down his weapon. Soon, a shootout was in progress and the guy attempted to cross the street, either to get away from the cops or intent on killing MK. The cops shot him dead.

Another bullet hit our windshield. Right between us. "Time to go!"

I wheeled the Hummer out of its space and into the street, nicking a brand-new Jag and knocking out its taillight.

"We were forced outside," I yelled into the phone jammed between my shoulder and ear.

The Hummer had been parked in the wrong direction, so we were backing toward the public market, away from the bicycle cops and hopefully away from that damn long gun. A patrol car raced toward us from the direction of the Battery. Maybe they'd take some of the heat off.

"We're still under fire and taking a yellow Hummer."

"You're not taking Belle's car?" asked McPherson.

"Not an option, and a rifleman's trailing us, so be careful when you close the net."

I let the phone drop from my shoulder onto the seat. "Don't worry, MK," I said, flashing what I thought was a reassuring smile. "All we have to do is reach the police lines and we're golden."

"Police lines?"

"Yeah. You don't think I'd let the last victim of Jack the Ripper go shopping alone, not today of all days."

She'd been watching me back down the street. Now she nodded in acknowledgment. "This is what you meant about the game being played out, whether I want to participate or not."

"Exactly."

Over the speaker of my cell phone, we heard McPherson issuing orders. "Chase and Belle are in a yellow Hummer. Make sure no one fires on any yellow vehicle. They're leaving now." McPherson spoke to me. "That's correct, isn't it?"

"You've got it!" I yelled in the direction of the phone. Backing into the next cross street, I became very busy with the traffic.

Likewise, McPherson was busy with his troops. "Chase says there's a rifleman in the vicinity. Be on the lookout!"

Cars jammed on brakes and drivers hit their horns, and we screeched to a stop. I glanced in the direction we'd just come from and saw the rifleman using the paralleled-parked cars for cover. He rose up and pointed the rifle in our direction, then saw the bicycle cops approaching the body lying in the middle of the street. He fired at the bicycle cops and continued in our direction.

Seconds later, someone came on the command net screaming: "Officer down! Officer down!" And gave the location.

Behind the rifleman, the patrol car from the direction of the Battery screeched to a stop when it reached the body in the middle of the street. Cops tumbled out, checking first the dead man, and then hustled over to their fallen comrade.

I shifted gears and put the pedal to the metal. Good that I did. A bullet from the rifleman shattered glass in the seat behind me. Mary Kate yelped and both of us ducked, but we were gone, and before we reached

East Bay, I'd brought Mary Kate up to date.

"Remember the information fed to the web by way of the Ripper's cell phone when he grabbed me in Catherine Eddowes' apartment? You saw it on one of the computers in my neighbor's apartment: the murder of Eddowes, the bloody apron, and what was written on the wall. All that's been taken as gospel by those playing the game, and your new friends are trying to collect the hundred grand promised to the one who kills Mary Jane Kelly. He'll be declared the winner of the game."

"Then I'm changing my name," said Mary Kate, looking behind us.

When the guy with the rifle ran around the corner, MK put the butt of the Walther on the top of our seat, leveled her eye behind the sight, and fired through the busted-out rear window.

"Take that, sucker!"

I couldn't help but smile.

As I turned on East Bay, she held out the Walther and examined it. "Hey, that felt pretty good, and it doesn't have much kick." She hefted the pistol. "Nice and light. I'll have to get one of these."

We barreled past the customs house and the public market, and tourists leaped out of the way, one of them shooting us the bird. So much for Charleston hospitality.

"I can't believe one of my grandmothers is trying to get me killed just because I bear her name."

"And Kelly, your ex-husband, too, so you'd better cancel your magazine subscriptions, anything with Mary Jane Kelly on it." I glanced at MK. She had become very somber.

"Mary Jane Kelly," said Mary Kate. "She's the prostitute who had the skin peeled off her by Jack the Ripper, wasn't she?"

"The most savage mutilation of them all."

"And then he was gone."

"Gone forever and never heard from again."

"Until today," muttered MK.

Sirens wailed. There was a nip in the air, and very few people were headed toward the South Carolina Aquarium. Still, one of them pulled out a cell phone, stepped into the street once we blew by, and tried to get a tag number. A few blocks ahead of us, another patrol car raced in our direction.

Mary Kate had been staring out the back window. Now, she shifted around, picked up the phone, and told McPherson that a police car had stopped down the street, blocking East Bay.

"Blocking you?" asked McPherson. "They're supposed to let you through. Tell me, Miss Belle, and make it quick, how many officers are in that unit."

"Er . . . there's only one, and he's getting out."

"Only one? There are two officers in each unit this morning, along with a paramedic."

All that was lost on us as the cop raised his shotgun and held up his other hand for us to stop. When I didn't show any intention of slowing down, the cop aimed the shotgun at us.

"Get down!" I shouted.

We did, and the blast blew out the windshield.

I raised my head and set a course so the Hummer would pass between a telephone pole and the front end of the patrol car. There would be barely enough room to pass.

Another blast blew out the remaining windshield, and this time shot rattled around in the cab. Mary Kate squirmed and squealed as the hot steel pellets found bare skin.

"No! Stay down!" I pushed her below the dash.

Ahead of us, the phony cop leaped behind the telephone pole when I aimed the Hummer between the pole and the front end of his vehicle. We had one set of tires on the curb, but enough of our front end in the street to jolt his car across the street.

Stunned, I lost control of the wheel for a moment and Mary Kate fell into the foot well, gripping the seat with one hand and the dash with the other. She stared up at me.

But I was concentrating on East Bay. "What's he doing, MK?"

She was rubbing her neck when she took a seat beside me. "Why'd he do that, Susan?"

"Mary Kate, what's he doing?"

She turned around. "He's . . . he's back in his car now. Oh, my gosh, Susan. He's coming after us." She glanced at the dash. "Can you make this thing go any faster?"

"Tell McPherson we're taking the bridge to Mount Pleasant."

"What—what?"

I repeated myself.

Mary Kate nodded and found the phone.

I ran the light at the post office and headed for the ramp to the new Ravenel Bridge. While I pushed the Hummer down East Bay, MK brought McPherson up to date.

"That's not possible, Miss Belle." I heard the captain of detectives say over the cell's speaker. "Everyone's been ordered not to shoot at any yellow vehicles."

"Well," I hollered, slowing through a red light and looking both ways before turning onto the ramp, "you'd better have all units report in. You may have officers down."

"Er—Susan," said Mary Kate, looking out the rear window, "that police car—it's coming real fast."

"Units are on the way," said McPherson. "We'll cut him off before you reach the bridge."

"Too late! We're already there." And I wheeled the Hummer onto the ramp.

I leaned on the horn and flashed my lights. Using the breakdown lane, I whipped by everyone, barely missing cars on my right, the retaining wall on our left. Trash set in motion whirled in the air behind us. Horns blared, people cursed, and behind everything was that damned patrol car, lights flashing and vehicles moving out of its way.

"Faster, Susan! Faster!"

We left the ramp and reached the bridge. The speedometer showed us doing, sixty, seventy miles an hour. Jiminy. I didn't know a Hummer could boogie like this, and all the time I leaned on the horn and flashed my lights. Pedestrians and runners slowed to a stop on the sidewalk crossing the bridge and stared at us.

Since police cars are faster than Hummers, it wasn't long before the phony cop was alongside us, light bar flashing, siren wailing, and scattering cars ahead of us. I could see him waving his pistol around and trying to get a shot off, but being in a patrol car he sat lower than the Hummer. I swung my heavy vehicle over into his lane, but he easily dodged away.

After he did this again, I yelled at Mary Kate, "Fasten your seatbelt!" I knew what the phony cop would have to do to stop us, and sooner or later, he'd be doing it.

"What?" asked Mary Kate.

She was leaning across me trying to get a shot off, which, if you think about it, was rather game of her.

"Because he's going to . . ."

There was another shot from the patrol car, then a second, and the left front tire blew and I lost control of the vehicle. The front end dipped, the rim bit into the surface of the bridge, and the steering wheel jerked out of my hands. The patrol car should've slowed down, but the driver was too intent on catching us, and in that way he played a large part in how we crossed the median and into the oncoming traffic.

He was running beside us when the Hummer jerked left and rolled over him, crushing the light bar and landing on the other side of the concrete median. Though we were dodged by several oncoming vehicles, one of them a police car, an eighteen-wheeler couldn't slow down fast enough and knocked us toward the far side of the bridge. At the highest point, we rolled between the struts, and taking a light pole with us, sailed out over the Cooper.

THE FINAL CHAPTER

Mary Kate screamed and I did, too. Plunging toward the Cooper, the Hummer completed another half turn and gave us a glimpse, through the busted-out windshield, of the new Ravenel Bridge.

Then we hit, and hit hard.

We were slammed into our seats and headrests. Both of us screamed again, then everything went black.

I don't remember anything until I was coughing, spitting up water, and felt a hard surface under me. Chad was about to give me another shot of mouth-to-mouth when I coughed up a mixture of river and saltwater, and he jerked back.

He was soaking wet, as was I.

"Suze," he said with obvious relief, "I couldn't believe it was you that I dragged out of that Hummer."

I coughed and coughed and eventually cleared my throat, trying to sit up. I could barely raise my head. "Mary Kate?"

Chad gestured at the pale woman huddled on the deck of the schooner, arms wrapped around herself. MK's black hair streamed down her pale face and she shivered. Overhead, I saw the sails of the boat, the clear blue sky, and the new Cooper River Bridge as we passed underneath. I saw it all, and shuddered in relief that I still could.

Chad was crying, or more water was running down his face. "I—I thought I'd lost you. When I went back down I had a hard time finding you. We got lucky, babe, really lucky, because it was yellow." Puzzled he asked, "Where did you get that Hummer anyway?"

I coughed and was finally able to sit up, with a little help from my man. "What is this boat?" It appeared to be an old wooden schooner in need of a lot of work.

He held a hand behind my back and grinned at me. "It's the boat I've been working on while you've been out chasing Jack the Ripper. I was planning on giving it to you as a wedding gift."

Again I looked around, taking in the lack of varnish, the worn lines, and the sail with a rip starting near the mast. "It's beautiful."

"No, it's not," he said, continuing to smile, "but this morning I finally got it seaworthy."

A tug came alongside, then the harbor patrol. Both wanted to know if everything was okay. Chad said both girls were fine.

I coughed in protest, and when I could catch my breath said, "I—I don't think that was a couple of girls who went off that bridge, and anytime—"

"No, no," said Chad, laughing. "I don't want to be able to do anything you do. I'm not man enough for that."

"But man enough for me." I put my arms around him and held him tight.

We hugged, and then he held out my hand as water ran down my arm. "Still got your ring?" he asked.

I held it out proudly. "And I'll never take it off!"

Again we hugged and kissed, and Chad looked to Mary Kate, then back to me. "If you ladies don't mind my asking, just where the hell were you two headed?"

"Any—anywhere," said Mary Kate, teeth chattering as she tried to hug herself warm. "Just trying to get out of Charleston."

Chad laughed again. "Well, you almost made it."

Mary Kate shivered. "Don't you have any blankets on this tub? What's the name of this boat anyway?"

Chad gave me one of those special smiles meant only for me. "Well, since young marrieds need every dime they can get, for the house, the kids, and the kids' education, it's called *Susan's Folly.*"

ABOUT THE AUTHOR

Author of six previous novels featuring Susan Chase, Steve Brown is one of South Carolina's most versatile writers, having also written *Radio Secrets*, a novel of suspense set in Columbia and the Lake Murray area; *The Belles of Charleston*, a historical novel set in 1856 Charleston; and *Carolina Girls*, a portrait of what it was like to vacation on the Carolina beaches in the sixties and the seventies.

You can reach Steve through www.chicksprings.com.